First Comes Scandal

BY JULIA QUINN

The Bridgerton Prequels
FIRST COMES SCANDAL
THE OTHER MISS BRIDGERTON
THE GIRL WITH THE MAKE-BELIEVE HUSBAND
BECAUSE OF MISS BRIDGERTON

The Bridgerton Series
THE DUKE AND I
THE VISCOUNT WHO LOVED ME
AN OFFER FROM A GENTLEMAN
ROMANCING MISTER BRIDGERTON
TO SIR PHILLIP, WITH LOVE
WHEN HE WAS WICKED
IT'S IN HIS KISS
ON THE WAY TO THE WEDDING
THE BRIDGERTONS: HAPPILY EVER AFTER

The Smythe-Smith Quartet
JUST LIKE HEAVEN
A NIGHT LIKE THIS
THE SUM OF ALL KISSES
THE SECRETS OF SIR RICHARD KENWORTHY

The Bevelstoke Series

THE SECRET DIARIES OF MISS MIRANDA CHEEVER

WHAT HAPPENS IN LONDON

TEN THINGS I LOVE ABOUT YOU

The Two Dukes of Wyndham

THE LOST DUKE OF WYNDHAM

MR. CAVENDISH, I PRESUME

Agents of the Crown

TO CATCH AN HEIRESS

HOW TO MARRY A MARQUIS

The Lyndon Sisters

EVERYTHING AND THE MOON

BRIGHTER THAN THE SUN

The Splendid Trilogy

SPLENDID

DANCING AT MIDNIGHT

MINX

First Comes Scandal

A Bridgerton Prequel

Julia Quinn

HARPER LARGE PRINT

An Imprint of HarperCollinsPublishers

FIRST COMES SCANDAL. Copyright © 2020 by Julie Cotler Pottinger. All rights reserved. Printed in the United States of America. No part of this book may be used or reproduced in any manner whatsoever without written permission except in the case of brief quotations embodied in critical articles and reviews. For information, address HarperCollins Publishers, 195 Broadway, New York, NY 10007.

HarperCollins books may be purchased for educational, business, or sales promotional use. For information, please e-mail the Special Markets Department at SPsales@harpercollins.com.

FIRST HARPER LARGE PRINT EDITION

ISBN: 978-0-06-297943-8

Library of Congress Cataloging-in-Publication Data is available upon request.

20 21 22 23 24 LSC 10 9 8 7 6 5 4 3 2 1

For Abi, and her year of grit,
determination, and resilience.

And also for Paul. It *is* lovely to have a doctor in the
family, but not as lovely as it is just to have you.

Chapter 1

Kent, England
1791

At least no one had died.

Beyond that, Nicholas Rokesby had not a clue why he'd been summoned home to Kent.

If someone had died, he reasoned, his father would have said as much in the message he'd dispatched to Nicholas in Edinburgh. He'd sent it by swift rider, so it was obviously a matter of some urgency, but if someone had died, surely Lord Manston would have written more than:

Please return to Crake with all possible haste. It is critical that your mother and I speak with you as soon as possible.

My regrets for interrupting your studies.
Your loving father,
Manston

Nicholas glanced up at the familiar canopy of trees as he embarked upon the final leg of his journey. He'd already traveled from Edinburgh to London by mail coach, London to Maidstone by stagecoach, and was now completing the last fifteen miles on horseback.

The rain had finally stopped—thank the good Lord—but his mount was kicking up a bloody ridiculous amount of mud, and between that and the pollen, Nicholas had a feeling that by the time he made it home to Crake he'd look like he had impetigo.

Crake. Less than a mile to go.

Hot bath, warm meal, and then he'd find out just what had his father in such a lather.

It had better be something serious. Not death, of course, but if he found out that he'd been called across two countries merely because one of his brothers was getting an award from the king, he was going to take someone's bloody arm off.

He knew how to do it too. All of the medical students were required to observe surgeries when the opportunity arose. It was not Nicholas's favorite part of the program; he much preferred the more cerebral aspects of medicine—assessing symptoms and solving the ever-changing puzzles that led to a diagnosis. But in this day and age it was important to know how to amputate a limb. It was often the doctor's only defense against infection. What could not be cured could be stopped in its tracks.

Better to cure, though.

No, better to prevent. Stop problems before they started.

Nicholas gave a mental eye-roll as Crake finally came into view. He had a feeling that whatever problem had brought him down to Kent on this rainy spring day, it was well underway.

Also, his brothers weren't getting awards from the king. They were stand-up gentlemen, all three of them, but *really*.

He slowed his horse to a trot as they rounded the final corner of the drive. The trees slipped from his peripheral vision and suddenly there was his home, stately and solid, all two-and-a-half centuries of it rising from the earth like a limestone goddess. Nicholas had always marveled at how such a large and ornate building could be so well hidden until the final moment of approach. He supposed there was something poetic about it, that he could continually be surprised by something that had always been a part of him.

His mother's roses were in full bloom, red and pink and riotous, just the way they all liked them, and as Nicholas drew close, he felt their scent in the damp air, drifting lightly over his clothes and under his nose. He'd never been particularly fond of the smell of roses—he preferred his flowers less fussy—but when everything came together in moments like this: the roses and the mist, the damp of the earth . . .

It was home.

It didn't seem to matter that he hadn't meant to be here, at least not for another few weeks. This was home, and he was home, and it set him at peace, even as his brain pricked with unease, wondering what manner of disaster had called him back.

The staff must have been alerted to his impending arrival because a groom was waiting in the drive to see to his mount, and Wheelock had the door open before Nicholas even took the front step.

"Mr. Nicholas," the butler said. "Your father would like to see you immediately."

Nicholas motioned to his mud-spattered attire. "Surely he will want me to—"

"He did say immediately, sir." Wheelock's chin dipped, almost imperceptibly, just enough to indicate the back of the house. "He is with your mother in the gold-and-green."

Nicholas felt his brow draw down in confusion. His family was less formal than most, especially when they were here in the country, but a greatcoat streaked with mud was never acceptable attire in his mother's favorite drawing room.

"I'll take that," Wheelock said, reaching for the coat. The man always had been a freakishly good mind reader.

Nicholas glanced down at his boots.

"I would just go," Wheelock said.

Good God, maybe someone *had* died.

"Do you know what this is about?" he asked, turning so that Wheelock could take the coat from his shoulders.

"It is not for me to say."

Nicholas glanced back over his shoulder. "So you do know."

"*Sir.*" Wheelock looked pained.

"I would have been down in less than a month."

Wheelock avoided Nicholas's gaze as he made a show of brushing dried bits of mud off the coat. "I believe time is of some essence."

Nicholas rubbed his eye. Good God, he was tired. "Do you enjoy being cryptic?"

"Not particularly."

Which was an utter lie. Wheelock loved the special

brand of understatement that was available only to butlers who were very secure in their positions. But Nicholas could tell that Wheelock was not finding anything
to love in this particular conversation.

"I'm sorry," Nicholas said. "It is badly done of me
to put you in such a position. No need to announce me.
I'll take my muddy boots and find my parents."

"Gold-and-green," Wheelock reminded him.

"Of course," Nicholas murmured. As if he'd forget.

The entrance to the gold and green drawing room
was at the end of the hall, and Nicholas had spent
enough time making that short journey to know that
his parents had to have heard him enter the house.
The floors were marble, always polished to perfection.
Stockinged feet slid like skates on ice and shoes clicked
with enough volume to percuss a small orchestra.

But when he reached the open doorway and peered
inside, neither of his parents were so much as glancing
in his direction. His father was by the window, staring
out over the verdant lawn, and his mother was curled
in her favorite spot on the mint green sofa.

She'd always said the left side was more comfortable than the right. All five of her children had tested
this hypothesis, scooting from one side to the other,
and no one had managed to reach the same conclusion. To be fair, no one had reached *any* verifiable

conclusion. Mary had declared that both sides felt the same, Edward pointed out that the only way to be truly comfortable was to put one's feet up, which was not generally permitted, and Andrew had hopped back and forth so many times he'd busted the seam on one of the cushions. George had declared the entire exercise ridiculous, but not before making his own perfunctory test, and as for Nicholas . . .

He had been but five during this family experiment. But he'd sat himself down in every spot before rising back to his feet and declaring, "Well, we can't prove her wrong."

That seemed to cover a lot of life, he'd come to realize.

Proving something right wasn't the same as proving the opposite wrong.

And if the left side of the sofa made his mother happy, who was he to say otherwise?

He hesitated for a moment in the doorway, waiting for one of his parents to notice his presence. They didn't, so he stepped inside, pausing at the edge of the rug. He'd already left a trail of mud in the hall.

He cleared his throat, and finally they both turned.

His mother spoke first. "Nicholas," she said, stretching her arm in his direction. "Thank God you're here."

He looked warily from parent to parent. "Is something wrong?"

It was the stupidest of questions. Of course something was wrong. But no one was wearing black, so . . .

"Sit down," his father said, motioning to the sofa.

Nicholas took a seat next to his mother, taking her hand in his. It seemed the right thing to do. But she surprised him by tugging it away and rising to her feet.

"I will leave the two of you to your discussion," she said. She laid her hand on Nicholas's shoulder, signaling that he did not need to rise. "It will be easier if I am not here."

What the devil? There was a problem that needed sorting and his mother was not just *not* taking charge, she was voluntarily exiting the scene?

This was not normal.

"Thank you for coming down so quickly," she murmured, bending to kiss him on the cheek. "It comforts me more than I could ever say." She looked back at her husband. "I will be at my writing desk, should you need me to . . ."

She seemed not to know what to say. Nicholas had never seen her so uncomposed.

"Should you need me," she finally finished.

Nicholas watched as his mother departed, silent and likely slack-jawed until she shut the door behind her. He turned back to his father. "*What* is going on?"

His father sighed, and a long, heavy moment passed before he said, "There has been an incident."

His father always had been a master of polite understatement.

"You should have a drink."

"*Sir.*" Nicholas didn't want a drink. He wanted an explanation. But this was his father, so he took the drink.

"It concerns Georgiana."

"Bridgerton?" Nicholas asked in disbelief, as if there was another Georgiana to whom his father could possibly be referring.

Lord Manston nodded grimly. "You haven't heard, then."

"I've been in Edinburgh," Nicholas reminded him.

His father took a sip of his brandy. A rather larger sip than was normal this early in the morning. Or any time of the day, for that matter. "Well, that's a relief."

"Respectfully, sir, I would ask you to be less opaque."

"There was an incident."

"Still opaque," Nicholas muttered.

If his father heard him—and to be honest, Nicholas rather thought he had—he made no reaction. Instead he cleared his throat and said, "She was kidnapped."

"What?" Nicholas sprang to his feet, his own glass

of brandy sliding from his fingers to the priceless carpet below. "You didn't think to *begin* the conversation with that? Good God, has anyone—"

"Calm yourself," his father said sharply. "She has been recovered. She is safe."

"Was she . . ."

"She was not violated."

Nicholas felt something unfamiliar slide through his veins. Relief, he supposed, but something else along with it. Something acrid and sour.

He'd met women who'd been forced into sexual congress against their will. It did things to them. To their bodies, which he thought he might understand a little, and then to their souls, which he knew he could not understand at all.

This feeling inside . . . it was sharper than relief. It had teeth, and it came with a slow thrum of rage.

Georgiana Bridgerton was like a sister to him. No, not quite a sister. Not exactly. But her brother Edmund *was* like a brother to him, closer than his own, to be honest.

Lord and Lady Manston had thought they were finished having children when Nicholas happened along. He was a full eight years younger than his next closest sibling; by the time he was old enough to do more than toddle about in nappies, they were all off at school.

But Edmund Bridgerton had been around, just a few miles away at Aubrey Hall. They were almost precisely the same age, born just two months apart.

They'd been inseparable.

"What happened?" Nicholas asked his father.

"Bloody fortune hunter went after her," his father bit off. "Nithercott's son."

"Freddie Oakes?" Nicholas said, with no small amount of surprise. They'd gone to school together. For a few years, at least. Freddie hadn't finished. He was popular, personable, and insanely good at cricket, but it turned out that the only thing worse than failing one's exams was cheating on them, and he'd been booted from Eton at the age of sixteen.

"That's right," Lord Manston murmured. "You know him."

"Not well. We were never friends."

"No?"

"Never *not* friends," Nicholas clarified. "Everyone got on with Freddie Oakes."

Lord Manston gave him a sharp look. "You defend him?"

"No," Nicholas said quickly, although without any facts, he had no idea what had truly happened. Still, it was difficult to imagine a scenario that involved Georgiana being at fault. "I'm just saying that he was always very popular. He wasn't *mean,* but you didn't really want to cross him."

"So he was a bully."

"No." Nicholas rubbed his eyes. Damn, he was tired. And it was near impossible to explain the intricacies of school social hierarchy to someone who hadn't been there. "Just . . . I don't know. As I said, we weren't really friends. He was . . . shallow, I suppose."

His father gave him a curious look.

"Or maybe he wasn't. I honestly could not say. I never really spoke with him about anything more than what was for breakfast or who was going home for half term." Nicholas thought for a moment, sifting through his memories of school. "He played a lot of cricket."

"You played cricket."

"Not well."

It was a sign of his father's distress that he did not immediately leap to correct him on this. In the Earl of Manston's mind, all four of his sons had been made in his image—splendid athletes who dominated the sporting fields of Eton College.

He was only twenty-five percent wrong.

Nicholas was not an incompetent athlete. To the contrary, he was a rather fine fencer, and he could outshoot any of his brothers with either rifle or bow. But put him on a field with a ball (of any sort) and a few other men and he was hopeless. There was a skill to knowing where one was in a crowd. Or maybe it was an instinct. Regardless, he did not have it. Cricket, the Field Game, the Wall Game . . .

He was terrible at them all. All of his worst memories of school took place on the playing fields. That sense of being watched and found wanting . . . the only thing worse was waiting while teams were chosen. It did not take boys long to figure out who could kick a ball or throw a googly.

And who could not.

He supposed it was the same in academics. He'd only been at Eton a few months before everyone knew he was the one with the perfect marks in the sciences. Even Freddie Oakes had come to him for help from time to time.

Nicholas knelt to finally retrieve the glass tumbler he'd dropped. He regarded it for a few seconds, trying to decide if the moment required a clear head or a softening around the edges.

Probably something in between.

He looked at his father. "Perhaps you had better tell me what has happened," he said, crossing the room to refill his glass. He could decide later if he wanted to drink it.

"Very well." His father set his own glass down with

a heavy clunk. "I'm not sure when they met, but Oakes had made his intentions clear. He was courting her. Your mother seemed to think that he was likely to propose."

Nicholas could not imagine why his mother thought she could read the mind of Freddie Oakes of all people, but this was clearly not the time to point this out.

"I don't know if Georgiana would have said yes," Lord Manston continued. "Oakes gambles too much—we all know that—but he'll eventually have the barony, and Georgie's not getting any younger."

At twenty-six, Georgie was precisely one year younger than Nicholas, but he was well aware that women did not age at the same rate as men, at least not as pertained to the customs and mores of English marriage.

"Anyway," his father continued, "Lady Bridgerton and your mother were up in London—shopping, I suppose; I didn't ask—and Georgiana went with them."

"But not for the Season," Nicholas murmured. As far as he knew, Georgie had never had a proper London Season. She'd said she hadn't wanted one. He'd never inquired further. A Season in London sounded as appealing to him as having his teeth pulled, so who was he to question her?

"Just a visit," his father confirmed. "I'm sure they went to some event or another. But nothing official.

Season's almost over, anyway. But Oakes called several times, and he took Georgiana out."

Nicholas splashed a bit of brandy into his glass and turned back around to face his father. "With Lady Bridgerton's permission?"

Lord Manston nodded grimly and took a long swallow of his drink. "It was all as it should be. Her maid accompanied them. They went to a bookstore."

"That sounds like Georgie."

His father nodded. "Oakes snatched her on the way out. Or rather, he made off with her. She got into the carriage willingly, because why shouldn't she?"

"What about the maid?"

"Oakes pushed her to the pavement before she could get into the carriage."

"My God, is she all right?" If she hit her head, it could be quite serious.

Lord Manston blinked, and it occurred to Nicholas that his father probably hadn't considered the question of the maid's health. "She's probably fine if you haven't heard anything," Nicholas said.

His father was silent for a moment, then said, "She is home now."

"Georgie?"

His father nodded. "She was in his custody for only a day, but the damage was done."

"I thought you said she wasn't—"

His father slammed his glass onto the side table. "She doesn't have to have been violated for her reputation to be destroyed. Good God, boy, use your head. It doesn't matter what he did or didn't do to her. She's ruined. And everyone knows it." He looked up at Nicholas with a withering expression. "Except, apparently, you."

There was an insult there somewhere, but Nicholas decided to let it slide. "I was in Edinburgh, sir," he said, voice tight. "I did not know that any of this had transpired."

"I know. I'm sorry. This is very distressing." Lord Manston raked his hand through his hair. "She is my goddaughter, you know."

"I do."

"I swore an oath to protect her. In church."

As his father wasn't a particularly religious man, Nicholas wasn't certain why the location of the vow held such importance, but he nodded all the same. He brought his glass to his lips but did not drink, instead using the tumbler to partially obscure his own expression as he watched his father.

He had never seen him quite like this. He was not sure what to make of it.

"I cannot see her ruined," his father said firmly. "We cannot see her ruined."

Nicholas held his breath. Later he realized his lungs knew what his brain did not. His life was about to take a drastic turn.

"There is only one thing to be done," his father said. "*You* must marry her."

Chapter 2

Quite a few things looped through Nicholas's mind upon his father's announcement.

What did you just say?

Are you mad?

You must be mad.

Yes, I'm sure you're mad.

Wait, did I hear that correctly?

All culminating in: *ARE YOU OUT OF YOUR BLOODY MIND?*

What he said, however, was, "I beg your pardon?"

"You must marry her," his father said again.

Proving that A) Nicholas had not misheard him and B) his father was indeed out of his bloody mind.

Nicholas downed his brandy in one gulp. "I can't marry Georgiana," he said.

"Why not?"

"Because—Because—" There were so many reasons Nicholas could not possibly coalesce them into a single statement.

His father raised a brow. "Are you married to someone else?"

"Of course not!"

"Have you *promised* to marry someone else?"

"For the love of God, Father—"

"Then I see no reason you cannot do your duty."

"It is not my duty!" Nicholas exploded.

His father stared at him, hard, and he felt like a child again, scolded for some minor infraction.

But this was not minor. This was marriage. And while marrying Georgiana Bridgerton might—*might*—be the right and honorable thing to do, it certainly was not his *duty.*

"Father," he tried again, "I am not in a position to marry."

"Of course you are. You are twenty-seven years old, of sound mind, and in good health."

"I live in a rented room in Edinburgh. I don't even have a valet."

His father waved a hand. "Easily remedied. We can get you a house in the new part of town. Your brother knows several of the architects involved with the planning. It will be an excellent investment."

For a moment Nicholas could only stare. His father was talking about property investments?

"You may consider it a wedding gift."

Nicholas brought his hand to his forehead, using his thumb and middle finger to press into his temples. He needed to focus. Think. His father was still talking, going on about integrity and duty and ninety-nine-year leases, and Nicholas's brain hurt.

"Do you have any idea what is involved in the study of medicine?" he asked, his eyes closed behind his hand. "I don't have time for a wife."

"She doesn't need your time. She needs your name."

Nicholas moved his hand. Looked at his father. "You're serious."

His father gave him a look as if to say, *Haven't you been listening?*

"I can't marry someone with the express intention of ignoring her."

"I hope that does not prove to be the case," his father responded. "I am merely trying to point out that your cooperation in this matter does not have to adversely impact your life at this crucial juncture."

"That was an awful lot of words to tell me, in effect, to be a bad husband."

"No, it was an awful lot of words to tell you, in effect, to be a young woman's hero."

Nicholas rolled his eyes. "After which I can go and be a bad husband."

"If that is your wish," his father said quietly.

Nicholas wasn't sure how long he stared at his father in disbelief. It was only when he realized he was slowly shaking his head that he forced himself to turn away. He walked to the window, using it as an excuse to set his attention elsewhere. He did not want to look at his father right now. He didn't want to think about him, or his mad proposition.

No, it wasn't a proposition, was it? It was an order. His father had not said, "Would you marry Georgiana?"

He'd said, "You *must* marry her."

It was not the same.

"You can leave her in Kent," his father said after whatever he must have deemed an appropriately considerate stretch of silence. "She doesn't need to accompany you to Edinburgh. In fact, she probably doesn't want to accompany you to Edinburgh. I don't think she's ever been."

Nicholas turned around.

"It would be up to you, of course," his father said. "You're the one making the sacrifice."

"It is so odd to think that this is how you mean to convince me," Nicholas said.

But it was clear they were having two separate conversations, because his father then said, "It's only mar-riage."

At that, Nicholas full-on snorted. "Say that to Mother and then come back and say it again."

His father's expression grew peevish. "This is Geor-giana we're talking about. Why are you so resistant?"

"Oh, I don't know . . . Perhaps because you sum-moned me away from my studies, across two countries, and then when I arrived, you did not *suggest* that I might have the means to solve a difficult situation. You did not *ask* me how I felt about the idea of marriage. You sat me down and ordered me to marry a woman who is practically my sister."

"But she is *not* your sister."

Nicholas turned away. "Stop," he said. "Please just stop."

"Your mother agrees that it's the best solution."

"Oh my God." They were ganging up on him.

"It is the only solution."

"A moment," Nicholas muttered. He pressed his fingers to his temples again. His head was starting to pound. "I just need a moment."

"We don't have—"

"For the love of God, could you be quiet for one bloody second so I can *think*?"

His father's eyes widened, and he took a step back.

Nicholas looked down at his hands. They were shaking. He'd never spoken to his father in such a manner. He wouldn't have thought it possible. "I need a drink," he muttered. A proper one this time. He strode back to the sideboard and filled his glass, nearly to the brim.

"The entire journey down from Scotland I wondered," Nicholas mused, "what on earth could be the reason for such a mysterious yet blatantly unignorable summons. Had someone died, I wondered."

"I would never—"

"No," Nicholas interrupted. He did not desire his father's commentary. This was *his* speech, his sarcasm, and by God he was going to get through it in his own good time.

"No," he said again. "No one could have died. My father would never compose such a cryptic note for that. But what else could it be? What could possibly have led him to call me down at such an astoundingly inconvenient time?"

Lord Manston opened his mouth, but Nicholas quelled him with another hard stare.

"Although *inconvenient* doesn't really quite cover it. Did you know I'm missing my exams?" Nicholas paused, but not for long enough to indicate that the question was anything but rhetorical. "My professors agreed to re-administer them when I return, but of course I had to admit to them that I didn't know *when* I would return." He took a long drink of his brandy. "Now, *that's* an awkward conversation."

Nicholas looked over at his father, almost daring him to interrupt. "I don't think they wanted to grant the delay," he continued, "but this is one of those cases where being the son of an earl does come in handy. Not to make friends, of course. Because no one really likes the fellow who pulls rank to get out of exams. Even if that fellow has every intention of taking those exams at a later, although as I may have already mentioned, unspecified, date."

"I have already apologized for pulling you away from your studies," Lord Manston said in a tight voice.

"Yes," Nicholas said blandly, "in your highly detailed letter."

His father stared at him for a moment, then said, "Are you finished with your petulance?"

"For the time being." Nicholas took a sip of his drink, then reconsidered. He still had one last thing to say. "I will tell you, though, of all the scenarios that played through my mind on the journey home, I never dreamed that I would arrive to find my father had all but promised my hand in marriage."

"Your hand in marriage," his father repeated with a slightly uncomfortable huff. "You make yourself sound like a girl."

"I rather feel like one right now, and I have to tell you, I don't like it." He shook his head. "I have new respect for all of them, putting up with us telling them what to do."

Lord Manston snorted. "If you think I have ever managed to tell your mother or sister what to do, you are sadly mistaken."

Nicholas set down his glass. He'd had enough. It wasn't even noon. "Then why are you doing so with me?"

"Because I have no other choice," his father shot back. "Georgiana needs you."

"You would sacrifice your son for the benefit of your goddaughter."

"That's not at all what I'm doing, and you know it."

It felt like it, though. It felt like his father was choosing a favorite child, and it was not Nicholas.

It was not even a Rokesby.

But even Nicholas had to admit that the lives of the Rokesbys and the Bridgertons were thoroughly entwined. They had been neighbors for centuries, but it had been this current generation that had truly cemented the bond. The lords and ladies were the closest of friends, and each had been entrusted with a godchild in the other family.

The whole thing had been made even more official when the oldest Rokesby son married the oldest Bridgerton daughter. And then the third Rokesby son had married a Bridgerton cousin.

Honestly, give someone a ball of yarn and the family tree and one could make quite an incestuous cat's cradle out of the whole thing.

"I need to think about this," Nicholas said, because it was clearly the only thing he could say at the moment that would put a temporary halt to his father's pressure.

"Of course," his father said. "I do understand that this comes as a surprise."

To put it mildly.

"But time is of the essence. You'll need to make your decision by tomorrow."

"Tomorrow?"

His father had the grace to sound at least a little bit regretful when he said, "It can't be helped."

"I have traveled for nearly two weeks, through at least six torrential downpours, cut short my studies, and been all but ordered to marry my neighbor, and you cannot even give me the courtesy of a few days' time to *think* about it?"

"This isn't about you. It's about Georgie."

"How is this not about me?" Nicholas all but roared.

"You won't even know you're married."

"Are you bloody gone in the head?" Nicholas was quite sure he'd never spoken to his father in such a way; he'd never have dared to. But he could not believe the words coming forth from his father's mouth.

His father had to have gone mad. It was one thing to suggest he marry Georgiana Bridgerton; there was a quixotic sort of logic to it. But to suggest that the act was meaningless . . . that Nicholas could carry on as if he had not taken her hand in marriage . . .

Did he know his son at all?

"I can't talk to you right now," Nicholas said. He stalked to the door, suddenly glad he'd never removed his muddy boots.

"Nicholas . . ."

"No. Just, no." He laid one hand against the frame of the door, pausing to take a steadying breath. He did not trust himself to look back at his father, but he said, "Your concern for your goddaughter is commendable, and I might—I *might* have listened to you had you framed your wishes as a request."

"You are angry. I understand."

"I don't think you do. Your utter disdain for the feelings of your own son—"

"False," his father snapped. "I assure you that your

best interests have never been far from the forefront of my mind. If I have not made that clear, it is because I am worried for Georgiana, not for you."

Nicholas swallowed. Every muscle in his body felt ready to snap.

"I have had a great deal longer to become accustomed to the idea," his father said quietly. "Time does make a difference."

Nicholas turned around to face him. "Is this what you would hope for me? A loveless, sexless marriage?"

"Of course not. But you already have affection. And Georgiana is a fine girl. I have every confidence that in time the two of you will find that you're very well suited."

"Your other children married for love," Nicholas said quietly. "All four of them."

"I had hoped for the same for you." His father smiled, but it was a sad, wistful thing. "I would not rule it out."

"I'm not going to fall in love with Georgiana. My God, if I were, don't you think it would have happened by now?"

His father gave him an amused smile. Not mocking, just amused.

But Nicholas wasn't having it. "I can't even imagine kissing her," he said.

"You don't have to kiss her. You just have to marry her."

Nicholas's mouth fell open. "You did not just say that to me."

"Very few marriages begin with passion," Lord Manston said, suddenly all friendly, fatherly advice. "Your mother and I—"

"I do *not* want to hear about you and Mother."

"Don't be a prude," his father said with a snort.

It was at that moment Nicholas wondered if he were, in fact, dreaming this entire conversation. Because he could not conceive of any other scenario that involved his father sharing any sort of intimate details about his mother.

"You're going to be a physician," his father said dryly. "Surely you know that your mother and I could not have produced five childr—"

"Stop!" Nicholas practically howled. "My God, I don't want to hear about that."

His father chuckled. He chuckled!

"I will think about it," Nicholas finally said, not bothering to mask the sullen tone of his voice. "But I cannot give you an answer tomorrow."

"You must."

"For the love of God, are you listening to me?"

"We don't have time for me to listen to you. Georgiana's life is ruined."

They were talking in circles. It was like they were out on the lawn, treading the same path until the grass was worn down to dirt. But Nicholas was too weary by this point to try to break free of the circuit, so he just asked, "And this is going to change if I take a few days to think about it?"

"If you don't marry her," Lord Manston said, "her parents need to find someone who will."

Which led to a *terrible* thought. "Have you discussed this with Lord and Lady Bridgerton?"

His father hesitated a moment before saying, "I have not."

"You would not lie to me about this . . ."

"You dare to question my honor?"

"Your honor, no. Your judgment, I no longer have any idea."

His father swallowed uncomfortably. "I would have suggested it, but I did not want to raise their hopes in the event you refused."

Nicholas eyed him skeptically. "You did not give the impression that refusal was an option."

"We both know I can't force you to marry the girl."

"You'll just be profoundly disappointed in me if I don't."

His father said nothing.

"That's answer enough, I suppose," Nicholas muttered. He sank back into a chair, exhausted. What the hell was he going to do?

His father must have realized that he'd had enough, because he cleared his throat a few times, then said, "Why don't I get your mother?"

"Why?"

Nicholas hadn't meant to sound quite so truculent, but really, what was his mother going to do?

"She has a way of setting me at ease when I'm troubled. Perhaps she can do the same for you."

"Fine," Nicholas grunted. He was too tired to argue any longer.

But before Lord Manston could leave the room, the door opened, and Lady Manston stepped quietly inside. "Is it settled?"

"He's going to think about it," her husband replied.

"You did not need to leave the room," Nicholas said.

"I thought it would be easier if I was not here."

"It was going to be difficult either way."

"I suppose that is true." She laid her hand on his shoulder and gave it a little squeeze. "For what it is worth, I am sorry that you have been put into this position."

Nicholas gave her the closest thing he could manage to a smile.

She cleared her throat. It was an awkward sound. "I

also wanted to inform you that we are having dinner at Aubrey Hall tonight."

"You have got to be joking," Nicholas said. Aubrey Hall was the home of the Bridgerton family. He could only assume that *all* the Bridgertons would be in attendance.

His mother gave him a regretful smile. "I'm afraid not, my son. It has been planned for some time, and I did mention to Lady Bridgerton that you would be home."

Nicholas groaned. Why would his mother do such a thing?

"She's terribly eager to hear about your studies. Everyone is. But you're tired. It's your choice."

"So I don't have to go?"

His mother smiled sweetly. "Everyone will be there."

"Right," Nicholas said, in a voice just one shade shy of bitterness. "So really, no choice at all."

Sounded just like the rest of his life.

Chapter 3

Georgiana Bridgerton had lost many things in her life—a leather-bound notebook she'd been particularly fond of, the key to her sister Billie's jewelry box, two left shoes—but this was the first time she'd lost her reputation.

It was proving far more difficult to replace than the notebook.

Or the shoes.

She'd taken a hammer to the jewelry box, and while no one had been pleased with the ensuing carnage, Billie's emerald bracelet had been safely recovered.

And never lent out again, but Georgie deserved no less.

But reputations . . .

Those were slippery, fickle things, resistant to repair

and repatriation, and it didn't matter if one had absolutely NOTHING TO DO with the aforementioned loss. Society was not kind to females who broke the rules.

It wasn't kind to females, full stop.

Georgie sent a stare down the length of her bed to her three cats, Judyth, Blanche, and Cat-Head. "It's not fair," she said.

Judyth placed one silvery-gray paw on Georgie's ankle, as sympathetic a gesture as one could expect from the most aloof of the three felines.

"It wasn't my fault."

This wasn't the first time she'd said those four words, in that order.

"I never said I would marry him."

Or those.

Blanche yawned.

"I *know*," Georgie responded. "I didn't even *break* the rules. I never break the rules."

It was true. She didn't. Which was probably why Freddie Oakes thought it would be so easy to break them for her.

She supposed she'd encouraged him—not to *kidnap* her, mind you, but she'd behaved as any proper young lady might when shown interest by an eligible young gentleman. She hadn't discouraged him, at any rate.

They'd danced once at Lady Manston's soirée and then twice at the local assembly room, and when Georgie had gone to London with her mother, he'd called upon her quite properly at Bridgerton House.

There had been nothing—*nothing*—in his behavior to suggest that he was an amoral, bankrupt cad.

So when he'd suggested an outing to Pemberton's bookshop, she'd accepted with delight. She loved bookshops, and everyone knew the best were in London.

She'd dressed exactly as an unmarried lady might for such an excursion, and when Freddie had arrived in his family's carriage, she'd joined him with a smile on her face and her maid Marian at her side.

Ladies didn't get into closed carriages with gentlemen without a chaperone. And Georgie never broke that sort of rule.

From the bookshop they'd walked to the Pot and Pineapple for tea and cakes, which were delicious, and again everything that was acceptable and expected in a young lady's behavior and agenda.

Georgie really wanted to make this clear, not that anyone was listening aside from her cats. She had done nothing wrong.

Nothing. Wrong.

When it was time to depart, Freddie was all graciousness and solicitude, carefully handing her up into the carriage before climbing in himself. The Oakes's groom was right there to offer the same courtesy to Marian, but then Freddie slammed the door in both of their faces, pounded his fist against the ceiling, and they'd taken off like a shot, right down Berkeley Street.

They'd almost run over a dog.

Marian had been hysterical. So had the Oakes's groom, for that matter. He'd not been in on the scheme and had feared both immediate termination of his position *and* eternal damnation.

The groom hadn't been sacked, and neither had Marian. The Oakeses and the Bridgertons both knew who was to blame for the scandal and were liberal enough not to take it out on the servants.

But the rest of society . . . Oh *ho*, they'd had a grand time with the news. And the consensus was, Georgiana Bridgerton had got nothing more than she deserved.

Uppity spinster.

Ugly hag.

She should thank him. It's not as if she had anyone else lined up to offer for her.

It was all false, of course. She wasn't an uppity spinster *or* an ugly hag, and as it happened, she *had* had a proposal of marriage, but when she'd chosen not to accept it she'd also chosen not to embarrass the man by advertising the fact.

She was nice that way. Or at least she tried to be.

She probably *was* a spinster, though. Georgie wasn't certain what age marked the line between dewy-fresh and long-in-the-tooth, but at six-and-twenty, she'd likely crossed it.

But she'd done so by choice. She hadn't wanted a London Season. She wasn't shy, or at least she didn't think so, but the thought of those crowds, day-in-and-night-out, was exhausting. Tales of her older sister's time in London had done nothing to convince her otherwise. (Billie had *literally* set someone on fire, though not on purpose.)

It was true that Billie had gone on to marry the future Earl of Manston, but that had nothing to do with her truncated disaster of a Season. George Rokesby lived just three miles away, and they'd known each other all their lives. If Billie could find a husband without leaving the southeast of England, surely Georgie could, too.

It had not been difficult to convince her parents to let her skip a traditional London debut. Georgie had been a sickly sort of child, always coughing and short of breath. She'd grown out of it, mostly, but her mother still fussed, and Georgie *might* have used that to her advantage once or twice. And it wasn't as if she'd lied. The choked and polluted London air could not possibly be good for her lungs. For anyone's lungs.

But now half of London thought she'd skipped the Season because she thought herself above it and the other half because she clearly had some sort of hideous defect her parents were trying to hide from society.

Heaven forfend that a lady might decide not to go to London because she *didn't want to go to London.*

"I'm thinking in italics," Georgie said aloud. That could not possibly be entirely sane. She reached toward her feet and scooped up Blanche. "Am I ruined?" she asked the mostly black cat. "Of course I am, but what does it mean?"

Blanche shrugged.

Or it could have just been the way Georgie was holding her. "Sorry," she muttered, setting her back down. But she put a little pressure on the cat's back, nudging her into prime snuggling position. Blanche took the hint and curled up next to her, purring as Georgie scratched the back of her neck.

What was she going to do?

"It's never the *man's* fault," she said out loud.

Freddie Oakes wasn't holed up in his bedroom, trying not to hear his mother sobbing over his misfortune.

"They're probably fêting him at his club. *Well done, you,*" Georgie snipped out in the overblown accents of the English elite. Which was to say, *her* accent, but it was easy to make it sound like something grotesque.

"Making off with the Bridgerton chit," she mimicked. *"That's forward thinking of you. She's got four hundred thousand a year, I've heard."*

She didn't.

Have four hundred thousand a year, that was. No one did. But exaggeration made the story better, and if anyone had a right to embellish it was she.

"Didja tup her? Do the deed? Poke her good?"

Dear God, if her mother could hear her now.

And what would Freddie say to such a question? Would he lie? Would it matter? Even if he said they hadn't had intercourse—

And they hadn't. Georgie's knee to his ballocks had more than made sure of that.

But even if he told the truth and admitted that they had not slept in the same bed, it did not matter. She'd been alone in a carriage with him for ten hours, then alone in a room with him for another three before she'd managed to metaphorically dismember him. She could possess the world's most intact maidenhead and she'd still be deemed deflowered.

"My hymen could be three feet thick and no one would think me a virgin."

She looked over at the cats. "Am I right, ladies?"

Blanche licked her paw.

Judyth ignored her.

And Cat-Head . . . Well, Cat-Head was a boy. Georgie supposed the old orange tabby wouldn't understand, anyway.

But all the indignation in the world could not stop Georgie's imagination from running back to the clubs of London, where the future leaders of the nation were undoubtedly still gossiping about her downfall.

It was horrible, and awful, and she kept telling herself that maybe they weren't talking about her, that maybe they'd moved on to things that really mattered, like the revolution in France, or the state of agriculture in the north. You know, things they *should* be bothering with, since half of them were going to be taking up seats in the House of Lords at some point.

But they weren't. Georgie knew they weren't. They were writing her name in that damned betting book, setting the odds that she'd be Mrs. Oakes by the end of the month. And she knew enough of callow young men to know that they were writing ditties and laughing uproariously.

Georgiana Oakes, princess of the pokes.

God, that was awful. And probably accurate. It was exactly the sort of thing they'd say.

Little Miss Bridgerton, isn't she a . . . a . . .

Nothing rhymed with Bridgerton. Georgie supposed she should be grateful for that.

She'll have to marry you now, oh ho ho.

Georgie's eyes narrowed. "Like. Hell."

"Georgiana?"

Georgie tipped her ear toward the door. Her mother was coming down the hall. Wonderful.

"Georgiana?"

"I'm in my room, Mama."

"Well, I know that, but—" Her mother knocked.

Georgie wondered what would happen if she did not respond with the expected, *Come in.*

Another knock. "Georgiana?"

Georgie sighed. "Come in."

She really wasn't that contrary. Or maybe she just didn't have the energy.

Lady Bridgerton entered, shutting the door carefully behind her. She looked lovely, as she always did, her eyes made especially blue by the cornflower silk shawl draped over her shoulders.

Georgie loved her mother, she really did, but sometimes she wished she wasn't quite so effortlessly elegant.

"Who were you talking to?" her mother asked.

"Myself."

"Oh." This did not seem to be the answer her mother was looking for, although in truth Georgie could not imagine what would have been preferable—that she was in deep discussion with the cats?

Her mother managed a small smile. "How are you feeling?"

Surely her mother did not want an honest answer to that question. Georgie waited a moment, then said, "I'm not really certain how to answer that."

"Of course." Lady Bridgerton sat gingerly on the edge of the bed. Georgie noticed that her eyes were a little puffy. She swallowed. It had been nearly a month, and still, her mother was crying every day.

She hated that she was responsible for this.

It wasn't her fault, but she was responsible. Somehow. She didn't really feel like working out the details.

Georgie picked up Judyth and held her out. "Want a cat?"

Lady Bridgerton blinked, then took her. "Yes, please."

Georgie stroked Blanche, and her mother stroked Judyth. "It helps," Georgie said.

Her mother nodded absently. "It does."

Georgie cleared her throat. "Was there something in particular you wished to tell me?"

"Oh. Yes. We are expecting guests for dinner."

Georgie avoided a groan. Just. "Really?"

"Please don't take that tone."

"What sort of tone does one take at a moment like this?"

Her mother set Judyth down. "Georgiana, I understand that this is a very difficult situation, but we must forge on."

"Can't I forge on tomorrow?"

"Darling." Her mother took her hand. "It's just family."

"I'm not hungry."

"What does that matter?"

Georgie stared at her mother. "Is that not what the partaking of a meal is all about?"

Lady Bridgerton's lips tightened, and under any other circumstances, Georgie would have awarded her mother points for not rolling her eyes.

"Everyone is coming to dinner, Georgiana. It would look very odd if you weren't there."

"Define everyone."

"Everyone who cares about you."

"Anyone who cares about me will understand why I am not hungry. Ruination, Mother. It's quite the appetite suppressant."

"Georgiana, don't."

"Don't what?" Georgie demanded. "Make light of it? It's all I *can* do."

"Well, I can't."

"You don't have to. But you have to let me do it. Because if I don't I'm going to cry."

"Maybe you should."

"Cry? No. I refuse." Besides, she already had cried. All it had done was make her eyes hurt.

"It can make one feel better."

"It didn't make me feel better," Georgie retorted. "Right now all I want to do is sit on my bed and say hateful things about Freddie Oakes."

"I support your hateful musings, but eventually we will have to take action."

"Not this afternoon," Georgie muttered.

Lady Bridgerton shook her head. "I'm going to have a word with his mother."

"What will that accomplish?"

"I don't know," Lady Bridgerton admitted. "But some-one should tell her what a terrible person her child is."

"She either already knows or she won't believe you. Either way, all she's going to do is advise you to make me marry him."

That was the rub. Georgie *could* make all of her problems go away. All she had to do was marry the man who'd destroyed her life.

"We certainly won't force you to marry Mr. Oakes," Lady Bridgerton said.

But there was a wistful hint left unspoken—that if Georgie decided she *did* want to marry him, they wouldn't stand in her way.

"I suppose everyone is just waiting to see if I turn up pregnant," Georgie said.

"Georgiana!"

"Oh, please, Mama. You know that's what everyone is wondering."

"*I'm* not."

"Because I *told* you I didn't lie with him. And you believe me. But no one else will."

"I assure you that is not true."

Georgie gave her mother a long stare. They'd had this conversation already, and they both knew the truth, even if Lady Bridgerton was loath to say it out loud. It did not matter what Georgie said. Society would assume Freddie Oakes had had his way with her.

And how could she prove them wrong? She couldn't. Either she showed up in nine months with a baby and everyone congratulated themselves on being right about that Bridgerton chit, or she kept her svelte figure and they all said that it didn't prove a thing. Lots of women didn't get pregnant on the first try.

She was still soiled goods, baby or no.

"Well." Her mother stood, clearly deciding that the conversation was more than she could bear. Frankly, Georgie couldn't blame her. "Dinner is in two hours."

"Do I have to go?"

"Yes. Your brother is coming, as is Violet, and I believe they are bringing the boys to spend the night in the nursery."

"Can't I go eat with them?" Georgie asked, only half jesting. At least Anthony and Benedict didn't realize she was a pariah. Up in the nursery she was still jolly Aunt Georgie.

Her mother gave her a steely look, indicating that she heard the comment and was choosing to ignore it. "Lord and Lady Manston are coming as well, as are George and Billie. And I believe Nicholas is down, too."

"Nicholas? Isn't he meant to be in Edinburgh?"

Lady Bridgerton gave a delicate shrug. "All I know is what Helen told me. He came down early."

"That's very odd. The term ends next month. I should think he would have exams."

Her mother looked at her curiously.

"I pay attention to details," Georgie said. Honestly, didn't her mother know this about her by now?

"Regardless," Lady Bridgerton said, setting her hand on the doorknob, "you cannot cry off now. He's come all this way."

"Not to see me."

"Georgiana Bridgerton, you cannot molder in your room."

"I wasn't planning to. Toasted cheese with the boys

sounds marvelous. We'll build a fort. And I'll bring the cats."

"You can't bring the cats. They make the baby sneeze."

"Very well, I won't bring the cats." Georgie smiled magnanimously. "But we *will* build a fort. Nicholas can join us if he wants. He'd probably prefer it to dinner with you lot."

"Don't be ridiculous."

"I'm not, Mama. I'm really not."

"You are an adult, and you are having dinner with the adults, and that is final."

Georgie stared at her mother.

Her mother stared back.

Georgie gave in. Or maybe she gave up. "Fine."

"Good." Her mother pulled the door open. "This will be good for you. You'll see." She started to exit, but then Georgie stopped her.

"Mama?"

Lady Bridgerton turned around.

Georgie realized she didn't know why she'd called out. Somehow, despite all the ways her mother had been driving her absolutely batty—she just hadn't been ready to let her go.

"Do you think . . ."

Georgie went quiet. What did she want to know? What would help? Anything?

Her mother waited, quiet. Patient.

When Georgie finally did speak, her voice was small. Not weak, but small. And tired. "Do you think that somewhere there is a society where men can't do things like this to women?"

Her mother went still, which to Georgie seemed odd, because it wasn't as if she'd been moving before. But somehow the stillness spread. From her body to her eyes to her very soul.

"I don't know," her mother said. "I hope so. Or at least I hope there will be."

"But not now," Georgie said. They both knew it was the truth. "Not here."

"No," her mother said. "Not yet." She turned to go, then paused to look back over her shoulder. "You will come to dinner?"

It was a request, not an order, and Georgie felt an unfamiliar prick of tears behind her eyes. Not the tears—those were familiar. She'd cried a lifetime's worth of tears in the past few weeks. Tears of sorrow, of frustration, of rage.

But this was the first time in a long time she'd felt gratitude. It was amazing how nice it felt to be asked rather than told. To have someone recognize the fact that she was a human being and deserved the right to make her own choices, even if it was about something as trivial as dinner.

"I'll be there," she told her mother.

She might even enjoy herself.

She picked up one of the cats as her mother left the room. Who was she kidding? She wasn't going to enjoy herself. But she supposed she could try.

Chapter 4

Georgie was trying to decide just how long she could put off heading downstairs after dressing for dinner when what sounded like a small herd of lead-footed foxes ran past her room.

She grinned. For real. Her nephews were here.

She bounded off her bed and pulled open the door just as her sister-in-law walked by. Violet immediately pivoted and bustled into the room, baby Colin in her arms. "Georgie!" she exclaimed. "It is so *good* to see you. How are you? Tell me everything. What can I do?"

"I—Well . . ." Where to start?

"Here. Hold the baby, would you?" Violet thrust Colin forward, and Georgie had no choice but to take him.

He immediately began to scream.

"I think he's hungry," Georgie said.

"He's *always* hungry. Honestly, I don't know what to do with him. He ate half of my meat pasty yesterday."

Georgie sent a horrified look at her little nephew. "Does he even have teeth?"

"No," Violet replied. "He just gummed the whole thing down."

"You little monster," Georgie said affectionately. Colin gurgled, clearly judging this to be a compliment.

"I'm so sorry I haven't been over," Violet said. "Colin was ill, nothing too serious, but he was coughing, and it was just a terrible sound, hoarse and barky. I didn't want to leave him."

"It's all right, Violet," Georgie assured her. "Your children must come first."

"Also, your mother said you wanted to be alone."

"She wasn't wrong."

"Four weeks of being alone is enough, though, I think. Don't you?"

"We'll find out tonight."

Violet smirked at that. "Has everyone else arrived? What am I saying? I don't even know who is coming."

"Billie and George. Lord and Lady Manston. Andrew and Poppy, perhaps?"

"No, they're visiting her family in Somerset. One of her brothers just got married."

"Oh, I hadn't realized."

Violet shrugged. "I don't know which one. She has so many of them. I can't imagine having such a big family."

As if on cue, Anthony and Benedict ran past the doorway, their nurse in hot pursuit.

"Three does seem to be a handful," Georgie said.

Violet flopped down in a chair. "You have no idea."

Georgie smiled. She knew Violet wouldn't trade motherhood for anything. Honestly, she wouldn't be surprised if she and Edmund decided to extend their family beyond their current three boys. Her sister-in-law was always harried but always happy. It lifted Georgie's spirits to see her, even as it occurred to her that this was something she was now unlikely to have in her own life.

Freddie Oakes had seen to that.

"I'm trying to decide who he looks like," Georgie said, bobbing baby Colin in her arms. He didn't have much hair yet, but it looked like it was coming in darker than Violet's dark blond locks.

"Edmund. They all look like Edmund."

"No, I don't think so. I think all three are a combination of both of you."

"You're very kind, but I know the truth." Violet sighed dramatically. "I'm but a vessel for the Bridgerton family."

Georgie laughed out loud. "Honestly, I think they mostly look like each other."

"They do, don't they?" Violet smiled to herself. "A matched set. I don't know why that makes me so happy."

"Me too." Georgie held Colin out a few inches for a better look at his face. "Look at those cheeks," she said. "And his eyes. I think his eyes are going to be green."

"The color of gluttony," Violet muttered.

"Not envy?"

"That, too." She shuddered. "He never stops eating."

Georgie grinned and kissed Colin's nose. "Is it too much to ask for one of you to favor your Aunt Georgie and come out a little bit gingery? Just a little? I could use another redhead in the family."

"Lone wolf that you are," Violet quipped. "I thought redheads were supposed to have tempers."

"Alas, no. I am a model of serenity."

Violet pointed a finger in Georgie's direction. "Mark my words, Georgiana Bridgerton. Someday you're going to explode, and when you do, I don't want to be anywhere nearby."

"Not even to watch?"

"Only if it's not directed at me."

Georgie looked back at the baby. "Do you think your mother could ever make me that angry? No? I don't think so, either."

Colin burped and pitched forward, almost causing Georgie to lose her balance. By the time she had a firm grip on him again he was gnawing on her shoulder. "I really think he's hungry," she said to Violet.

"Eh." Violet waved a hand.

"I can't believe you," Georgie said with a laugh. "When Anthony was a baby you fussed over him like he was made of porcelain."

"I didn't know any better. They're really quite sturdy."

Georgie smiled at her little nephew. "Well, I think you're adorable," she told him. He grinned back.

"He smiled at me!" Georgie exclaimed.

"Yes, he's quite charming when he wants to be."

"I didn't know babies could smile at this age."

"Anthony didn't. Benedict . . ." Violet frowned. "I don't remember. Does this make me a terrible mother?"

"You could never be a terrible mother."

"You're too kind, and I do love you for it." Violet stretched out her arm, but when Georgie walked over she realized her sister-in-law wasn't reaching for the baby. Instead she took Georgie's hand and gave it a quick squeeze. "You were born with a sister," Violet said, "but I wasn't. I hope you know that's what you are to me now."

"Don't." Georgie sniffled. "You're going to make me cry, and I've done far too much of that already."

"If it makes you feel better, you don't look as if you've been crying."

"You didn't see me last week." Georgie tipped her head toward the open door. She thought she heard voices. "It sounds as though people are arriving. We should go down soon."

Violet stood and took Colin from her. "Edmund told me a little of what happened," she said as she led the way to the nursery. "I have never seen him so angry. I thought he would call Mr. Oakes out."

"Edmund would never be so stupid," Georgie said.

"You're his sister," Violet said, "and your honor has been impugned."

"Tell me he didn't use the word *impugned*."

"It was something considerably more profane."

"That sounds more like my brother," Georgie said with a roll of her eyes. "And he needs to learn that I can fight my own battles. In fact, I did."

Violet's eyes lit with glee. "What did you do?"

Georgie gathered her skirts just high enough to show Violet the exact motion she'd used to knee Freddie Oakes in the ballocks.

"And you say you don't have a temper," Violet said. "Good for *you*. Did he cry? Please tell me he cried."

He did, but not half so much as Georgie had the following day, when she realized that the only way to save her reputation was to marry the man who'd abducted her.

"What happened next?" Violet asked.

Georgie followed her into the nursery. "I tied him up."

"Brava," Violet said admiringly. She handed Colin off to the nurse, then poked her head back out into the hall. "Anthony! Benedict! Now!" Then, barely missing a beat, she pulled Georgie aside. "Then what happened? I'm feeling particularly bloodthirsty."

"I climbed out the window."

"Resourceful."

Georgie gave a modest nod although in truth she was insanely proud of herself for having escaped.

"But couldn't you have just gone out the door?"

"We were on the ground floor, so it wasn't quite as awful as it might have been. And there were some rough looking men in the inn. I didn't want to go back through the front room by myself."

"Good thinking," Violet said approvingly. "Were you terrified? I would have been terrified."

"I was," Georgie admitted. "I didn't even know where we were. All I knew was that we were heading north—he'd told me we were bound for Gretna Green—and that we'd been traveling for hours and hours."

"Edmund said you were in Bedfordshire?"

"Biggleswade," Georgie confirmed.

"Biggles-what?"

"It's a village on the Great North Road. There are quite a few coaching inns there." Georgie stretched her mouth into a flat, self-effacing line. "I know this now."

Violet considered this. "I don't suppose you ever had cause to travel north before."

"I don't suppose I did."

"But wait . . . Edmund said you were saved by Lady Danbury of all people?"

"She was at the same inn. Heading north, but she turned around to take me back to London." Georgie could not even begin to describe the relief she'd felt upon seeing Lady Danbury's familiar face outside the inn. Lady D was a leader of the *ton*, and Georgie wasn't sure she'd ever exchanged two words with her, but she'd practically thrown herself at her, begging her to intercede.

"I don't know what I would have done without her," Georgie said. Or more truthfully, she didn't want to think about what might have happened without her.

"She terrifies me," Violet said.

"She terrifies everyone."

"But surely *she's* not the reason everyone found out," Violet remarked. "She would never spread such gossip."

"No," Georgie said bitterly. "Mr. Oakes took care of that. He told all of his friends when he returned to London—minus the part about my, er, unmanning him."

"And tying him up."

"No, not that part, either."

Violet let out an appropriately sympathetic snort of disgust.

"But even if he hadn't," Georgie continued, "there was such a commotion in Berkeley Square when he pushed Marian out of the carriage. From what I understand, the gossip was all over town by nightfall."

Violet ground her teeth together. "It makes me so angry I can't even tell you. I have never struck another human being, you know, at least not on purpose, but if I saw that—that *bastard*—"

The nurse gasped.

"I would blacken his eye," Violet said.

"Do you know," Georgie said slowly, "I believe you would."

Violet poked her head out the door again. "Anthony! Benedict!" She looked over at the nurse, who was still recovering from Violet's uncharacteristically coarse language. "Do you happen to know where they've gone off to?"

The nurse shook her head.

Violet let out a sigh. "I'm sorry to leave you like this, but we've got to go down to dinner."

"We can ask one of the footmen to hunt them down," Georgie assured the nurse. "They know all the boys' favorite hiding places."

"I can't possibly be paying that nurse enough," Violet said once they were in the hall. She smoothed her dress, a royal blue round gown that complemented her eyes. "Do I look presentable?"

"You look beautiful."

Violet pulled her chin toward her chest as she tried to examine her shoulders. "Are you sure? The baby spit up in the carriage. I was wearing a cloak, but . . ."

"You look perfect," Georgie said. "I promise. And even if you didn't, no one would care."

Violet smiled gratefully. "I think I asked you already, but has everyone else arrived?"

"I think so?" Georgie said. She wasn't certain. She'd heard at least one carriage in the drive, but she hadn't looked out the window. It could have held two people or five. "Oh, I forgot to tell you. Nicholas is coming."

"Nicholas? Why? He's not supposed to be here. He is in the middle of his examinations."

"He's obviously not in the middle of his examinations because he's here in Kent. Mama told me this afternoon."

"That's very odd. I hope nothing is wrong. Edmund received a letter from him just last week, no, maybe a little before that, but still, he didn't mention anything."

Georgie shrugged as she followed Violet down the stairs. "I only know what Mama told me. And as far as I can tell, she only knows what his mother told her."

"Pack of gossips, we are."

"We are *not*," Georgie said emphatically. "We are people who love and care about each other and are therefore logically interested in comings and goings. It is not at all the same as a pack of gossips."

"Sorry," Violet said with a wince. "There really ought to be a more benign word for people who love and care about each other and are therefore logically interested in the comings and goings."

"Family?" Georgie suggested.

Violet let out a loud bark of laughter just as they entered the drawing room. Edmund handed her the glass of sherry he'd already poured for her with an amused smile. "What's so funny?"

"You," she said. "Everyone in this room, actually."

He turned to Georgie.

"She's right," Georgie said.

"I may need to head back over to the less feminine side of the room," Edmund joked.

"Oh, please," Violet returned, linking her arm with

his. "Don't act as if you haven't the numbers at home. It's four against one."

He kissed her hand. "You're easily worth *five* of us."

Violet looked over at Georgie. "I'm not sure that was a compliment."

"I would take it as such, regardless of his intentions."

"Good evening to you, too, sister," Edmund said, offering Georgie his usual mischievous smile.

Georgie returned the gesture with a quick kiss on his cheek. "I take that back," she said to Violet. "Disregarding his intentions presupposes that he *had* intentions. Most of the time when he speaks, the words just spew forth like . . ." She rolled her hands in front of her face in a rough approximation of a verbal tumbleweed.

"You are evil," Edmund said approvingly.

"I learned from the best."

"Yes, you did, didn't you?"

"Has Nicholas arrived?" Violet asked. "Georgie mentioned he would be coming. Do you know why he's home?"

Edmund shook his head. "Billie and George are here, but they said that Lord and Lady Manston and Nicholas are coming separately."

George Rokesby was the heir to the earldom, and he and Billie also lived at Crake with their three children. Lord Manston often said that Billie was the finest thing to happen to the Rokesby family since they'd gained their title in 1672. She was passionate about farming and land management, and Crake's agricultural output had nearly doubled in the decade since she'd married George.

Billie was quite a bit older than Georgiana, though, and while they'd never been terribly close, that seemed to be changing as Georgie moved further into adulthood. The nine-year age gap that had been so daunting when Georgie was sixteen was not such a huge thing at twenty-six.

"I should go greet Billie," Georgie said, leaving Edmund and Violet to make their usual dove eyes at each other. It was hard sometimes to be around them. They were *so* much in love. Georgie had never met two people so obviously made for each other.

She loved them both, she really did, but tonight they were a reminder of all the things she would never have.

No husband. (Not unless she agreed to marry Freddie Oakes, and *that* wasn't going to happen.)

No children. (One needed a husband for those.)

No everything else that followed.

But she did have more than most people. She had a loving family, and she never had to worry where her next meal might come from, and she supposed if she gave herself enough time to ponder it, she'd find some sort of new purpose in life.

Her mother was right. She couldn't molder in her room forever. She probably *was* justified in taking a few more weeks of feeling sorry for herself, but after that she would have to move on.

"Georgie, darling," Billie said when Georgie reached her side. "How are you holding up?"

Georgie shrugged. "Eh."

"Is Mama driving you mad?"

"Just a little bit."

Billie sighed. She'd visited several times since the scandal had broken, often just to distract their mother so that she would not smother Georgie with her concern. "She means well."

"I know. That's what makes it bearable. And occasionally even nice."

Billie took her hand and squeezed it. "Have you heard anything from Mr. Oakes?"

"No," Georgie said with some alarm. "Why, have you heard something?"

"Not really. Just little rumblings that he might still be trying to press his suit."

"*That's* not new news." Georgie's mouth flattened into a grim line. She'd received a letter from Freddie

Oakes the day after she'd returned home to Kent. It had been full of drippings and drivel, and she could hear his smarmy voice in his words of undying love and devotion. The way he told it, he'd been overcome with the need to make her his.

Rubbish. All of it. If he'd wanted to make her his, he should have bloody well asked.

"We shall do our best to distract you this evening," Billie said. "There is nothing like the banded multitudes of Rokesbys and Bridgertons to make one laugh." She considered that. "Or cry. But tonight, I think laugh."

"Speaking of multitudes, do you know why Nicholas is home?"

Billie shook her head. "I saw him only briefly. He looked rather grim."

"Oh, dear. I hope nothing is wrong."

"If that's the case, I'm sure he'll tell us when he's ready."

"How unlike you to be so patient."

"It can't be anything too serious," Billie said. "I can't imagine there is trouble at school—he's always been so clever. But why else would he be down?"

Georgie shrugged. She hadn't seen Nicholas very often in the last few years. But given that a family was indeed a group of people who loved and cared about each other (and were therefore logically interested in comings and goings), she generally knew what he was up to.

"I think they've arrived," Billie said, looking over her shoulder toward the door that led out to the hall.

"The Earl and Countess of Manston," Thamesly announced, as if they didn't all know who was expected, "and Mr. Nicholas Rokesby."

This bit of formality was followed by Edmund's more jovial greeting. "Rokes!" he exclaimed. "What the devil are you doing in Kent?"

Nicholas laughed and made the sort of noise that revealed nothing. Georgie thought it remarkable that this seemed to satisfy Edmund, but the two men began to chat as if nothing was amiss.

"Did you see that?" she asked her sister.

"See what?"

"He just completely avoided the question, and Edmund didn't even notice."

"Oh, he noticed," Billie said. "He's just pretending not to."

"Why?"

Billie shrugged. "I don't know. Maybe he doesn't care."

"Of course he cares. Nicholas is his closest friend."

"Then he'll ask him later. Really, Georgie, why are you so curious?"

"Why aren't you?"

"Probably because I know I'll find out soon enough. It's not as if someone has died."

"Of course not," Georgie murmured, because what else could she say? Sometimes she truly did not understand her sister.

"I'm getting a glass of sherry," Billie said. "Can I get you one?"

"No, thank you. I'm going to say hello to Nicholas."

Billie gave her a look. "Don't interrogate him."

"I won't!"

But Billie clearly didn't believe her. She pressed her lips together and wagged her finger as she departed. It was rather like getting scolded for something one hadn't yet done. Georgie scowled in return—since there was nothing like an older sister to bring out one's inherent immaturity—and of course that was when she found herself face-to-face with—

"Nicholas!" she exclaimed.

Although really, *exclaimed* might be too optimistic a verb. The sound that came out of her mouth did not sound fully human.

"Georgiana," he said, giving her a polite bow. But the look he gave her was somewhat wary.

"I'm sorry," she said quickly. "You surprised me."

"My apologies. I did not mean to."

"No, of course not. Why would you?"

He did not have an answer to that. And, to quote herself, why would he? It was a stupid question.

"I'm sorry," she said. "Let us begin again. It is lovely to see you."

"And you."

If this wasn't the most awkward conversation they had ever shared, she didn't know what was. Georgie did not know what to make of it. She would never have called Nicholas Rokesby a confidante, but he was certainly a friend, and she'd never had difficulty chatting with him before.

"You look well," he said.

He looked tired. Exceedingly so. His eyes were the same blue shared by all of his brothers, but the purple shadows beneath seemed to be draining them of their usual sparkle.

But she couldn't very well say this to him after not having seen him for nearly a year, so instead she thanked him politely for the compliment. "Er, thank you. It's been a . . ." Oh, for heaven's sake, he had to have heard what had happened to her. "It's been an eventful few weeks," she finally said.

"Yes, I, er . . ." He cleared his throat. "I imagine so."

There was another awkward pause, and then another, which made her wonder if two awkward pauses in a row was really just one *long* awkward pause.

But what if one broke them up with a nonverbal motion such as shuffling one's feet? Did that ensure they were two separate pauses? Because she had definitely shuffled her feet.

She was doing it again, as a matter of fact.

Aaaaand now it was officially the longest pause in the history of long pauses.

"Ehrm . . ."

"Ahh . . ."

"Do you like Scotland?" she blurted out.

"I do." He looked relieved that she'd asked such a benign question. "It can be quite cold, of course, although not so much this time of year."

"It is far to the north."

"Yes."

She waited for him to ask her a question, because surely she could not be expected to take care of *all* the boring questions, but he just stood there with a queasy expression on his face, and every so often he'd dart a glance over at his parents.

That was odd.

Lord and Lady Manston were talking with her parents, which was *not* odd. Except that half the time she could swear Lord Manston was sneaking glances in their direction. And when he wasn't, Lady Manston was.

Honestly, the entire exchange was downright bizarre.

She decided to make one last attempt at polite conversation and gave Nicholas her best sunny smile. "Did I hear that you arrived only this morning?"

"Indeed."

"We are very lucky you decided to come to dinner, then."

His brows rose, just a tiny bit.

Georgie dropped her voice to something closer to a murmur. "Or would it be correct to assume that you had no choice?"

"None whatsoever." He quirked a wry smile, and Georgie had a feeling it was his first authentic expression of the evening.

"I sympathize utterly," she replied. "I begged Mama to let me have toasted cheese with Anthony and Benedict in the nursery."

"Are they getting toasted cheese?" He sounded undeniably jealous.

"They *always* get toasted cheese," Georgie replied. "Why don't we ever get it, that's what I'd like to know. Because you know it's what we all really want."

He scratched his jaw. "I am quite fond of your cook's famous rack of lamb . . ."

She leaned in. "But it would be better with a side of toasted cheese."

He smiled. There, that was better, Georgie decided. Maybe she'd imagined the odd way he'd been looking at her.

Toasted cheese fixed everything. She'd been saying it for years.

Chapter 5

As it turned out, toasted cheese did not fix everything.

Georgie knew this now because her mother, in a rare display of whimsy over decorum, had requested that it be served alongside the soup, and now everyone was happily munching away, commenting on what a lovely, comforting surprise this was, and why didn't they always have toasted cheese with dinner?

It should have been delightful.

It *would* have been delightful, except . . .

Georgie stole a glance to her right.

He was looking at her again.

Georgie wasn't sure what was more aggravating— that Nicholas Rokesby kept looking at her with a strange expression or that she kept *noticing* that he was looking at her with a strange expression.

Because this was *Nicholas.*

Rokesby.

If ever existed a gentleman who should not make her feel awkward and out of place, it was he.

But he kept stealing sidelong glances, and while Georgie's experience with gentlemen was limited, she could tell these weren't *admiring* sorts of sidelong glances.

Freddie Oakes had given her plenty of those. Insincere ones, but still.

But Nicholas . . . He was looking at her differently. Almost like he was assessing her.

Inspecting her.

It was disconcerting in the extreme.

"Are you enjoying the soup?" she blurted out.

"What?"

"The soup," she said. She tried to sound sweet and accommodating, but from the look on his face, she'd clearly failed. "How is it?"

"Er . . ." He looked down at his bowl with a perplexed expression. Georgie supposed she couldn't blame him considering her query had come out more like a barked command than anything else.

"It's delicious," he finally said. "Are . . . you enjoy-ing it?"

His voice rose more than was normal on the final word, as if the question itself was a question.

Georgie could only imagine what he was thinking. *Should he talk to her? Had she gone a little bit feral?*

She wondered what he'd do if she bared her teeth.

Had he been told of her downfall? He must have been; she could not imagine that his parents would have not told him. And Lord and Lady Manston had to know; she couldn't imagine that her parents wouldn't have told *them*.

So he knew. He had to. And he was judging her.

Was this what her life had come to? Being judged by Nicholas Rokesby?

God*damn* this made her angry.

"Georgie, are you all right?"

She looked up. Violet was staring at her from across the table with a vaguely alarmed expression.

"I'm fine," Georgie said in a clipped voice. "Splendid."

"Well, we know that's not true," Edmund said.

Violet elbowed him. Hard.

"What?" Edmund grunted. "She's my sister."

"Which means you should be more careful of her feelings," Violet hissed.

"I'm fine," Georgie ground out.

"Splendid," Lord Bridgerton said, having obviously missed the first half of the conversation. He turned to his wife. "The soup is delicious, darling."

"Isn't it?" Lady Bridgerton gushed. "Cook tells me it's a new recipe."

"It's the toasted cheese," Edmund said, still chewing. "It makes the soup taste better."

"Whatever you do, *don't* say that to Cook," his mother replied. "And the toasted cheese was Georgie's idea."

"Well done," Edmund said with a wink.

"If you must know, I wanted it in the nursery with your children," she said to him.

"And who could blame you, delightful little terrors that they are."

"Stop," Violet said. "They're perfect."

"She forgets so quickly," Edmund murmured.

"They take after *you*," Lord Bridgerton said to his son. "It's no more than you deserve."

"To have a child just like me? I know, you've been saying as much for years."

"They are delightfully perfect little terrors," Violet said.

While that conversation spiraled into something both adorable and nauseating, Georgiana turned back to Nicholas. For once he wasn't staring at her, or pretending not to be staring at her. But he did look, well . . . odd.

"Are you all right?" she asked. Because maybe this wasn't about her. Maybe he was ill.

He winced. Or not a wince, because he didn't actually make a sound. But he did one of those things where the corners of his mouth twitched to the side without actually forming a smile. "I'm fine," he said. "It was a long journey."

"Of course."

She said it politely, but she knew he was lying. Not about being tired. That was clearly the truth. But whatever it was that had him acting so strangely, it wasn't a lack of sleep.

Frankly, she was starting to find this entire dinner tedious. If she could slap a happy expression on her face and keep up her end of the conversation, why couldn't he? The only thing that had changed since the last time they'd seen each other was her social ruin.

Surely he did not condemn her for that?

Not Nicholas.

It was as if the entire world had been set to a ten-degree slant, and he was the only person to notice.

At first glance, everything seemed normal. Every-thing *was* normal. Nicholas knew that.

But it didn't feel right.

Seated around the table were the people Nicholas knew best in the world, the people with whom he had always felt the most at ease. His parents, his older brother George and his wife Billie, Edmund and Violet, Lord and Lady Bridgerton, even Georgiana.

And yet he could not tamp down the sensation that everything was wrong. Or if not wrong, then at least a little bit not right.

A little bit not right.

Coming from a man of science, it was the most ridiculous statement imaginable.

But there it was. Everything was off. And he did not know how to fix it.

All around him the Rokesbys and Bridgertons were acting with complete normality. Georgiana was seated to his left, which was perfectly normal; he couldn't begin to count the number of times he'd sat next to Georgiana Bridgerton at a dining table. But every time he looked at her—

Which was to say far more often than he normally looked at her.

Which was also to say that every glance was abnormally quick because he was painfully aware that he was looking at her far too often.

Which was to say *bloody hell,* he felt awkward.

"Nicholas?"

He couldn't stop thinking that—

"Nicholas?"

He blinked. Georgie was talking to him. "Sorry," he grunted.

"Are you sure you're feeling well?" she asked. "You look—"

Strange?

Mad?

Strangely mad?

"Have you slept?" she asked.

Madly strange it was, then.

"You must be terribly tired," she said, and he could not help but wonder what was in his eyes to make her say that, since he had not managed to respond to either of her queries.

She cocked her head to the side, but he noticed that her eyes took on a different expression. She was no longer looking at him in that oddly penetrative manner, thank God.

"How long does it take to travel to Kent from Edinburgh?" she asked.

"It depends on how you do it," he told her, grateful for a fact-based question. "Ten days this time, but I took the mail coach from Edinburgh to London."

"That sounds uncomfortable."

"It is."

It was. But not as uncomfortable as he was right now, conversing with the lady he had a feeling he was going to end up marrying, despite his very great number of reservations.

"I was surprised to hear you would be joining us this evening," she said. "Actually, I am surprised you are here at all. Weren't you meant to come down next month?"

"Yes, but"—Nicholas felt his cheeks grow warm—"Father had some business to attend to."

She stared at him with an open, curious expression.

"That he needed me for," he added.

"Of course," she murmured. But she didn't look the least bit put off by his words. If she was blushing, it was with such delicacy that he could not detect it in the candlelight.

It occurred to Nicholas that he'd forgotten to ask his father one very crucial question: Had anyone told *Georgiana* that he'd been summoned from Scotland to marry her?

"I hope whatever he called you down for was worth it," she said breezily. "If I were studying something as interesting as medicine I wouldn't wish to be disrupted for an annoying family triviality."

No, then. She didn't know.

"What do you like best about it?" Georgie asked, dipping her spoon into her much-discussed soup. "Studying medicine, I mean. I think it sounds fascinating."

"It is." He thought for a moment about how to answer her question. "There is always something new. It is never the same thing."

Her eyes lit with interest. "I watched Anthony get a wound stitched last month. It was splendidly gruesome."

"Is it healing well? No infection?"

"I believe so," she replied. "I saw him before dinner and he seemed perfectly healthy to me. Violet would surely have said something if there had been a complication."

"I would be happy to take a look at it after dinner."

"He'll be asleep, I'm sure. Violet insists upon an early bedtime."

"Tomorrow, then." It was good to talk about medicine, to remind himself that there existed an area of his life where people looked up to him. Where he could say something and have it assumed that he knew what he was talking about.

In Edinburgh he was his own man.

He was still learning, of course. Nicholas was not so

conceited to think that the breadth of his knowledge exceeded that which was left to learn. He doubted he'd ever know more than what was left to learn. It was part of why he so enjoyed the pursuit.

He looked past Georgie toward the head of the table. Violet was chatting with Billie, but Edmund's attention was not hard to catch. "How is Anthony's—"

He looked to Georgie.

"Hand," she supplied.

"Hand," Nicholas repeated. "Georgie said he needed stitches?"

"All healed," Edmund said with a grin. "Or at least I assume so. He tried to take a punch at Benedict yesterday and it didn't seem to bother him to make a fist."

"Nor when you grabbed said fist to put a halt to the altercation," Violet said with the sort of smile exclusive to mothers of boys.

"I'll give it a look tomorrow if you like," Nicholas said. "There can be less obvious signs of infection."

"I'm fairly certain he's healthier than a horse," Edmund said, "but by all means."

"It's so lovely to have a doctor in the family," Violet said to no one in particular. "Wouldn't you agree?"

"It would have been helpful back when Billie was small," Lady Bridgerton said. "She broke both her arms, you know."

"Not at the same time," Billie said, with just enough amused boredom to remind everyone that this was not a new exchange.

"Have you set any bones?" Georgie asked him.

"A few times," Nicholas said. "We are all required to learn. But it's not like reading philosophy where one can open a book and study. We can't go about breaking bones just so we can learn to set them."

"That *would* be splendidly gruesome," Georgie murmured. Her eyes narrowed, and Nicholas allowed himself a moment just to watch her think. He'd long suspected she had a devious streak.

"What?" she said.

"I beg your pardon?"

"You're looking at me."

"You're sitting next to me. Where else am I to look?"

"Yes, but you were—" Her lips pressed together. "Never mind."

He felt himself smile, but waited until after the footmen had removed the soup bowls before saying, "You were trying to figure out how to break a bone, weren't you?"

Georgie's eyes lit with surprise. "How did you—"

"Oh, please, it was obvious."

"What are the two of you talking about?" Nicholas's mother trilled.

He gave her a look. He knew that tone. He'd heard it employed with his older siblings. And Georgie's older siblings.

His mother was playing matchmaker, but she was also trying to avoid the *appearance* of playing matchmaker. Trying, but failing, because she was too curious to hold her tongue when she thought she saw something happening. Because what if she could intervene and make things better?

He knew his mother. He knew his mother well.

"We're talking about how to break bones," Georgie said plainly.

Nicholas didn't bother to hide his grin.

"Oh." His mother looked disappointed. And perhaps a bit queasy.

"I recommend falling from a tree," Billie said. "Twice if you can manage it."

"But not at the same time," her mother said.

Billie turned to her with some exasperation. "How would one fall from two trees at the same time?"

"If it can be done, I have every confidence that you will be the one to figure out how."

"Such faith in your eldest daughter," Billie said in a dry voice. "It is positively uplifting."

Conversation slowed when the next course was

served—rack of lamb with mint jelly, herbed potatoes and French beans with butter, and duck terrine with *courgettes.*

Georgie turned to Nicholas with a look of pure camaraderie. "Toasted cheese *and* rack of lamb. We are outdoing ourselves tonight."

Nicholas nearly groaned with pleasure at the first bite. "I can't remember the last time I had such a good meal."

"Is Scottish food so very dreadful?"

"The Scottish food in my rooming house is."

"Oh," she said. "I'm so sorry."

"Did you think I traveled with a chef?"

"No, of course not. I thought—well, to be honest, I don't think I did think about it."

He shrugged. He would have been surprised if she had.

She cut her meat slowly, then used her knife to add a bit of jelly. But she had a faraway look in her eyes and did not bring the food to her mouth. "I can't stop thinking about it," she said.

His own fork paused about two inches above his plate. "My gustatorial deprivations?"

"No, of course not. That's just poor planning on your part. I'm still stuck on the broken bones."

"Why does this not surprise me?"

"As you said, one can't just open a book in the pursuit of medical inquiry."

"We do, actually, for much of it."

"Yes, but there must come a point when practical knowledge is required. As you also said, you can't go around breaking people's arms. You have to wait for it to happen."

"True, but there is rarely a shortage of ill and injured patients."

She seemed somewhat impatient with this explanation. "But what if they are not ill or injured in the way you *need*?"

"Will I regret it later if I ask what you mean by that?"

She waved off his (mostly) rhetorical question, and said, "It's such an interesting ethical dilemma."

"You've lost me."

"What if you *could* break someone's bones?"

"Georg—"

She cut him off. "For the pursuit of knowledge. What if you offered to pay?"

"Pay someone to have his bones broken?"

She nodded.

"That's inhumane."

"Is it?"

"Certainly unethical."

"Only if you do not have their consent."

"You can't ask someone permission to break their arm."

"Can't you?" She cocked her head to the side. "Consider this example. Imagine that I am a widow. I don't have very much money. In fact, I have almost none. And I have three children to support."

"Your life has turned very grim indeed," Nicholas murmured.

"I'm trying to make a point," she said, visibly peeved.

"My apologies."

She waited a beat, presumably to be sure he wasn't going to interrupt again, then said, "If a doctor offered me enough money to break my arm and then set it, I would do it."

Nicholas shook his head. "That's madness."

"Is it? I'm a penniless widow with three hungry children. It sounds to me as if my only other option is prostitution. Frankly, I'd rather have my arm broken." She frowned. "Although it would make it more difficult to care for my children."

Nicholas set down his fork. "Prostitution is *not* your only other option."

"What are you talking about *now*?" his mother

asked. She looked very concerned, and Nicholas suspected she'd heard the part of the conversation that included the word *prostitution*.

"Still on the broken bones!" Georgie said with a sunny smile.

Which slid right into a steely stare when she turned back to him. "It's easy for you to say that prostitution is not my only option. *You* have an education."

"So do you."

She snorted. "From my governess. It does not compare, and frankly I'm insulted that you'd even imply that it did." She stabbed a potato with enough force that Nicholas winced in sympathy.

"I beg your pardon," he said politely.

She waved this off, leaving him to wonder if she found this, too, to be mostly rhetorical.

"It doesn't matter, anyway," she said, "because we are talking about hypothetical me, not real me. Hypothetical me does not have the support of a loving and wealthy family."

"All right then." He could play along. "Hypothetical you has three children. Are they old enough to work?"

"Not old enough to earn a decent wage. Unless I send them into the coal mines, and frankly, that seems worse for their health than a broken bone."

"What *are* you talking about?" Edmund asked.

Nicholas ignored him. "Wait, so are you now saying you want me to break your children's bones?"

"Of course not. Not if you can break mine instead."

"This is precisely my point. You would never allow me to do such a thing if you were not being paid."

"I'm not stupid."

"Just desperate."

Something flashed in her eyes, something pained. Wounded.

"*Hypothetical* you is desperate," he said softly.

She swallowed. "It isn't pleasant to be without choices."

"No." He brought his napkin to his lips. He needed a moment. He wasn't sure what they were talking about any longer, or even if they were talking about the same thing.

"This is why you cannot pay someone to do something like this," he said quietly. "Consent can be coerced. Hypothetical you says she agrees to have her arm broken in exchange for money to feed her children. But is that really consent if your only other choice is the sale of your body?"

"Some would say that it's the sale of my body either way."

"Touché," he admitted.

"I understand your point," Georgie said. "I even

agree with it a little. There are some things in life that ought not be for sale. But on the other hand, who am I to decide that for another human being? It is easy for me to condemn a decision I would not make, but is it fair?"

"Are you still talking about broken bones?" Violet asked. "Because you look very serious."

"Our conversation has taken a turn for the philosophical," Georgie told her.

"And the morbid," Nicholas added.

"We can't have that." Violet nudged her husband. "They need more wine, don't you think?"

"Absolutely." Edmund nodded to a footman, who immediately refilled their glasses.

Not that there was much to refill, Nicholas noted. He and Georgie were both staggeringly sober.

"I am not sure," he said slowly, and in a tone only Georgie could hear, "if we have the right to condemn people for the decisions they make if we ourselves are never forced with a similar choice."

"Exactly."

He was quiet for a moment. "This *has* taken a turn for the philosophical."

"And are we in agreement?"

"Only in that there is probably no answer."

She nodded.

"Now the two of you look like you're going to *cry*," Violet protested.

Georgiana recovered first. "Philosophy does that to me."

"I concur," Edmund said. "My least favorite subject by far."

"You always did well in it, though," Nicholas said.

Edmund grinned. "That's because I can talk my way out of almost anything."

Everyone rolled their eyes at that. It was the absolute truth.

"I think baby Colin takes after you in that way," Georgie said.

"He's four months old," Edmund said with a laugh. "He can't even speak."

"There's something in the way he looks at me," Georgie said. "Mark my words. That boy is going to be a charmer."

"If he doesn't explode first," Violet said. "I swear, all that baby does is eat. It is unnatural."

"What are you talking about *now*?" Lady Manston asked, clearly exasperated by a seating arrangement that kept leaving her just barely out of earshot.

"Exploding babies," Georgie said.

Nicholas nearly spit his food across the table.

"Oh." His mother placed a hand over her heart. "Oh my."

He started to laugh.

"One baby specifically," Georgie said, elegantly flipping her wrist with perfect sardonic punctuation. "We would never talk about exploding babies in the *general* sense."

Nicholas started to laugh so hard it hurt.

And Georgie . . . Oh, she was in fine form. She didn't even crack a smile as she leaned ever so slightly in his direction and murmured, "That would be tasteless."

His laughter turned silent, the kind that shook the room.

"I don't see what's so funny," his mother said.

Which nearly made him fall out of his chair.

"Do you need to excuse yourself," Georgie said behind her hand. "Because I know when *I* laugh that hard . . ."

"I'm fine," he gasped. In fact, he was better than fine. His ribs were sore, and it felt *good*.

Georgie turned to answer a question her sister had asked her—presumably something about why Nicholas was acting like a loon. He took the moment to catch his breath and also to think about what had just happened.

He'd forgotten, for a moment, why he was here.

He'd forgotten that his father had summoned him home, all but ordered him to marry a girl he'd known all his life and never shown a whit of romantic interest in.

To be fair, she'd never displayed a whit in his direction, either.

But that hadn't mattered. Not while he was laughing so hard he probably *should* have taken Georgie's advice and excused himself. Now all he could think was—*this wasn't bad at all.*

Maybe he *could* marry her. It might not be love, but if this was what life with Georgie would be like, it was a damn sight better than most people had.

She laughed at something Billie had said, and his gaze dropped to her mouth. She was looking at her sister, but she was still enough in profile that he could see the shape of it, the fullness and curve of her lower lip.

What would it be like to kiss her?

He had not kissed many women. He'd usually chosen to study while his contemporaries caroused, and the one man—Edmund—with whom he might have gotten drunk and made foolish decisions had married young. No sowing of wild oats there.

Then he'd started his medical studies, and if ever there was a hard and fast lesson on why a man should keep himself in check, that was it. He'd told Georgie that there was rarely a shortage of illness, and that was true. He'd seen enough syphilis to curdle his brain.

He'd seen how syphilis curdled other men's brains.

So no, he did not have a wide range of sexual experience.

But he had thought about it.

He'd imagined all the foolish decisions he could have made, the things he might have done if he'd met the right woman. Usually the women in his fantasies were nameless, maybe even faceless, but sometimes they were real. A finely dressed lady he'd passed on the street. The woman serving ale at a public house.

But never, *never* Georgiana Bridgerton.

Until now.

Chapter 6

Crake House, later that night

By any standard, Nicholas's first non-platonic thoughts about Georgiana Bridgerton were disconcerting.

Almost to the point of bewilderment.

She was certainly pretty—he'd never have said otherwise if asked—but he'd also never really looked at her beyond her just being . . . her.

She was Georgiana Bridgerton, and she had blue eyes like her mother and gingery hair like no one else in her family. And that was the extent of what he'd noticed.

Wait. No. Her teeth were straight. He supposed he'd noticed that. She was of average height. He hadn't *really* noticed that, but if someone had asked him how tall she was, he could have made a reasonably decent estimation.

But then they had joked about exploding babies and she'd done that little twist with her hand. His gaze had fixed inexplicably on her wrist.

Her *wrist.*

He had been laughing, and looking at her, and she'd done that thing . . . A curve, a flip, a sweeping gesture—whatever it was that women did with tiny movements that spoke volumes and seemed to envelop them in a fine mist of Pretty. It was an innocent enough move, clearly executed with no coy forethought, simply done to punctuate her dry humor.

Simple, innocent.

And if his father had not suggested they marry, Nicholas was sure he'd never have looked at the inside of Georgie's wrist, much less *noticed* it.

But then he'd moved his gaze from her wrist to her face.

And he'd thought about kissing her.

Georgie.

Georgie.

He couldn't kiss Georgie. It would be like kissing his sister.

"Sister? No," he said to the nighttime air. He was sitting by his open bedchamber window, staring up at stars he could not see.

It was a cloudy night. The air was turbulent.

Georgie was not his sister. Of that he was certain. The rest of it, though . . .

Thinking about exploding babies felt a whole lot safer than thinking about Georgie's wrist. Or to be more precise, thinking about laughing about the ludicrousness of exploding babies felt safer than thinking about turning Georgie's wrist upward and pressing his lips to it.

Could he kiss her? He twisted one of his own hands palm up—or rather, fist up; he wasn't feeling terribly relaxed—and stared down at the inside of his own wrist.

Yes. Of course he *could*. But did he want to?

He looked into the night. Could he spend day after day and year after year with her? At her table, in her bed? Nothing in the stillness of the night assured him that this was anything but an impossible question, and yet again he felt the acuteness of time. Not of the seconds ticking but the hours, the days that led to her more permanent ruin.

He could not tarry much longer. His father spoke of Georgie's ghoulish schedule, of the husband she needed to find if he did not step forward for the position. But Nicholas, too, had a calendar he must keep. Even if he set out for Scotland the very next day, he'd have been away nearly a month. A month of classes, of missed exams. By his estimation, he could stay in Kent only a few days more—maybe a week—before he would fall too hopelessly behind to make up the material.

He needed to make a decision.

He looked at his bed. He could not picture her there.

Not yet, the night seemed to whisper.

Her profile and lips and her wrist—it all flashed in his brain. But when he tried to hold on to them, to keep these images still and in focus, it was the laughter he felt.

With his gaze still on the bed he couldn't picture her in he murmured, "I just don't know."

A breeze cooled his skin and he shivered.

Yes, you do.

He stood, giving his back to the night. It was time for bed.

Remarkably, he slept.

By morning he had accepted his fate.

Which sounded a lot more dramatic than it actually was. But given the events of the past twenty-four hours, he rather thought he'd earned a touch of self-serving hyperbole.

He'd borrowed his brother's valet for a good shave, made himself eat a hearty breakfast, and sent a footman to the stables with a request to ready a horse. He would go to Aubrey Hall, find Georgiana, and ask her to be his wife.

It wasn't his fault that Georgie had found herself in such dire straits. But it wasn't her fault, either, and he honestly wasn't sure he could look at his own face in the mirror knowing he'd abandoned her to an uncertain future.

It was actually rather simple: He had the means to make things right. He could save her. Wasn't that what he'd devoted his life to? Saving people? Surely such benevolence ought to start at home. Or in this case, at the rather stately home three miles down the road.

When he reached Aubrey Hall, however, he was informed by one of the footmen that Georgiana was not in; she had taken her nephews out for a walk. Anthony and Benedict Bridgerton did not strike Nicholas as the most romantic of props for a proposal of marriage, but then again, this would not be a particularly romantic proposal.

He could try, he supposed, but she'd see through that in a heartbeat. She knew he didn't love her. And her circumstances being what they were, she'd know exactly why he was proposing.

No one seemed to know exactly where Georgie and the boys had gone off to, but the lake seemed the most obvious spot. The bank was wide and only slightly sloped, perfect for an adult who wished to sit comfortably on a blanket while keeping an eye on two boys running about like berserker knights. The gentle incline also meant it was almost impossible to fall in.

Or if not impossible, then at least highly unlikely. Nothing was impossible when young children were determined to get wet, but if one wanted to actually dunk one's head beneath the surface, it required some forethought.

You had to climb a tree, Nicholas recalled. Climb a tree and crawl out along a horizontal limb until you were far enough out and then—*Plop!* That was how you did it.

But hopefully Anthony and Benedict had not figured this out yet.

He headed across the lawn, taking his time as he pondered his imminent task. Should he just come out and ask her? Should he give some sort of lead-in? Talk about how they'd known each other for so long, they'd always been friends, et cetera, et cetera.

Frankly, he thought that sounded like rubbish, and he suspected Georgie would, too, but it did seem like a man ought to say *something* before blurting out, "Will you marry me?"

He supposed he'd have to figure it out as he went along. It wasn't his style to do so; he'd always been the sort of student who studied twice as much as he needed to. But there was no preparation for this examination. There was only a question, and an answer, and the answer wasn't even his to give.

Nicholas kicked a pebble along the well-worn path that led to the lake as he made his way up the slope. He wasn't sure where he'd look next if Georgie wasn't there, but sure enough, when he reached the crest of the hill, he saw the three of them by the water's edge.

By all appearances, they'd settled in for a long spell in the breezy morning sunshine. Georgie sat on a dark blue blanket next to a hamper of food and what appeared to be a sketchbook. The two boys squealed and chased each other back and forth along the narrow strip of dirt that separated the water and the grass. It was a charming scene.

"Georgie!" he called out as he approached.

She turned and smiled. "Oh, Nicholas. Good morning. What brings you this way?"

"I came to see you, actually."

"Me?" She looked a little surprised, but honestly more amused than anything else. "Poor you."

"Poor me?"

She motioned to the boys with her hand and the hamper with her head. "There have got to be more exciting ways to spend your morning."

"Oh, I don't know. My other option involves my mother, her embroidery, and six different colors of thread."

"Six you say?"

"Almost a rainbow."

One side of her mouth made a wry curve. "I tell you this in all honesty, Nicholas. I have never felt so valued."

He choked out a laugh as he sat down beside her, stretching his legs straight and long in front of him. It was remarkable how at ease he felt now that he'd made up his mind to marry her. All of the angst and awkwardness of the previous night was gone, replaced with what had always been there—the familiarity and ease of lifelong friendship.

"Were you sketching?" he asked.

"Jabbing blindly with pencil at paper is more like it," she said. "I'm a terrible artist."

There were several loose sheets of paper tucked under the sketchbook, and Nicholas sifted through these, stopping on one of a bird in a tree. It was done in pencil, but somehow Nicholas could tell that it was a red-breasted robin, and not just from the shape of it. "I like this one," he said.

She rolled her eyes. "Benedict drew that."

"Oh. Sorry."

She gave a wave, clearly unperturbed by her own lack of talent.

"It's really quite good." Nicholas gave it a closer inspection. "*How* old is he?"

"Just five."

Nicholas felt his eyebrows rise. "That's . . . remarkable."

"I know. The boy has talent, although I think right now he's much more interested in torturing his brother."

Nicholas watched the two boys for a moment. Anthony was holding Benedict upside down by his ankles.

"Or trying to avoid being tortured," Georgie said.

"If that's the case, he's not doing a very good job of it."

"No," Georgie agreed. "Alas, the plight of the younger sibling."

"We would both know, wouldn't we?"

She nodded in absent agreement, keeping her eyes on her nephews, presumably to make sure they weren't about to kill each other. "Actually . . ." she began.

He waited a moment, then prompted, "Actually . . . ?"

She looked over at him with a wry smile. "We're both a little like onlys, aren't we?"

"Onlys?"

"You've how many years between you and Andrew?

Eight? Nine? Did he ever actually bother with you when you were growing up? Pay you any attention?"

Nicholas thought about that. Most of the time his older siblings had ignored him. Or more likely, simply forgotten his existence. "Not really, no."

"If you asked him," Georgie went on, "I'd wager he'd say he felt more like a youngest child than a middle one." She turned, looking at Nicholas over her shoulder. "Which makes *you* an only."

She had a point, but he hardly saw how it applied to her. She was one year younger than Edmund and one year older than Hugo, a middle child if he'd ever seen one. "And how does this work for you?" he asked.

"Oh, I'm entirely different," she said with an offhand wave. "It was because I was always so sick. No one ever treated me like a sibling."

"That's not true."

"Oh, please. My mother was convinced I would die if she let me play outside."

"That seems a little extreme."

"Well, yes, I agree, but that's what she thought, and there was hardly a way to convince her otherwise. I mean, I suppose I could go outside and *not* die, but that doesn't prove much." She shaded her eyes and frowned. "Not so close to the water, Benedict!"

Benedict pouted, but he stepped back.

"Speaking of going outside and not dying," Nicholas murmured.

"He can swim," Georgie said, "but I'm not sure how well."

Nicholas thought back to his childhood, back to all the times he and Edmund had swum in this lake. Georgie had never joined them. Not once. Come to think of it, he couldn't recall ever seeing her out of doors. Not in childhood, at least. She was always inside, propped up on a sofa with a book, or sitting on the floor setting up a tableau with her dolls.

"How do you feel now?" he asked. She did not look unhealthy. Her color was fine, and she did not seem to lack energy.

She shrugged. "I've mostly grown out of it."

"Were you really that ill?" Nicholas asked. Because in all honesty he couldn't recall the details. It seemed odd now, given his choice of profession, but he remembered almost nothing about Georgie's being sick as a child, except that she was. "You used to have trouble breathing, right?"

She nodded. "But not all the time. Most of the time I was fine. But sometimes . . ." She turned, looking at him more squarely. "Have you ever had difficulty catching your breath?"

"Of course."

"Imagine that, except that it doesn't get better. That's what would happen to me."

"And now?"

"I can't remember the last time it happened. Several years, at least."

"Did you ever see a doctor about it?"

She gave him a look. "What sort of question is that? You know my mother. I saw so many doctors we could have opened up a medical school here in Kent."

He gave her a lopsided smile. "That would have made my studies considerably more convenient."

"Indeed," she said with a laugh. "I'm surprised your parents let you go off to Edinburgh. It's so far away."

"It's not up to them to let me or not let me," he replied, bristling at the remark. "And at any rate, I'm sure it seemed positively local after Edward off and went missing in the Colonies."

Nicholas had been at Eton when his brother had served in the army, first as a lieutenant and then as a captain in the 52nd Regiment. He had been missing and presumed dead for many months before finally returning home.

"True," Georgie said. "I suppose that is a convenience of having older siblings. They do ease the way."

He frowned.

"Oh, not for me," she said. "Stop breathing just once

in front of your parents and it doesn't matter if your sister broke both her arms and accidentally set someone on fire. My mother didn't take her eyes off me for three years straight."

Nicholas leaned in. He'd heard the story many times but never with satisfactory detail. "Did Billie *really* set someone on fire?"

Georgie laughed with delight. "Oh, Nicholas, I adore that *that's* what you want to know more about."

"It might be the only thing that could have drawn my attention away from the part about your not breathing."

"Well, you *are* a doctor. One would hope you'd find the part about not breathing interesting."

"Almost a doctor," he corrected. "I won't be finished for another year. Fourteen months, actually."

Georgie acknowledged this with a nod, then said, "I'm *told* she didn't do it on purpose, but witnesses are few."

"Suspicious indeed."

She chuckled at that. "Actually, I believe her account. It happened just before she was presented to the queen. Have you seen the sort of dresses ladies must wear to be presented? Hoops out to here." She stretched her arm out as far as it went. "Farther, actually. You can't reach the end of your skirts. You can't walk through doorways without turning sideways, and even then it's a close thing. It's ludicrous."

"What did she do, knock over a candelabra?"

Georgie nodded. "But the girl she set on fire was also wearing court dress. The candle fell onto the other girl's hoop, which was so far from her body that she did not immediately realize she'd been set aflame."

"Dear God."

"Oh, how I *wish* I'd seen it."

"Rather bloodthirsty, aren't you?"

"You have no idea," she muttered.

While Nicholas was pondering what that might mean, she flopped onto her back and said, "Keep an eye on them, would you?"

"Are you planning to take a nap?" he asked, somewhat amused.

"No," she said contentedly. "Just enjoying the sun on my face. Don't tell my mother. She fears freckles. Says I'm more likely to get them because of my hair."

Her hair did mark her as a bit of a changeling in the Bridgerton clan. Everyone else he'd met—cousins included—had brown hair, generally somewhere between chestnut and dark. But Georgie was most definitely a redhead. Not that bright orange that stuck out like a beacon, but rather something soft and delicate. People called it strawberry blond, but Nicholas had never liked that term. It didn't seem at all accurate, and as he stole a glance at her basking in the sun, he marveled at how the light seemed to reflect off each individual strand.

She sighed contentedly. "Have they killed each other?"

Nicholas turned back to watch the boys, which was what he was supposed to be doing. "Not yet."

"Good. It got quiet there for a moment." Her expression turned suspicious, even as she lay there with her eyes closed. "Too quiet."

"They're just running back and forth," Nicholas said. "I'm trying to figure out if it's a game, and if so, if it has rules."

"There are definitely rules," Georgie said. "Benedict tried to explain it, but I'm not sure he was speaking English."

"I bet I could figure it out."

She opened one eye to give him a dubious look.

"I was a seven-year-old boy once, you know."

"Obviously."

"Get up," he said, nudging her again. "Watch Anthony. See how he's picking up a rock?"

Georgie sat up instantly. "Anthony Bridgerton, do not throw that at your brother!" she yelled.

Anthony ground to a halt, planting indignant hands on his hips. "I wasn't going to!"

"Oh, he was going to," Georgie said.

"I don't think he was," Nicholas said thoughtfully. "See, look. He's making a pile over there."

Georgie frowned as she craned her neck. "So he is. What's he building, a cairn?"

"Nothing so organized, I assure you. But . . . Watch Benedict now. *He's* trying to get the rocks from Anthony's pile—"

"Oh, that's not going to happen," Georgie cut in. "Anthony has six inches on him. And that boy is strong."

"He'll have to be sneaky," Nicholas agreed.

They watched as Benedict charged his older brother with all the finesse of a wild boar.

Georgie chuckled. "Although brute force is always an option."

"Always an option," Nicholas agreed.

Anthony charged back.

"But not a wise one," Georgie said.

"No."

She frowned as they watched the boys go down in a tangle of limbs. "Are we concerned?"

"It does look as if it might end badly."

"But will there be blood? That's really all I need to know."

Nicholas took a more assessing look. The boys were making an astonishing amount of noise, but mostly they were rolling around like wet puppies. "Not above the skin."

She shot him a look. "What does *that* mean?"

"That's all a bruise is, you know. Bleeding under the skin."

"Huh." She sounded vaguely intrigued. "I suppose that's right. I hadn't really thought about it."

"Well, there you go. We call it an ecchymosis."

"You can't just call it a bruise?"

"Of course not. Then anyone would think they can be a doctor."

He grinned when she batted him on the shoulder, then said, "But to answer your question the way you intended it, I don't *think* there will be blood, but they may yet surprise me."

Benedict made a sound that was not quite a shriek. But it was close. Very close.

"Would blood really be that surprising?" Georgie asked.

Anthony growled, and Nicholas began to reassess. "In what quantities?"

"Quantities that would either worry their parents or reveal me to be a bad monitor of small children."

"Is this an either/or?"

She shoved him with her elbow.

He grinned. "Sorry, no. I don't think so. Based

upon my copious experience as a former seven-year-old boy."

"It's odd how you say that," she mused, turning away from him to open the hamper.

"What do you mean?"

" 'My copious experience as a seven-year-old boy,' " she mimicked. "Such a dry tone you used there. As if you *didn't* have copious experience."

"Well, it *was* a long time ago."

She shook her head and pulled out a wedge of cheese. "Frankly, I'm amazed any of you reached adulthood."

"So am I," he said with all honesty. "So am I. Although it must be said, it was your sister who broke two arms."

She laughed at that, and they sat in companionable silence, taking turns breaking off chunks of cheese. "I have bread, too," Georgie told him. She peered into the hamper. "And jam."

"Strawberry?"

"Raspberry."

He sniffed disdainfully. "Then I'm not interested."

She gave him a look, then sputtered with laughter. "What does that mean?"

He grinned again, rather enjoying the feel of it on his face. "I have no idea."

He was comfortable with her. He could make the sort of stupid comments that were only a little bit funny and made no sense. The kind one made when one didn't have to weigh every word and worry about judgment or scorn.

That's how it had always been with Georgie—well, except for the night before. And even that had turned out fine in the end.

There were worse fates than marrying one's friend.

He propped himself into a more upright position, pushing slightly past her to peer into the hamper. "I'd love some jam. Whatever the flavor."

"Bread?" she asked.

"We're not savages."

She raised a brow. "Speak for yourself."

"You eat jam straight from the jar?"

"You don't?"

He gave her a sideways glance. "Raspberry or strawberry?"

She threw a chunk of cheese at him.

He laughed and popped it in his mouth. "Fine, yes, I admit it. I've eaten jam straight from the jar. But I used a spoon."

"So proper, you are. Next you'll be telling me you've never drunk whiskey straight from a bottle."

"I haven't."

"Oh, there's no way," she scoffed. "I've seen you and Edmund after a night out at the tavern."

"Where we drank from mugs and glasses," he said pointedly. "Gad, Georgie, do you know what an entire bottle of whiskey would do to a man?"

She shook her head. "I've never had whiskey."

"How can that be?" he asked. It would be highly unusual for a well-bred lady such as Georgiana to drink whiskey on a regular basis, but surely somewhere along the way she'd had a sip.

Georgie started spreading jam on a slice of bread. "Well, I don't live in Scotland, for one thing."

"I suppose that would make it difficult. Your father doesn't drink it?"

She shook her head. "Not that I'm aware."

Nicholas shrugged. Whiskey was so ubiquitous in Edinburgh he'd forgotten that people didn't drink much of it in England, especially this far south.

Georgie handed him a slice of bread and got to work preparing one for herself. "Here you go."

"Aunt Georgie!"

They both looked up. Anthony was sidling over, one hand behind his back.

"Aunt Georgie, do you like worms?"

"I adore them!" She looked over at Nicholas. "I

hate them." And then back at the boys: "The more the better!"

Anthony conferred with his younger brother. They both looked disappointed.

"Clever girl," Nicholas said.

"At least more clever than a seven-year-old."

They watched as the two boys surreptitiously dropped a few worms on the ground. "Lofty goals," Nicholas murmured.

She munched her bread and jam. "You do know how to flatter a lady."

"Right," he said, clearing his throat. It seemed as good an opening as any. "Speaking of which . . ."

She gave him an amused glance. "Speaking of flattering me?"

"*No.*" Good God. This was not going well and he hadn't even started.

Her eyes turned to mischief. "So you *don't* want to flatter me."

"No. Georgie . . ."

"My apologies. I couldn't resist." She set her bread carefully down on a napkin. "What was it you needed?"

What was it he *needed*? He needed to go back to Edinburgh and resume his life. But instead he was here, about to propose a marriage of—he assumed— convenience.

Not *his* convenience.

Not hers, either. Not really. Nothing about her life had been convenient lately.

"Sorry," he muttered. "I wanted to talk to you, actually. It's why I came out here this morning."

"Not for the worms?" she asked cheekily.

This, more than anything, cemented his belief that she had no idea what was afoot.

He cleared his throat.

"Tea?"

"What?"

She picked up a flask he had not noticed. "Would you like some tea? It's cold by now, but it will take care of your throat."

"No. Thank you. It's not that."

She shrugged and took a sip. "I swear by it."

"Right. Georgie. I really do need to ask you something."

She blinked, regarding him with an expectant expression.

"When I came down from Edinburgh it was, as I told you, because my father wished to consult with me about something. But—"

"Oh, sorry, hold on one moment," she said before turning toward the lake and yelling, "Anthony, stop that this minute!"

Anthony, who was sitting rather cheerfully on his brother's head, said, "Do I have to?"

"Yes!" Georgie looked for a moment as if she might get up to enforce her will, but Anthony finally rolled off his brother and went back to poking holes in the dirt with a stick.

Georgie rolled her eyes before returning her attention to Nicholas. "Sorry. You were saying . . ."

"I have no bloody idea," he muttered.

Her expression was somewhere between perplexed and amused.

"No," he said. "That's not true. I do know what I meant to say."

But he didn't say it.

"Nicholas?"

In the end, he blurted it out, just like he'd told himself not to do.

"Will you marry me?"

Chapter 7

"I'm sorry," Georgiana said slowly. "I thought you just asked me to marry you."

Nicholas's mouth moved in an odd manner, as if he didn't quite understand what she'd said. "I did."

She blinked. "That's not funny, Nicholas."

"It wasn't meant to be funny. It was meant to be a proposal of marriage."

She stared at him. He didn't *look* as if he'd been struck by a temporary bout of insanity. "But *why*?"

Now he was looking at her as if *she* had been the one struck by a temporary bout of insanity. "Why do you think?"

"Oh, I don't know. Most of the time marriage is proposed because two human beings have fallen in love with one another, but since we both know *that* isn't true . . ."

Nicholas let out an impatient snort. "First of all, you know damn well that most of the time the two human beings are not in love, and—"

"*This* human being would like to be," she snapped.

"So would *this* human being," he snapped right back, "but alas, we don't always get what we want."

Georgie felt herself nod. It was all beginning to make sense. "So," she said, "you're asking out of pity."

"Friendship."

"Pity," she corrected. Because that's what it was. That's all it could be. A man didn't abandon his studies and travel for ten days just to make a kind gesture to a friend.

He didn't love her. They both knew that.

And then she realized. "Oh my God," she said with a horrified gasp. "This is why you came down from Scotland. It was because of me."

He did not meet her eyes.

"How did you even know what had happened to me?" she asked. Had the gossip reached Scotland? How far would she need to travel to escape it? North America? Brazil?

"My father," Nicholas said.

"Your father?" she choked out. "Your father told you? What, in a letter? The Earl of Manston has nothing better to put in a letter to his youngest son than the tale of my *ruin?*"

"Georgie, it wasn't like that. I didn't even know the details until yesterday."

"So then what did he say?"

But she knew. She knew before Nicholas could reply, and then it became clear that he wasn't going to reply. Because he was embarrassed. And that made her furious because he had no right to feel embarrassed. He didn't get to blush and look at his feet when he had rained such complete mortification down on her. If he was going to do this to her, then damn him he had to take it like a stoic and watch.

She couldn't stay still any longer. She jumped to her feet and began pacing back and forth, hugging her arms to her body. Tight . . . so tightly, as if she could hold her emotions inside with brute force.

"Oh no oh no oh no oh no," she said to herself. Was this what her life had come to? Men were being begged to marry her?

Or bribed? Was Nicholas being *bribed* to ask for her hand? Had her dowry been doubled to sweeten the pot?

Her parents—they had promised they wouldn't force

her to marry Freddie Oakes, but they'd also made it clear they didn't want her to choose the life of a spinster.

Had *they* asked Lord Manston to call Nicholas down from school? Did *everyone* know? Were they all plotting behind her back?

"Georgie, stop." Nicholas grasped her arm, but she shook him off, casting a quick glance toward the lake to make sure Anthony and Benedict weren't watching.

"It wasn't even your idea, was it?" she whispered hotly. "Your father summoned you."

He looked away. The aggravating little weasel, he couldn't even meet her eyes.

"He asked you to ask me," Georgie said with growing horror. Her hands covered her face. It had been bad enough that Freddie Oakes had tried to haul her off to Gretna Green, but this—this—

It was the pity. That was what she could not bear.

She had not done anything wrong.

She should not be pitied. She should be admired. A man had kidnapped her. Kidnapped her! And she'd got away.

Why wasn't that something to celebrate?

There should be parties in her honor. A gala parade. Look at the brave and intrepid Georgiana Bridgerton! She fought for her freedom and won!

When *men* did that entire countries were created.

"Georgie," Nicholas said, and his voice was awful. Condescending and superior and all those things men were when they thought they were dealing with a hysterical female.

"Georgie," he said again, and she realized that actually his voice wasn't any of those things. But she didn't care. Nicholas Rokesby had known her his entire life. He didn't want to marry her. He felt *sorry* for her.

Then she nearly choked on her thoughts. Because she knew Lord Manston. He was her godfather, her own father's closest friend. And she'd seen him with his sons often enough to know exactly how the conversation must have gone.

He had not *asked* Nicholas to marry her.

She forced herself to look at him. "Your father ordered you to marry me, didn't he?"

"No," he said, but she could tell he was lying. He'd never been a good liar. She couldn't imagine why his father thought he could fake his way through a proposal of marriage.

Honestly, he was the *worst*.

"He can't order me to marry you," Nicholas said somewhat stiffly. "I'm a grown man."

She scoffed. "Some grown man. Your father sent for you and you came trotting down like a good little boy."

"Stop it," he snapped.

"Don't pretend any of this is your idea. You are doing nothing but your father's bidding."

"I am doing you a favor!"

Georgie gasped.

"I didn't mean it that way," Nicholas said quickly.

"Oh, I know how you meant it."

"Georgie—"

"Consider this a refusal," she said, each word a little snip of fury.

"You're saying no." He didn't ask it like a question. It was more of a statement of disbelief.

"Of course I'm saying no. How can you possibly think I would accept such an offer?"

"Because it would be the reasonable thing to do."

"*Because it would be the reasonable thing to do,*" she scoffed. "Were you laughing at me?"

He grabbed her arm. "You know that we weren't."

"I can't believe this," she ground out, yanking herself from his grasp. "Do you understand— No, you couldn't possibly understand what it feels like to be so utterly without choices."

"You think not?"

"Oh, you think this"—she waved her arm wildly—"this counts as having no choice? Being ordered to marry me? At least you get to feel good about yourself."

"I feel splendid right now, let me tell you."

"You get to call yourself a hero, saving poor little ruined Georgiana Bridgerton. Whereas I—I get to decide between the man who ruined me and a man who pities me."

"I don't pity you."

"But you don't love me."

He looked ready to tear his hair out. "Do you want me to?"

"No!"

"Then for the love of God, Georgie, what is the problem? I'm trying to help."

She crossed her arms. "I am not a charity. I don't want to be your *good works*."

"Do you think I wanted to sacrifice my life for you?"

Oh, that stung.

"I didn't mean it that way," Nicholas said quickly.

Her brows rose. "That's the second time you've had to make that statement in the past few minutes."

He cursed under his breath, and she was shallow enough that she took pleasure in his discomfort.

"I hereby release you from all obligation," she said in her most annoyingly supercilious voice. "You asked. I said no. You have done your duty."

"It is not my duty," he bit off. "It is my choice."

"Even better. That means you will respect *my* choice. To say no."

He took a breath. "You are not thinking clearly."

"I'm not *thinking clearly*?" God help a man who told a woman she was not thinking clearly. Freddie Oakes had said the same thing in the carriage heading north to Gretna Green. If Georgie heard it one more time, she wasn't sure she could answer to the consequences.

"Keep your voice down," Nicholas hissed. He jerked his head toward Anthony and Benedict, who had halted their games and were now looking their way.

"Did you find more worms?" Georgie called out. She had no idea how she managed to sound so cheerful. She didn't sound so cheerful when she *was* cheerful.

"No," Anthony said, but he looked suspicious. "They're not fun if they don't bother anyone."

"Right, well, carry on then." She smiled so broadly her cheeks hurt.

"You're going to injure yourself," Nicholas muttered.

"Shut up and smile so they stop looking at us."

"You look deranged."

"I feel deranged," she practically hissed. "Which should worry *you*."

He held up his hands and took a step back, a motion so patronizing she nearly went for his throat.

"Aunt Georgie, why do you look like you're going to strike Uncle Nicholas?"

Georgie froze, only then realizing she'd made a fist. "I'm not going to strike anyone," she said to Benedict, who was regarding her with undisguised curiosity. "And he's not your uncle."

"He's not?" Benedict looked from Nicholas to Georgie and back again. He opened his mouth, closed it, and then turned back to Georgie, this time with a slightly suspicious expression. "Are you sure?"

Georgie planted one of her hands on her chest. This had to be some sort of elaborate practical joke. Even Shakespeare could not have conceived of such a farce.

"Papa says we should call him Uncle Nicholas," Benedict said, his little nose wrinkling. "I know Mummy told us we're to mind you this morning, but I can't go against my father."

"Of course not," Georgie said.

Meanwhile, Nicholas was standing off to the side, doing a terrible job at hiding his amusement.

"You must do as your father says," she said to Benedict.

He nodded. "I think Uncle Nicholas should be my uncle."

Georgie wanted to scream. Even the children were conspiring against her.

"Uncle George is Uncle Nicholas's brother," Benedict explained, "so it only makes sense that he's our uncle too."

"Uncle George is your uncle because he is married to Aunt Billie," Georgie explained. "And Aunt Billie is your aunt because she is your father's older sister."

Benedict stared up at her with huge, unblinking eyes. "I know."

"A person isn't your uncle just because his brother is."

Benedict considered this for about half a second. "But a person *can* be your uncle if his brother is."

"It's like squares and rectangles," Anthony interjected, with all the authority of an oldest child. "All squares are rectangles, but not all rectangles are squares."

Benedict scratched his head. "What about circles?"

"What *about* circles?" Anthony countered.

Benedict looked up. "Aunt Georgie?"

She shook her head. *This*, she could not handle right now. No one should have to deal with an unwanted marriage proposal *and* geometry in the same morning.

"You don't know anything about circles," Anthony said.

Benedict crossed his arms. "Yes, I do."

"If you did, you wouldn't have asked about them, because they have *nothing* to do with—"

"Boys, stop," Georgie ordered. "Now."

"He does this all the time," Benedict protested. "He thinks because he's bigger than me—"

"I am bigger than you."

"Not forever you're not."

"Says who?"

"Says me!"

"Stop!" Georgie yelled.

"I hate you," Benedict seethed.

Anthony stuck out his tongue. "I hate you more."

"Boys, stop this at once," Nicholas said sternly.

God above, if they listened to Nicholas when they wouldn't listen to her, Georgie was going to scream.

"He started it!" Benedict whined.

"I did not! You asked about circles!"

"Because I wanted to know about them!"

"Enough!" Nicholas put his hand on Benedict's shoulder, but the little boy yanked himself away.

And Georgie's faith in the universe was restored. Nicholas wasn't having any success at managing them, either.

Benedict stamped his foot. "Anthony Bridgerton, I hate you the *most*." And then he drew back his fist.

Georgie leapt forward. "Do not hit your brother!"

But Benedict had no intention of hitting his brother.

Instead, his little hand swung through the air, releasing a heretofore unnoticed patty of pure lakefront mud.

It would have hit Anthony in the face if Georgie had not tried to intervene.

Anthony gasped with pure schadenfreude as it slopped down on Georgie's shoulder. "Oh, Benedict," he breathed. "You are going to be in *so much trouble.*"

"Benedict!" Nicholas said sternly.

"I didn't mean to!" Benedict cried. "I was aiming for Anthony."

Nicholas took him by the upper arm, pulling him a step back for a scolding. "That does not make it any better."

And then Georgie—honestly, she could not say what came over her. She would never know what mad devil plucked her hand from her side. It was like she'd been attacked by malevolent marionette strings.

She scooped the mud from her shoulder and let fly.

Right into Nicholas's neck.

"I was aiming for Benedict," she said sweetly.

Then she made the mistake of looking at the boys. They were staring at her with identical expressions—eyes wide, mouths wider—and then Benedict said in almost reverent tones, "Aunt Georgie, you are going to be in so much trouble."

Nicholas—damn him—swooped in to save the day. "Boys," he said with deceptive calm, "I think your aunt isn't feeling well."

Georgie would have snapped, "I'm fine," except that she wasn't fine, and she wanted this to be over more than she wanted to prove him wrong.

"Run along home," Nicholas said to the boys. "We will be right behind you."

"Is Benedict in trouble?" Anthony asked hopefully.

"No one is in trouble."

"Is Aunt Georgie in trouble?"

"*Home*," Nicholas said sharply.

They took one look at his face and started to run.

Georgie grit her teeth. "I'm sorry about the mud."

"No you're not."

"You're right. I'm not."

His brows rose. "That was a refreshingly quick capitulation."

"I'm not a good liar."

"Neither am I," he said with a shrug.

"Yes, I know."

Then his mouth started to twitch, and by God, that was the final straw.

"Don't laugh," she practically growled.

"I'm not."

Her eyes narrowed.

Nicholas looked like he might throw his hands in the air. "I'm not! Believe me, I find no humor here."

"I think you should—"

"Although I *am* flattered that Edmund has granted me uncle status."

He wanted to laugh. She was sure of it.

"Stop looking so self-righteous," Nicholas said testily. "We're both covered in mud."

She gave him one long stare and then marched away.

"Georgie, stop!" He caught up instantly. "We are not finished."

"I am," she ground out. She was *done.* "You can tell your father," she said, each syllable more clipped than the last, "that you have done your duty and asked me to marry you. And then you can tell him that I said no."

"You're not thinking."

"Don't you *dare.*" She stepped forward, jabbing her finger toward him. She poked it through the air, and then she poked him right in the chest. "Don't you ever tell me I don't know my own mind. Do you hear me?"

"That's not what I meant."

"Again! Do you hear yourself? If you have to say 'that's not what I meant' three times in a single conversation, perhaps you should consider the inclarity of your words."

"Inclarity?" he repeated.

Now he was correcting her grammar? Georgie wanted to scream. "I think you should go," she said, trying for a hushed tone. The boys weren't that far ahead of them on the path.

"At least let me—"

She thrust one of her arms out, vaguely in the direction of Crake. "Go!"

Nicholas crossed his arms and looked her hard and square in the eye. "No."

She drew back. "What?"

"No," he said again. "I'm not going to go. Not until I am convinced that you have actually heard what I've had to say."

"Will. You. Marry. Me," she said, ticking the words off on her fingers. "I heard you quite clearly."

"Don't be deliberately obtuse, Georgiana. It does not become you."

She stepped forward. "When did you become so condescending?"

He stepped forward. "When did *you* become so short-sighted and full of pride?"

At this point they were nearly nose to nose, and Georgie was seething. "A gentleman would accept a lady's refusal with grace."

He countered with, "A lady would consider the proposal before rejecting it out of hand."

"That's not what I'm doing."

"I am not asking you to marry me because I pity you," he said in a furiously tight voice. "I am asking because I have known you for as long as I have known my own memory. I *like* you, Georgiana. You are a good person, and you do not deserve to spend the rest of your life in isolation because of the misguided actions of a jackass."

Her comeback died in her throat. Because now *she* felt like a jackass.

A jackass who had no idea what to say.

She swallowed, hating that the lump in her throat tasted like tears. Hating that he didn't understand why she was so angry. And hating that he was actually a good person and he *still* didn't understand.

But most of all, she hated that she'd fallen into this awful position where someone could make a kind gesture, born of nothing but care and good intentions, and all she wanted to do was scream.

"Thank you, Nicholas," she said, picking through her words with careful cadence. "It was very thoughtful of you to ask."

"Thoughtful," he repeated, and she got the feeling that he was startled by the milkish, nondescript word.

"The answer is still no," she said. "You don't need to save me."

He bristled. "That's not what I'm doing."

"Isn't it?"

He stared at her for a moment before capitulating. "Yes, fine, I suppose it is, but it's *you*, Georgie."

"Me?"

"You must know I wouldn't do it for anyone else."

Her heart pricked. She wanted to cry. She wanted to cry *so hard* and she didn't know why. Or maybe it was that there were simply too many reasons and the prospect of sifting through them made her want to cry the hardest of all.

She shook her head. "Did it ever occur to you that I don't want to spend the rest of my life feeling grateful?"

"Don't be ridiculous. It wouldn't be like that."

"You can't know that."

He didn't quite roll his eyes, but she could tell he wanted to. "You can't know the opposite," he said.

She took a steadying breath. "I can't be your sacrifice."

"That's absurd."

"*Don't be ridiculous. That's absurd.*" Her voice turned to steel. "Kindly do me the honor of not disparaging my every word."

He gaped at her. "You know—"

Georgie waited, breath held, as he turned on his heel

and took a step away from her. Every line of his body was rigid with frustration—or maybe fury—even as he whirled back around. "Forget I said anything," he said hotly. "Forget I tried to be a friend. Forget you're in a difficult spot. Forget I tried to give you a way out."

He started to walk away, but she could not bear to see him leave in such a temper, so she called out, "Don't be like that, Nicholas. It's not about you."

He turned around. "What did you just say?" he asked, his voice chillingly soft.

She blinked with confusion. "I said it's not about you," she repeated.

And then he just laughed. He laughed so uproariously that Georgie couldn't think of a thing to say. She just stood there like an idiot, wondering what on earth had led to this moment.

"Do you know," he said, wiping his eyes, "that is exactly what my father said."

She shook her head. "I don't understand."

"No. Neither did he." He stopped and bowed; they had reached the spot where the path broke in two. One way to the house, the other to the stables, where she presumed he had left his mount. "I bid you good day."

Good day, indeed.

Chapter 8

Well, that went well.

Funny how it had never occurred to Nicholas that she might say no.

"It's a relief," he said to himself as he handed his mount over to the grooms at Crake's stables. "I didn't want to marry her anyway."

"I've done my duty," he announced to the empty lawn as he marched over to the house. "I asked, she refused. There is nothing more to be done."

And finally, when he yanked open Crake's massive front door and stamped into the hall, he muttered, "It was a cock-up of an idea, anyway. Good God, what was I thinking? *Georgiana Bridgerton.*"

"Sir?"

It was Wheelock, materializing from thin air, as was his habit. Nicholas nearly jumped a foot.

"My apologies if I surprised you, sir."

Nicholas could not begin to count the number of times Wheelock had uttered this exact sentence. It was approximately equal to the number of times he had not meant it. Wheelock lived to sneak up on Rokesbys.

"I went out for a ride," Nicholas said. It wasn't a lie. He *had* gone for a ride. To Aubrey Hall, where he'd asked a woman to marry him, been hit in the neck with a pile of mud, and been turned down, although not strictly in that order.

Wheelock eyed Nicholas's muddy sleeve, the one he'd used to wipe his neck.

"What?" Nicholas snapped. He'd regret it later, talking to Wheelock with such incivility, but he could not manage anything else just now.

Wheelock paused before replying, for the exact amount of time necessary to make it clear that one of them was the epitome of serenity and calm and one of them was not. "I merely wished to inquire if I should call for refreshment," he said.

"Yes," Nicholas said. "No." Gad, he didn't want to see anyone. But he *was* hungry. "Yes, but have it sent to my room."

"As you wish, sir, but might I add—"

"Not now, Wheelock."

"You will want to be aware that—"

"A bath," Nicholas announced. "I'm going upstairs, taking a bath, having a drink, and going to bed."

"At half eleven in the morning?"

"Is that what time it is?"

"Indeed, sir."

Nicholas bowed with a flourish. "Then I bid you farewell."

Wheelock looked at him as if he'd gone mad. Hell, he probably had.

But Nicholas made it only three steps before Wheelock called out again. "Master Nicholas!"

Nicholas groaned. "Sir" he might have been able to ignore. "Master Nicholas" threw him right back into childhood, when Wheelock's word was law. He turned slowly around. "Yes, Mr. Wheelock?"

"Your father is waiting in his study."

"My father is always waiting in his study."

"A most astute observation, sir, but this time he is waiting for you."

Nicholas groaned again, this time with purposeful volume.

"Shall I divert your refreshments to Lord Manston's study, then?" Wheelock asked.

"No. To my room, please. I won't be there long enough to eat."

Wheelock looked dubious, but he nodded.

"You're going to send them to my father's study, aren't you?" Nicholas asked.

"To both locations, sir."

Nicholas should have seen that coming. "Good God, you're impressive."

Wheelock nodded graciously. "I do my best, sir."

Nicholas shook his head. "If butlers ruled the world . . ."

"We can only dream of such a utopia."

Nicholas smiled, despite his hideous mood, and took himself to his father's study. The door was open, so he gave the wall a little knock and went inside.

"Ah," Lord Manston said, looking up from his desk. "You're back."

"As you can see."

His father's brow wrinkled as he tipped his head toward Nicholas's shoulder. "What happened to you?"

As Nicholas had no intention of telling the truth he merely said, "It's muddy."

His father glanced toward the window. It looked as if it might rain, but they both knew it had been dry all morning. "I see," he murmured.

"I was down by the lake," Nicholas said.

His father nodded, fixing a placid smile to his face.

Nicholas let out an exhale and waited. He knew why he was here. *Three, two, one . . .*

"Did you ask her?"

There it was.

"Not yet," he lied. He wasn't sure why. Probably because he felt like a fool. A rejected fool.

"Isn't that why you went to Aubrey Hall?"

"She was minding Anthony and Benedict. It was hardly an ideal moment."

"No, I suppose not." Lord Manston chuckled. "Edmund wasn't joking when he called them right little terrors. Were they running her ragged?"

"Not really. She seemed to have them well in hand."

Lord Manston's eyes moved pointedly to the mud.

"It was an accident," Nicholas said. He certainly wasn't about to tell his father that Georgiana had thrown it.

His father gave a little shrug. "These things happen."

"Indeed they do." Nicholas wondered how long they could keep up such an utterly inconsequential conversation.

"She'll be a good mother."

"She probably will," Nicholas replied. For some other man's children. Not his.

She'd said no.

No.

That was all there was to it. He could go back to Scotland tomorrow. Or at least as soon as he told his father that Georgie had rejected his proposal.

But first, a bath. "If that is all, sir—"

"My man is back from London with the special license," his father said.

Nicholas nearly groaned. "How expedient."

"The archbishop owed me a favor."

"The archbishop owes you a favor," Nicholas repeated. It was not often one heard those words said in that order.

"Owed," his father corrected. "We are even now."

Nicholas could not imagine a series of events that had led to the Archbishop of Canterbury owing his father a favor. "I hope you have not wasted your indulgence."

His father gave him a look. "You yourself told me you need to get back to Edinburgh. Do you really want to wait for three weeks of banns?"

Nicholas took a breath. "Has it occurred to you that she might not accept?"

"Don't be daft. Georgiana is a sensible girl. She knows how the world works."

"I thought *I* knew how the world worked," Nicholas muttered.

"What was that?"

Nicholas shook his head. "Nothing."

And then to himself: "Absolutely nothing at all."

It took Georgie precisely one hour to realize that she was being an idiot.

Two hours after that, she decided she had to do something about it.

She was sitting in the drawing room with her mother, as was her habit most afternoons. Her mother was working on her embroidery. Georgie was doing the same, which was *not* her habit most afternoons. She always had her basket at her side; she had to give the impression that she was at least thinking of attacking the embroidery, but she usually ended up staring out the window or reading a book.

Today, however, she'd been inspired to work on her stitches. *Needle up, needle down. Needle up, needle down.*

Nothing fancy or floral, just a neat, straight line of stitches. Needle up, needle down. She felt almost mechanical. It was oddly satisfying.

Her conversation with Nicholas at dinner the night before had reminded her how impressed she'd been by the doctor's work on Anthony's hand. The stitches had been as even and tidy as any she'd ever seen in an embroidery hoop. And on a howling, squirming child to boot.

She wondered how much training it took to reach that level of proficiency.

Needle up, needle down.

Georgie frowned. Would her work be good enough to stitch a wound? Probably not. Her line was straight and even, but fabric was not skin. If she were stitching an actual wound, she wouldn't be able to reach underneath, as she could with muslin stretched across an embroidery hoop.

"My goodness, Georgiana," her mother said. "I have never seen you so focused on your embroidery. What are you working on?"

Georgie had no choice but to show her the row of stitches, neat and tidy and forming nothing more interesting than a straight line.

Her mother looked perplexed, but Georgie did not think she was feigning interest when she asked, "Er, what is that meant to be?"

"Nothing," Georgie admitted. "I thought I would challenge myself to see how many identical stitches I could do in a row."

"Oh. Well, that seems an admirable goal. One must master the basics before moving on to the more creative aspects of needlework."

Georgie tried to peer over at her mother's hoop. "What are you working on?"

"Just a few flowers." Lady Bridgerton held her work up. Just a few flowers indeed. It was nothing short of a masterpiece. Pink peonies, purple irises, delicate white somethings—all interwoven with leaves of every possible shade of green.

It was clear where Benedict got his artistic talent.

"That is gorgeous," Georgie said.

Her mother flushed with pleasure. "Thank you, dear. I spent several days designing it on paper before working on the fabric. I used to try to be more spontaneous, but I've realized I must plan things out."

"You get a lot of joy out of your needlework, don't you?"

"I do. I really do."

Something in her mother's tone piqued Georgie's curiosity. "You sound almost surprised."

"Not surprised . . ." Lady Bridgerton's brow furrowed and a faraway look settled onto her face, the sort one got when one was deep in one's own mind. "I suppose I never really thought about it," she said, "but there is great satisfaction to be had in creation."

"Creation?"

"And completion. And the knowledge that one is responsible for both."

Georgie looked down at the neat row of stitches

marching across her embroidery hoop. She'd used blue thread, for no reason other than the fact that it was in her basket near the top of the pile, but now she found she liked it. It was soothing.

And endless. Blue was the ocean, the sky. And the thread that, if she loosened the fabric from the hoop, could go on forever.

All she had to do was remove the boundaries.

She loved Aubrey Hall. She really did. And she loved her family, too. But the walls here had been closing in on her for years, so slowly she had not even realized it.

Nicholas had offered her a choice. Maybe it wasn't the right choice; but she had been foolish to dismiss his offer out of hand. She'd chosen pride over reason, and she hadn't even given him a chance to explain himself.

Yes, it stung that the only reason he'd proposed was that his father had called him down from Scotland to do so, but maybe . . .

Maybe . . .

Maybe there was more?

Or maybe not, but maybe there *could* be?

And even if there wasn't, even if she wasn't destined to find love and passion and hearts and flowers and whatever else it was that cupids and cherubs sang of on high . . .

Maybe it would still be worth it.

So how did one go about un-rejecting a marriage proposal?

Georgie stood up. "I'm going to Crake."

Her mother regarded her with palpable surprise. "Now?"

"Yes." Now that she'd made her decision Georgie was determined to be on her way. "I'm going to take a cart."

"Really? A cart?"

"It's faster than walking."

"Are you in a rush?"

"No."

Yes. What if Nicholas left for Scotland this afternoon? Highly unlikely, all things considered, but possible. And wouldn't she feel like a fool?

Her mother turned to the window and frowned. "It looks like rain, dear. I don't think you should go."

What she really meant was—*You shouldn't go out in the rain because you could catch a chill, stop breathing, and die.*

Georgie gave her mother a reassuring smile. "It has been over a year since I had an episode, Mama. I really do think I've grown out of them."

Her mother did not reply, and Georgie half-expected her to order a steaming bowl of oversteeped tea for

Georgie to hover over with a heavy linen over her head. It had been a common ritual in Georgie's youth—one her mother no doubt was sure had saved her life many times over.

"Mama?" Georgie prompted, after the silence stretched into the awkward.

Her mother let out a sigh. "I would not recommend that anyone go out in this weather," she said. "At least not in what I think the weather is going to be in a few minutes."

As if on cue, a fat raindrop hit the windowpane.

Both Bridgerton ladies went still, staring out the window, waiting for another drop to fall.

Nothing.

"False alarm," Georgie said brightly.

"Look at that sky," Lady Bridgerton countered. "It grows more ominous by the second. Mark my words, if you go to Crake right now, you're either going to catch your death on the way over or be stranded there overnight."

"Or catch my death on the way home," Georgie quipped.

"What a thing to joke about."

Splat.

Another raindrop.

They both looked out the window again. "I suppose

you could take a carriage," Lady Bridgerton said with a sigh.

Splat. Splatsplatsplat.

The rain started to pelt the house, the initial fat droplets giving way to sharp little needles.

"Are you sure you want to go *now?*" Lady Bridgerton asked. Georgie nodded.

"I'm not even sure Billie's home this afternoon," her mother said. "She said something about barley fields and well, honestly, I don't know what. I wasn't really listening. But I got the impression she had a lot to do."

"I'll take my chances," Georgie said, not bothering to correct her mother's assumption that she intended to visit her sister.

Ping!

Lady Bridgerton turned to the window. "Is that *hail?*"

"Good God," Georgie muttered. The minute she decided to take action, the universe just went all in against her. She wouldn't be surprised if it started to snow.

In May.

Georgie walked over to the window and looked out. "Maybe I'll wait just a bit," she said, chewing on her lower lip. "In case the weather improves."

But it didn't.

It hailed for an hour.

Then it rained.

Then it stopped, but by then it was dark. If Georgie was a more intrepid sort of female, or maybe just a more foolish one, she might have told her family that she was taking the carriage (they would never have allowed her to drive herself in a cart on dark muddy roads).

But that would have invited far too many questions, both at home and at Crake, where her nocturnal arrival would have been most unorthodox.

"Tomorrow," she said to herself. Tomorrow she would head over to Crake. Tomorrow she would tell Nicholas that she'd been a fool, and while she wasn't quite ready to say yes, would it be all right if she didn't say no?

She took her dinner in her room, plotted out what she might say to Nicholas when she next saw him, and eventually crawled into bed.

Where she'd thought she'd stay until morning.

She thought wrong.

Chapter 9

Georgie sat up suddenly in bed, muddled and groggy. She had no idea what time it was, or why she had woken up, but her heart was pounding, and her pulse was racing, and—

Tap.

Instinctively, she shrank back against the head of her bed. She was still too disoriented to identify the sound.

Tap.

Was it one of her cats?

Taptaptap.

She caught her lower lip between her teeth. That last noise was different, like a bunch of little taps all at once. Or rather, almost all at once. And it definitely wasn't a cat.

Taptaptaptap.

There it was again, coming from . . . her window?

That was impossible. Maybe a bird? But why would a bird tap repeatedly in one spot? It made no sense. It had to be a human, except it *couldn't* be a human. She was too high up. There was a ledge, and she supposed it was wide enough for a person to stand on, but the only way to get there was to go up the massive oak her father always complained grew too close to the house. But even so, you'd have to crawl out on a branch.

A branch she didn't think would support a person's weight all the way out to the house.

Even her sister Billie, who had been known to take phenomenally stupid risks in the pursuit of treetops, had never attempted that one.

Plus, it had only stopped raining a few hours earlier. The tree would be wet and slippery.

"Oh, for the love of heaven," Georgie said. She hopped down from her bed. It had to be an animal. An extremely intelligent animal or an extremely foolish human.

Tap. Tap. Tap.

Or pebbles. Someone was throwing pebbles at her window.

For a second she thought—*Nicholas*. But Nicholas would never be so stupid. Plus, why would he sneak?

And again. Nicholas was not stupid. It was one of the things she liked best about him.

She approached the window slowly, although for the life of her, she didn't know why. If someone was throwing pebbles, it meant he couldn't get in on his own. Still, she grabbed a candlestick for good measure, pushed the curtains aside, and peered out. But it was too dark to see, so she tucked the candlestick under her arm and then used both her hands to wrench the window up.

"Who's out there?" she whispered.

"It's me."

She froze. She knew that voice.

"I've come for you, Georgiana."

Bloody hell. It was Freddie Oakes.

Judyth, who had jumped on silent paws up to the windowsill, immediately hissed.

It was a cloudy night, but there was enough light coming from the lanterns on the house that she could see him in the tree, perched on the long branch right where it met the trunk.

Georgie tried to shout her whisper. "What in the name of God are you doing here?"

"Did you get my letter?"

"Yes, and perhaps you noticed I didn't write back." Georgie grabbed the candlestick out from under her arm and jabbed it angrily in his direction. "You need to go away."

"I won't leave without you."

"He's mad," she said to herself. "He is stark, raving—"

"Mad for you," he finished. He smiled, and all she could think was—*what a waste of straight white teeth.* By any measure, Freddie Oakes was a handsome young gentleman. The problem was, he knew it.

"I love you, Georgiana Bridgerton," he said, smiling that too-confident smile again. "I want you to be my wife."

Georgie groaned. She didn't believe that for a second. And she didn't think that he believed it, either.

Freddie Oakes wasn't in love with her. He just wanted her to think that he was so that she'd let him marry her. Did he really think she was that gullible? Had he had such previous success with the ladies that he thought she'd fall for such obvious bunk?

"Is that your cat?" he asked.

"One of them," Georgie replied, pulling Judyth back. The silver gray cat was hissing loudly now, her little paws pinwheeling through the air. "She's a very good judge of character."

Freddie seemed not to get the insult. "Did you get my second letter?" he asked.

"What? No." She plunked Judyth down on the floor. "And you shouldn't be writing to me."

"I memorized it," he said. "In case I arrived before it did."

Dear God.

"Freddie," she said, "you need to go before someone sees you."

"*My dearest Georgiana,*" he intoned.

"Stop! Now." She twisted her head to look up at the sky. "I think it's going to rain again. It's not safe in that tree."

"You *do* care about me."

"No, I was simply stating that it's not safe in that tree," she retorted. "Although heaven knows why I bother. Only a fool would climb it in this weather, and I could certainly do with fewer fools in my life."

"You wound me to the quick, Miss Bridgerton."

She groaned.

"That wasn't in the letter," he explained.

"I don't care what was in the letter!"

"You will when I finish reciting it," he said.

Georgie rolled her eyes. God save her.

"Here is what I wrote." He cleared his throat in that way people did before a grand speech. "*It distresses me more than I can say that I have not heard back from you.*"

"Stop," she begged.

But he sailed on, as she knew he would. "*I bared my heart to you in my letter. I wrote words of love and devotion and heard only silence. I can only believe that you never received my letter, for surely you are too gentle-hearted and lovely to wound me with silence.*"

He looked up expectantly.

"I already told you I got the first letter," Georgie said.

This deflated him. But only momentarily. "Well," he said, in the sort of tone one uses when deciding to ignore logic and fact, "I also wrote: *I am sorry if I frightened you with my ardor. You must know it is because I love you so desperately. I have never felt this for another lady.*"

Georgie let her forehead fall into one of her hands. "Stop, Freddie. Just stop. You're embarrassing both of us. But mostly you."

"I am not embarrassed," he said, placing a dramatic hand over his heart. The motion caused him to sway, and Georgie gasped, convinced he was going down. But he must have had a better grip on the tree than she'd realized, because he remained solidly in his perch, legs wrapped around the long branch that stretched toward her window.

"For the love of heaven, Freddie, you need to get back down before you kill yourself."

"I'm not getting out of this tree until you agree to marry me."

"Then you should consider building a nest, because that is never going to happen."

"Why are you being so bloody stubborn?"

"Because I don't want to marry you!" Georgie jerked to the side as first Judyth, and then Blanche hopped up onto the windowsill. "Honestly, Freddie, can't you find someone else to marry?"

"I want *you*."

"Oh, please. We both know you don't really love me."

"Of course I—"

"*Freddie*."

Judyth hissed. Blanche followed suit, but Blanche always did whatever Judyth did. At that point Cat-Head jumped up, and now there were three hostile cats in a row, all glaring at Freddie.

"Fine." His mouth came together in a hard line, and his entire demeanor changed. "I don't love you. I don't love anyone. But I do need to get married. And you're the best woman for the job."

"One would think the best woman for the job would be a woman who actually *wants* the job."

"I don't have the luxury of finding that woman," he retorted. "I need to get married now."

"How far in debt *are* you?"

"Quite," he said. "You're the perfect combination of dowry and tolerability."

"This is how you think to convince me?"

"I *tried* to go about it the nice way," he said.

"Kidnapping?"

He waved dismissively, causing Georgie to once again gasp for his safety. But he did not slip. She recalled that someone had once told her Freddie was a natural athlete, that he'd ruled the cricket fields at Eton. Thank God for that, because she had a feeling it was the only reason he hadn't yet tumbled to the ground.

"I did everything properly," he said. "I danced with you. I took you to a bookshop."

"From which you kidnapped me."

He shrugged. "My creditors advanced my calendar considerably. Now please, if you would. You haven't a choice. Surely you must know that. Your reputation is in tatters."

"Thanks to you!"

"Then let me make it up to you. Once we're married, it will all go away. You will have the protection of my name."

"I don't want the protection of your name," Georgie seethed.

"You will be Mrs. Oakes," he said, and Georgie honestly couldn't tell if he was willfully ignoring her or too caught up in his own greatness to notice that she'd spoken.

He leaned toward her. "When my father passes you will be Lady Nithercott."

"I'd rather remain Miss Bridgerton."

"Miss Bridgerton is a spinster." He started scooting down the branch. "You don't want to be a spinster."

"Stop it, Freddie!" Georgie eyed him with growing panic. Surely he didn't think the branch would hold him all the way to her window.

"I'm coming in."

"You are not."

"Accept your fate, Georgiana."

"I will scream," she warned.

He actually laughed at her, the cretin. "If you were going to scream, you would have done so by now."

"The only reason I haven't is because my brother is here tonight, and he will disembowel you if he finds you anywhere near me."

"So you do care."

Dear God, this man was stupid. "About my brother," she hissed. "I have no wish to see him jailed for murder. And I don't need another scandal. You've already ruined my life."

"So let me fix it."

"Your plan all along, I assume."

He shrugged again as he nudged himself forward a few inches. "You're not going to do better."

"Freddie, don't! It won't support your weight."

"Toss me a rope."

"I don't have a rope! Why would you think I had a rope in my bedroom? And for the love of God, back up."

He didn't listen.

"Do not come closer," Georgie warned. She was starting to worry that maybe the branch *would* hold his weight. It wasn't bowing nearly as much as she would have thought.

"You *will* marry me," he growled.

"Would it be easier if I just *gave* you money?"

He paused. "You would do that?"

"No!" She picked up the closest object she could put her hands on—a book—and hurled it at him.

"Ow!" It clipped him on the shoulder. "Stop that!"

She threw another book.

"What the hell are you doing?"

"Defending my honor," she ground out. She tried to lean forward, but the cats were in the way. Without taking her eyes off Freddie she picked them up one by one and tossed them down. "If you have any care to your well-being," she warned him, "you'll remember what happened last time you tried to convince me to marry you."

"Don't be a—Jesus Christ!"

She knobbed him on the head with an inkpot.

"I've got another right here," she growled. "I write a lot of letters."

His face curled into something unpleasant. "I'm beginning to think you're not worth the trouble."

"So I've been *telling you*," she hissed. She hurled the second inkpot at him, but as he moved to dodge it, Cat-Head (who had never been the brightest of her three cats) hopped back up onto the sill, let out an unholy *scraw*, and launched himself out the window.

"Cat-Head!" Georgie lunged forward, trying to get hold of him, but the cat was on Freddie's face before she even had her arms out the window.

"Get it off me!" Freddie shrieked.

"Cat-Head! Cat-Head, come back!" Georgie hissed, trying to keep her voice down. The other bedrooms were around the corner, so with any luck no one would have heard Freddie's cry of distress.

Freddie clawed at the cat, trying to dislodge it, but Cat-Head held firm, wrapped around Freddie's head like half of a furry octopus.

Half of a furry octopus with claws.

"You bloody—" Freddie's words disintegrated into a furious grunt as he seized the cat by its midsection.

"Don't you dare throw my cat!" Georgie warned.

But Freddie already had him by the belly. Cat-Head let out a mighty cat-scream, and Freddie tossed him away.

It did not go well for Freddie.

Cat-Head fared splendidly. After a terrifying moment when he seemed to be suspended in mid-air, fur sticking out in every direction, he got his claws into a clump of leaves hanging down from another branch and then swung himself to safety.

Freddie, on the other hand, lost his balance completely. He let out a howl of distress as he clawed for purchase, but it was to no avail. He slid from the branch and fell, bumping against several lower branches as he tumbled to the ground.

"Oh my God." Georgie's words came out in a tiny horrified squeak as she leaned out the window. "Oh my God." Was he dead? Had she killed him? Had her cat killed him?

She ran out of her room, grabbing a lantern from a table in the hall.

"OhmyGodOhmyGodOhmyGod . . ." All the way down the stairs, skidding through the hall and out the front door in her bare feet. "Oh my God."

He was at the base of the tree, lying very still. His head was bleeding, and already one of his eyes appeared to be swelling shut.

"Mr. Oakes?" she asked hesitantly, inching toward him. "Freddie?"

He moaned.

Oh thank God. He wasn't dead.

She leaned in a little closer, nudging his hip with her toe. "Mr. Oakes, can you hear me?"

"Bitch."

So, that was a yes.

"Are you hurt?"

He gave her a malevolent stare. A one-eyed malevolent stare, which was somehow worse.

"Er, *where* are you hurt?" she amended.

"Everywhere, you bloody moron."

"You know," she said, "considering this is entirely your own fault, and I'm the only one here with the ability to summon help, you might think about being a little more polite."

She held the lantern closer. There was a lot of blood on his head, although in the dark it was difficult to say how much of it might have been from the inkpot. But that wasn't the worst of it. His left arm was twisted at an angle that wasn't just unnatural, it was positively inhuman.

She winced. "I think you broke your arm."

His reply was a string of vile curses, all of them directed at her.

"Miss Georgiana? Miss Georgiana!"

It was Thamesly, hurrying down the front steps in his dressing gown. Georgie wasn't surprised that the butler would be the first to arrive on the scene. He had always had freakishly good hearing.

"Miss Georgiana, what has happened?"

"There has been an accident," she said, wondering if she should avert her eyes. She didn't think she'd ever seen Thamesly in anything less than full uniform. "Mr. Oakes was injured."

His eyes widened. "Did you say Mr. Oakes?"

"I did."

Thamesly looked down at the man on the ground. "He appears to have broken his arm."

Georgie nodded.

"It looks quite painful."

"It is, you bloody idiot," Freddie snapped from the ground, "and if you don't—"

Thamesly took a small step forward and stepped on Freddie's hand. "It's rather late to seek medical attention," he said to Georgie. "I hate to bother a doctor when the injuries are so clearly not life threatening."

Georgie's eyes welled with tears. She had never loved the family butler as much as she did right at that moment.

"He appears to have cut his face, as well," Thamesly

said. He glanced down, and then back up. "That'll leave a scar."

"Not if he gets it stitched properly," Georgie said.

"Middle of the night," Thamesly said with a patently false sigh of regret. "Alas."

Georgie had to cover her mouth to choke down a nervous laugh. She reached out and took the butler by the arm, pulling him away from (and off of) Freddie. "I adore you for this," she whispered, "but I do think we need to get him help. If he dies . . ."

"He won't die."

"But if he does, it will be on my conscience."

"Surely you don't take responsibility for this idiot climbing the—" Thamesly looked up. "I assume he fell from the tree."

Georgie nodded. "He was trying to get into my room."

Thamesly's nostrils flared ominously. "I will kill him myself."

It was almost funny, delivered as it was in Thamesly's signature monotone. Almost.

"You will do nothing of the sort," Georgie whispered urgently. "His father is a baron. I might be able to get away with injuring him, but you most assuredly will not."

"He does not deserve your care, Miss Georgiana."

"No, but you do." Georgie looked up at him. She would not go so far as to say that Thamesly had been a second father to her, but he had been a calming, compassionate presence in her life for as long as she could remember, and she cared for him deeply.

"I will lose no sleep over him." Georgie flicked her head toward Freddie, who was still seething on the ground. "But if you were punished because we did not see to his injuries properly, I would never forgive myself."

Thamesly's pale blue eyes turned watery.

"We need to get him help," Georgie said, "and then we need to get him out of here."

Thamesly nodded. "I will summon your parents."

"No!" Georgie clutched his arm with surprising urgency. "It will be better if no one knows he was here."

"He should pay for what he's done."

"I agree, but we both know I'm the one who will pay. There is no way we'll be able to keep it quiet if anyone else becomes involved." Georgie twisted her mouth into a frown, looking quickly to the house and then off toward the stables. "Can you hitch a cart?"

"What are you thinking?"

"Can you hitch a cart?" she repeated.

"Of course," he replied. He sniffed, clearly offended that she'd questioned his skills.

"I'm going to run inside to get shoes and a coat and something we can use for bandages. You get a cart hitched and we'll take him somewhere out of the way."

"And then what?"

"And then we . . ." She thought, grimacing as she kicked a toe through the grass. "And then we . . ."

What was she going to do?

"My lady?"

She raised her head. There was really only one thing they could do.

"And then we get Nicholas."

Chapter 10

"**S**ir."

Nicholas batted away whatever insect was buzzing in his ear and rolled over.

"Sir! Sir!"

He came awake with a giant indrawn breath, shaking as he sat up straight. He never had woken well when his sleep was interrupted.

"What is it? What's wrong?"

. . . was what he thought he said. The reality was probably a great deal more garbled. He blinked his eyes open. Wheelock was standing next to his bed, holding a candle.

"Wheelock? What the devil?"

"You're needed," Wheelock whispered. "Thamesly was here."

If sleep was still fogging his brain, it was gone in an instant. "Thamesly? Why? What? Is someone hurt?"

"I was not able to obtain all the details," Wheelock said. "But I thought you should know that he asked that I wake you and only you."

"What the hell?" Nicholas mumbled to himself.

Wheelock held out a piece of paper. "He left this for you."

"He's no longer here?"

"No. He departed immediately. He said he could not leave Miss Georgiana alone for much longer."

"Georgiana!" Nicholas flew out of bed, stumbling to the wardrobe for his clothes. Wheelock was already there, holding out a shirt, but Nicholas wanted to read Thamesly's message first.

"What does he say?" Wheelock asked.

Nicholas read the few short sentences by the light of Wheelock's candle. "Not much. Just that he and Georgiana need my help and I'm to go to the old Millston farmhouse."

"I believe that's the one—"

"—where Billie sprained her ankle all those years ago, yes. I believe it is still in disrepair, is it not?"

"It is being used for storage, but no one lives there."

Nicholas yanked on his clothing with fear-fueled

haste. "Did Thamesly tell you *anything*? Is it Georgiana? Is she ill? Has she been injured?"

Wheelock shook his head. "I don't think so, no. He said that someone else was in need of medical attention."

"Someone else? Who the devil would be out with her at—" Nicholas looked up toward the clock, but it was too dark to make out the face. "What the hell time is it?"

"Half two, sir."

Nicholas swore under his breath. Something was very wrong.

"Your boots, sir." Wheelock held them up. "May I suggest you don them outside, so as to make less noise?"

Nicholas nodded, in both agreement and admiration. "You do think of everything, don't you?"

"It is my job to do so, sir."

They slipped out of the room on stockinged feet, moving silently down the grand staircase. Nicholas rarely walked through Crake this late at night. All the Rokesbys tended to turn in early in the country. It wasn't like London where myriad engagements and entertainments could keep one busy until the wee hours of the morning.

The house was different in the dark. Moonlight whispered through the great hall, casting pale stripes and shadows that slid along the floor and up the walls.

Absolute quiet reigned, but the air was oddly expectant, almost as if it were holding its breath, waiting for
something—or someone—to pierce the silence.

Nicholas wasn't sure if he liked it.

At the bottom of the stairs, Wheelock stopped him
with a hand to his arm. "Wait for me outside, sir," he
whispered. "I will be there in under a minute."

Nicholas wanted to argue that they had no time to
lose, but Wheelock had dashed off before he could
form words, and Nicholas wasn't about to risk waking
the house by calling after him. Instead he made his way
outside, pausing on the front steps to finally pull on his
boots. A moment later the butler reappeared, his own
shoes in hand.

"I am coming with you," Wheelock said.

"You are?" Nicholas hadn't expected this.

Wheelock drew back, deeply affronted. "Sir."

"Can you ride?" Nicholas asked.

"Of course I can."

Nicholas gave him an approving nod. "Then let's go."

About ten minutes later they approached the old farmhouse, and Nicholas saw a light—presumably from a
lantern—glowing from around the side. "This way, I
think," he said to Wheelock, who, it had to be said,
was a surprisingly proficient horseman.

They slowed their mounts, made their way around the corner, and Nicholas saw what looked to be three people near the old stone wall that ringed the property. Georgie and Thamesly were both crouching down, tending to a third person who was lying prone, unidentifiable from a distance.

"Georgiana!" he called in a shouted whisper. She looked up, relief evident in her posture.

"I'll see to the mounts," Wheelock said as they hopped down from their saddles.

Nicholas handed him the reins and hurried over.

"Georgiana," he said again. "What is going on? Are you all—" He looked down. "Bloody hell."

He pulled her aside. "Is that Freddie Oakes?"

Georgie nodded. "He broke his arm."

Oakes looked ready to spit. "The little b—"

Thamesly stepped on Oakes's leg. "What did we say about proper language in the presence of a lady?"

"Well done, Thamesly," Nicholas murmured.

"He also cut his head," Georgie said. "I've slowed the bleeding, but I can't seem to stop it entirely." She lifted a bandage she'd been holding against his forehead, near his hairline.

"Bring the light in," Nicholas said.

Thamesly brought the lantern closer. It was hard to tell with the dried and oozing blood, but Oakes appeared to have a not-too-serious laceration on his temple. The rest of his face was fairly well scraped up but not actively bleeding.

"It seems like he's lost quite a lot of blood," Georgie said. "It's been over an hour since it happened."

"It almost certainly looks worse than it is," Nicholas assured her. "The scalp is heavily vascularized. It always bleeds more than other parts of the body."

"Thank goodness," she said.

He looked up. "You are concerned for him?"

"I don't want him to *die*."

Nicholas did a quick assessment. He would not be able to make a proper judgment without a full examination, but for now, it looked as if Freddie Oakes was going to be just fine.

"He won't die," Nicholas told Georgie. "More's the pity. Although . . ." He took a closer look, waving Thamesly closer with the lantern. "I'm a little confused by the discoloration of his blood."

"Oh, that's ink," Georgie said. "I threw an inkpot at him. You can see it on his shirt, too."

"Zooks!" Oakes suddenly exclaimed. "Is that you, Rokesby?"

"Indeed," Nicholas replied, his voice tight. He could not recall if Georgie knew that he and Freddie Oakes had attended Eton at the same time, so he

looked over at her and said, "We went to school together."

"Best mates," Freddie said with one of his signature
grins.

"We were not best mates," Nicholas said.

But Freddie was having none of that. "Oh, the times
we had."

Nicholas shook his head. "We had no times. None
whatsoever."

"Aw, don't be a studge."

"Studge?" Georgie echoed.

Nicholas shrugged. He had no idea what it meant.
"Hold still," he said to Freddie. "I need to look at your
arm."

"Haven't seen you in a good few years," Freddie
went on. "What's it been . . . six? Eight?"

Nicholas ignored him.

"Ten?"

"Hold still," Nicholas bit off. "Do you want me to
treat your injuries or not?"

"Ye-es," Freddie said, drawing the word out into
two hesitant syllables. "Although I should probably say
I don't have a rat's idea what you're doing here."

"I live nearby," Nicholas said.

Georgie poked her head in. "He's studying to be a
doctor."

"Oh!" Oakes's countenance brightened instantly. "Should have said so." He looked back over at Georgie. "We're best mates."

"We are not best mates," Nicholas snapped. He looked over at Georgie. "He was kicked out for cheating."

"Asked to leave," Freddie corrected.

Georgie looked at Nicholas. "Isn't that the same thing?"

Nicholas shrugged. "Having never been asked to leave an educational institution, I wouldn't know."

"It wasn't my fault," Freddie said. "Winchie gave me the wrong answers, the stupid arse."

Nicholas rolled his eyes. God save him from idiots.

"But we *are* mates, right?" Freddie used his uninjured arm to give Nicholas a jolly slap on the shoulder. "Come round London some time. I'll take you to the club. Introduce you. I know all the people."

Nicholas gave him a sharp look. "I don't want to be your mate, and I don't want to be introduced to any of the people. I will, however, set your arm if you shut the hell up." He looked over at Georgie. "My pardon."

She gave him a wide-eyed little shake of her head. If anything, she looked fascinated by the exchange. "No pardon is necessary."

"Do you want to tell me what happened?" he asked quietly.

"Later," she said. "After we tend to his injuries."

Nicholas carefully palpated Oakes's injured arm.

"Gah!"

"Sorry," Nicholas said automatically.

"Can I help?" Georgie asked.

"I don't want her touching me," Freddie said.

"You were going to *marry* me," Georgie said in disbelief.

"Entirely different," Oakes grunted. "You didn't want to hurt me then."

"Oh, I've always wanted to hurt you."

Nicholas choked a little at that. "Do you really want to help?" he asked her.

"I do. I really do." Her entire face lit up. "It's like kismet. We were just talking about it."

"You were talking about my broken arm?" Freddie asked.

"Not *your* broken arm," Georgie said. She gave him a testy look. "For heaven's sake, Freddie, be reasonable."

"You threw me out of a tree!"

Nicholas glanced over at Georgie, impressed. "You threw him out of a tree?"

"I wish."

"I believe a cat was involved," Thamesly said, holding the lantern closer.

"Ah." Nicholas took another look at Freddie's face. "That explains the scratches."

"Some of them," Freddie said sullenly. "The rest were from the tree."

"Did the cat bite you?" Nicholas asked. Ironically, of all Freddie's injuries, a cat bite could prove the most dangerous.

"No. Damned sharp claws, though."

"He was scared," Georgie said.

"He should be shot," Freddie spat.

Thamesly stepped on his leg again.

"I wouldn't speak ill of Miss Bridgerton's cat," Nicholas recommended. "In fact, I'm going to ask that you not speak at all, unless it is to answer a direct question issued by me."

Freddie's mouth formed a flat line, but he nodded.

"Good. Now don't move. I'm going to cut your shirt off you."

Nicholas had brought a small medical kit home with him from Edinburgh—he never traveled without it— and he'd grabbed it before leaving Crake. He pulled out a small pair of scissors—hardly ideal for cutting through linen, but they would have to do. He could probably rip the fabric faster once he made the initial cut, but he didn't want to jostle Oakes's arm any more than he had to.

"I can do that," Georgie said.

He looked at her.

"His shirt. I can cut it off. That way you can tend to his face while I'm doing it."

"Good idea." Nicholas handed her the scissors.

Georgie grinned and got to work.

"It would go faster with proper shears," Nicholas said.

"I've got it," she assured him, and indeed she did.

Nicholas turned his attention back to Oakes's forehead. The main wound definitely needed cleaning. He took out the small flask of whiskey he kept in his medical kit and sloshed some on a handkerchief.

"This will—"

"Sting, I know," Freddie said grimly.

Nicholas gave him a vaguely approving nod. It was possibly the most sensible thing he'd said all night.

Freddie flinched while Nicholas cleaned the blood from his face, but that was to be expected. Nicholas had never seen someone not flinch when presented with whiskey on an open wound. At his side, Georgiana was still working diligently on the shirt, making tiny cuts with the tiny scissors, moving in a perfectly (and unnecessarily) straight line.

"Almost done," she said.

Nicholas could hear the smile in her voice.

"I'm not sure this needs stitches," he said to Freddie, peering more closely at the wound, "but you're probably not going to want to show your face at the club anytime soon," he said.

"That bad?" Freddie asked.

"It's more the ink. It doesn't come off as easily as the blood."

"He does look diseased," Thamesly said.

"And you're sure the cat didn't bite you, lick you, anything like that?" Nicholas asked.

"Is it dangerous to be licked by a cat?" Georgie inquired.

"Only if it's in an open wound."

"Thank goodness," she said. "I'd be dead in a week."

Freddie muttered something under his breath. Nicholas could not fully make out the words, but it was enough for him to splash a little extra whiskey into the wound.

"You were saying about the cat?" Nicholas murmured.

Freddie glared up at him. "I am quite sure it did not bite, lick, spit, piss—"

"Done!" Georgie announced, expertly cutting Freddie off as she made her final snip with a flourish. She looked over at Nicholas. "Now what do we do?"

"If you would avert your eyes," Thamesly said. He motioned wanly toward Freddie's now bare chest.

"I can't treat him if I can't see him," Georgie said.

"Mr. Rokesby is here to treat him."

"And I am his assistant." She gave Nicholas a rather fierce look. "I am your assistant, am I not?"

"Absolutely," he said. And he meant it. She was doing a brilliant job. "We'll need something to act as a splint." Nicholas looked up at the two butlers. Thamesly was holding the lantern, so he directed his request to Wheelock. "Could you find a stick or something about yea-long?"

Wheelock squinted as he took in the measurement Nicholas had indicated with his hands. "Right away, sir."

Nicholas turned back to his patient but spoke to Georgiana. "We need to set the bone before we splint it."

"And how do we do that?"

"Move closer to his head," Nicholas directed. "I need you to hold his upper arm. Firmly. It is vital that you keep him immobile. I'll pull on the lower part of his arm to create traction. That will separate the ends of the bone so that I can fit them back into the proper alignment."

She nodded. "I can do it."

"Could one of them"—Freddie flicked his head toward the butlers—"hold my shoulder?"

"It's Miss Bridgerton or no one," Nicholas said sharply. "Your choice."

Freddie hesitated a moment too long, so Nicholas said, "It's a two-person job."

It wasn't, strictly speaking, but it was certainly easier with two people than one.

"Fine," Freddie ground out. "Do your worst."

"I should think you'd want our best," Georgie quipped. She shot Nicholas an adorable little smile, and he realized—*She's enjoying this.*

No, she was *really* enjoying it.

He smiled back.

"Are you ready?" he asked her.

She nodded.

He looked down at Freddie. "It's going to hurt."

"It already does."

"It's going to hurt worse. Do you want something to bite down on?"

"Don't need it," Freddie scoffed.

Nicholas brought his face closer to that of his patient. *"Are you sure?"*

"I . . . think so?" Freddie was starting to look concerned.

Nicholas turned back to Georgie. "Are you ready?"

She nodded eagerly.

"On the count of three. One, two—"

Oakes let out a bloodcurdling scream.

"We didn't even do anything yet," Nicholas said in disgust.

"It *hurts*."

"Stop being such a baby," Georgie said.

"If I didn't know better," Freddie said, "I'd think you were enjoying this."

Georgie leaned in close, baring her teeth. "Oh, I *am*," she said. "I am definitely enjoying this."

"Bloodthirsty—"

"*Don't* say it," Nicholas warned.

"If it makes you feel better," Georgie said to Freddie, "my enjoyment is primarily of an academic nature. It has very little to do with you."

"Speak for yourself, Miss Georgiana," came the voice of Thamesly. "I am enjoying Mr. Oakes's pain and distress immensely."

Wheelock's head popped into view. "As am I."

"The merry band of butlers," Freddie muttered.

"Quite," Wheelock said. "In fact, I would go so far to say that I am as merry as I have ever been."

"Not such a difficult achievement," Nicholas was compelled to point out. "You are not generally known for your merry countenance."

Wheelock smiled, so broadly that Nicholas nearly flinched from the sight of it. "Good God," he said, "I didn't know you had so many teeth."

"All thirty-two, sir," Wheelock said, tapping against

an incisor with his knuckle. "One does not need to attend medical school to understand the importance of good oral hygiene."

"Can we get back to it?" Freddie asked, all piss and petulance.

"We haven't even started," Nicholas said. "You screamed last time before we could do anything."

"Fine. I'll take something to bite down on."

Everyone paused and looked about.

"I have a stick," Wheelock said. He held up a medium-sized twig. "I took the liberty of collecting it when I was looking for a splint. Which I also have." He held up medium-thick stick, a few inches shorter than Oakes's ulna. Nicholas nodded approvingly. It would be perfect.

Freddie jerked his head to indicate that he wanted the twig. Wheelock brought it to his mouth pointy-end first.

"Wheelock," Nicholas scolded.

Wheelock sighed and made a great show of turning the twig the proper way. Oakes took it between his teeth and grunted for Nicholas to continue.

"Ready, Georgie?"

She nodded.

"One . . . Two . . . *Three*."

There was a wrenching groan on the part of Freddie, but Nicholas got the bone into place on the first try. "Excellent," he said to himself, checking the limb to be sure. "Splint?"

Wheelock handed him the stick.

"Can one of you rip his shirt in two? We'll use one part for the stick and the other to fashion a sling."

"I can cut it," Georgie said.

"It'll be quicker this way," Nicholas told her. "I would have just torn it before, but I was concerned about jostling the break."

"Oh. Good. I would hate to think all my work was for nothing. Or worse"—she paused to make a snip in the edge of the fabric to make it easier to rip—"that you were just giving me something to do for the sake of giving me something to do."

"Not at all. You were indispensable."

She beamed, and for a moment Nicholas stopped breathing. It was the dead of night, pitch black save for the lantern and the moon.

And her smile.

When Georgiana Bridgerton smiled like that, he wanted to reach into the sky and grab down the sun, just to hand it to her on a platter.

If only to prove that it did not compare.

"Nicholas?"

What was happening to him?

"Nicholas?"

This was Georgie, whom he'd never thought to marry. Georgie, who, when he did think to marry her, had said no.

Georgie, who—

"*Sir!*"

He blinked. Wheelock was glaring at him.

"Miss Bridgerton has called your name at least twice," the butler said.

"Sorry," Nicholas mumbled. "I was just . . . thinking . . ." He shook his head. "I'm sorry. What is it?"

"The splint," Georgie said, holding up a piece of Freddie's shirt.

"Right. Of course." Nicholas took it from her and looked down, both eager and relieved to have something medical upon which to focus.

He wrapped the arm, using the cloth to hold the makeshift stick in place. "You'll want to see a doctor as soon as possible," he said to Freddie. "He'll be able to get you sorted with a proper splint."

"You don't think Mr. Oakes will wish to use a branch for the duration of his convalescence?" Georgie teased.

"It would work if it had to," Nicholas said with half a smile. "But he'll be more comfortable with something other than needs-must medicine."

"Well, I'm impressed," Georgie said, watching Nicholas as he fashioned a sling for Freddie's arm. "Anyone can set an arm in the comfort of their home."

"Anyone?" Nicholas murmured.

"Anyone with a little training," she amended. "It takes talent to do it in the dead of night with nothing but a stick and a lantern."

"And whiskey," Nicholas said, holding up the flask in salute.

"I thought that was for his face."

He took a swig. "And to salute a job well done."

"In that case . . ." She held out her hand.

"That's right," he said. "You've never had it."

"Mr. Rokesby," Thamsely said with palpable disapproval. "Surely you are not offering spirits to Miss Bridgerton."

Nicholas looked up at the butler. "We're outside in the dead of night, tending to a man without a shirt, and *that's* what you object to?"

Thamsely stared at him for a long beat and then snatched the flask right out of his hand. "As long as I have a drink first," he muttered. He popped one back, then handed it to Georgie. "Miss."

"Thank you, Thamsely," she said, her eyes darting back and forth between the butler and Nicholas as if to say—*Did that really just happen?*

She took a dainty sip before handing the flask back to Nicholas. "That's vile."

"You get used to it."

"Some for me?" Freddie asked.

"No," everyone said in unison.

"Buggers," Freddie said sullenly.

"Language, Mr. Oakes," Thamesly said.

"Please don't step on me again," Freddie moaned.

"Keep your mouth shut and we have a deal."

Nicholas caught Georgie's eye, and they both stifled a laugh.

"If I might interrupt," Wheelock said, "we do need to decide what to do with him. Much as I'd like to leave him to the wolves, we cannot simply abandon him."

"There are wolves?" Freddie asked.

"You're speaking, Mr. Oakes," Thamesly warned.

"There aren't wolves," Georgie said, somewhat impatiently. "Good heavens."

"One of us is going to need to see him home," Nicholas said. "Or at least to a coaching inn. I assume he can take care of himself from there." He turned to Freddie. "It goes without saying that you will never breathe a word of this to anyone."

"If you do," Georgie put in, "I'll tell everyone you were felled by a housecat."

Freddie looked ready to snarl, but Thamesly nudged him with his toe before he could speak.

"Load him into the cart," Thamesly said. "I'll take him to the Frog and Swan."

"Are you sure?" Georgie asked. "It's a two-hour drive at least. The Musty Duck is much closer."

"Best if he's out of the area," Thamesly said. "Plus, he'll be on the main road. It will be easier for him to hire transport to London."

Georgie nodded. "If you take the cart, though, how will I . . ." She looked over at Nicholas.

"I will see you home," he said. "Wheelock can ride with us, if it makes you more comfortable."

"It will make *me* more comfortable," Thamesly said.

"For heaven's sake, Thamesly," Georgie said. "Are you worried for me or for my reputation? Because if it's for me, surely you know that Mr. Rokesby is as honorable a man as you will ever meet. And if it is for my reputation, my God, what is left to ruin?"

Thamesly regarded her for a long moment, then stepped on Freddie's leg again.

"Bloody hell! I didn't say a word!"

"That one," Thamesly said, "was just for fun."

Chapter 11

"A word, Mr. Wheelock?" Georgie placed her hand on the butler's arm before he could go to help Nicholas and Thamesly load Freddie Oakes onto the cart.

"Of course, Miss Bridgerton. What is it?"

She gave her head a little tick, motioning to the side. "In private, if you don't mind." She didn't think that Nicholas could hear her, but better to be safe than sorry.

Wheelock nodded his assent, and they moved a few steps away.

"Ehrm . . ." *How to start? What to say?* She settled on: "I have an unusual request."

Wheelock said nothing, but his brows rose, signaling that she should continue.

Georgie cleared her throat. This was far more difficult than it should have been. Or maybe it was exactly as difficult as it should be. She'd made a big mistake this afternoon, and no one had ever said that fixing one's mistakes was supposed to be easy.

"You might be aware that Mr. Rokesby has asked me to marry him," she said.

"I was not aware," Wheelock replied, his face betraying no emotion, "but I am not surprised."

"Right, well . . ." She cleared her throat again, trying to decide how best to continue. She couldn't very well tell Wheelock that she had rejected the proposal. He loved Nicholas like a son. In fact, she'd always suspected that the youngest Rokesby was his favorite of the brood.

"I didn't give him an answer," she fibbed. Not the correct answer, at least.

Again, Wheelock's brows rose. This time, Georgie thought, because he judged her to be either insane or a fool for not having accepted Nicholas immediately.

"I should like to have the opportunity to speak with him about it this evening," she said.

"It cannot wait until morning?"

She shook her head, hoping he would not press for further clarification.

"May I assume that you do not plan to disappoint him?"

"You may," Georgie said quietly.

Wheelock gave a slow, considering nod. "It would be difficult for you to find the right moment if I accompany you to Aubrey Hall."

"That was my thought."

"But you don't want Mr. Thamesly to be aware of the lapse of propriety."

"That was also my thought."

Wheelock's lips pursed. "I try to live by a certain set of rules and standards, and this, Miss Bridgerton, goes against almost all of them."

"Only almost?" she said hopefully.

"Indeed," he said, quite clearly against his better judgment. He sighed, but it was overdramatized and obviously for her benefit. "I shall devise some sort of nonsense once Mr. Thamesly has departed with the cart. You shall have your moment alone with Mr. Rokesby."

"Thank you, Mr. Wheelock."

He stared down his nose at her. "Do not make me regret my decision, Miss Bridgerton."

"I would never," Georgie vowed.

True to his word, once Thamesly rolled away with a disgruntled Freddie Oakes sitting next to him in the seat of the cart, Wheelock "noticed" that his mount was favoring his right foreleg.

Nicholas looked over from where he was checking his own mount's saddle. "Are you certain? She seemed unhampered on the way over."

"I thought I—" Wheelock pointed. "There. Did you see that?"

Georgie didn't see a thing, and she was quite certain Nicholas didn't either, but Wheelock gave them no opportunity to contribute further to the conversation. "I will have to walk her back," he said. "We risk injury, otherwise. I don't think she can take my weight."

"No, of course not," Nicholas murmured. But he looked slightly conflicted since the original plan was for all three of them to ride to Aubrey Hall to drop off Georgie. "I suppose we can all walk to Aubrey Hall, but . . ."

"We don't have time," Wheelock said with a shake of his head. "It's already too close to sunrise. The servants will be rising soon."

"I trust you," Georgie said to Nicholas. It seemed like the right time to chime in. "And honestly, it's not like we've never been alone together."

His blue eyes met hers. "Are you sure?"

"Are you going to attack and ravish me?"

"Of course not!"

"Then I'm sure."

"Jesus, Georgie," Nicholas said under his breath.

"Don't *you* scold me for language." She let out a little huff. "After everything that's happened tonight, surely I'm entitled."

"Of this night," Wheelock pronounced, "we shall never speak."

"Thank you, Wheelock," Nicholas said. "Truly."

"It was my honor, sir. Now if you will excuse me, I must start back. It's best if I'm at Crake before the household rouses."

"Move as swiftly as is safe," Nicholas directed.

"Oh, but Wheelock? Could you give me a leg up before you go?" Georgie asked.

Nicholas gave her a look. "I can help you."

"We've only the one horse," she explained. "I assume you'll be in front. Won't it be easier if you mount first?"

He muttered something she could not quite make out, but he must have agreed with her because he swung himself up onto his horse.

"It must be nice to be so tall," Georgie grumbled. As if men didn't already have the advantage in, well, *everything*, they didn't need blocks just to get into a saddle.

Or the hands of a helpful butler. Poor Wheelock seemed somewhat chagrined to be performing such a menial task, but as in all things, he had no difficulty hoisting her up into the saddle.

"Can he do everything?" Georgie asked with no sarcasm whatsoever.

Nicholas chuckled. "As far as I can tell."

It was at that moment that Georgie realized just how risqué a position she'd put herself into. She could not recall the last time she'd ridden astride, and it was positively scandalous how far she had to hike up her nightshift to be able to spread her legs widely enough.

"Let me just adjust my dressing gown," she mumbled. It was split in the front, and so she was able to tuck it around her legs. Somewhat.

"Are you comfortable?" Nicholas asked.

"Yes," she lied.

Because she wasn't comfortable at all. As she wrapped her arms around his waist, the distance between them disappeared entirely, and when he spoke, she *felt* his voice. It pulsed through his body, humming against her skin before it sank into her bones. Her breasts were pressed against his back, and as she bobbed up and down in the saddle along with the movement of the horse, they began to feel sensitive in a way that was entirely new to her. Her nipples grew hard, like they did in the cold, but the similarity ended there. Instead of discomfort, she felt a tingling sensation, one that shot through her like sparks, stealing her breath.

Stealing her sanity.

Was this arousal? She'd seen the looks her brother and Violet shared when they thought no one was looking. Whatever it was that passed between them, it was different from love. It was flirty, and it was hot, and Georgie had never quite understood it.

Now she, too, was gripped by something unfamiliar. And strange, because this was Nicholas, and even though she had decided to accept his marriage proposal, she hadn't thought she'd feel this urge to hold him closer, this need to feel his body pressed hard against hers.

She felt hungry. At her center, at that part of her body she was not supposed to talk about.

Not hungry. Ravenous.

Dear God.

"Are you all right?" Nicholas asked, sending a brief glance at her over his shoulder.

"Yes," she somehow managed to say. "Of course. Why?"

"You made a noise."

Thank *God* they were on horseback, with sound muffled by the wind and the beating of the hooves. Because she had an awful suspicion that when the horse had shifted from a trot to a canter, she'd actually moaned.

"Just a yawn," she improvised. But she was glad for

his question. And for her embarrassment. She'd needed something to snap her out of her sultry haze.

"It's not much farther," Nicholas said.

She nodded against him, enjoying the warmth and the closeness, his clean masculine scent, and the slightly scratchy wool of his coat.

Nicholas had been magnificent this evening. There was something thrilling about a man who was capable, who could do things and fix things. She'd been mesmerized by his hands, by his flat, square nails, and the quiet confidence of his movements.

She could be happy with him. She was sure of it. Maybe it wouldn't be the great love story she'd seen her brother and sister find, but she would be happy. More than happy, even.

What lay between happiness and love?

If all went well, she'd marry this man and find out.

They reached the edge of Aubrey Hall's south lawn, and Nicholas brought the horse to a stop, keeping them veiled in a small copse of trees. "We shouldn't ride any closer," he said. "It will make too much noise." He dismounted, then reached up to help her down, his large hands spanning her hips.

Her feet touched the ground, and he let go, exactly as he should.

But she wished he hadn't.

She liked being near him. She liked his quiet strength, his sense of purpose. And when his hands had been on her hips, even just to help her down from the saddle, she'd liked the way it had made her feel like she was his.

"How do you propose to enter the house?" he asked, demonstrating that *his* mind wasn't on such fanciful thoughts. In fact, he looked terribly stiff and formal, clasping his hands in front of him in that way gentlemen were taught to do whenever they stood still.

Georgie felt a stab of disappointment. It served her right, though, she supposed, for having said no when he'd asked her to marry him.

"Thamesly and I left one of the doors ajar," she answered. "In the silver salon. It's far from the servants' quarters."

He nodded. "I will walk you to the house. It's still dark enough. No one will be about."

"It's not necessary. I can always say I went for a walk."

He looked down at her. "Dressed like that?"

"I've done stranger things." She shrugged, but she couldn't stop herself from tugging the collar of her dressing gown closer together.

He let out the tiniest of sighs. "Indulge me my gentlemanly tendencies and pray allow me to see you to the door."

For some reason this made her smile. "You'll be able to see me from here. Almost the entire way."

He did not look happy, but he did not argue.

She swallowed. It was now or never. "Before I go, I wanted to ask you . . ."

His eyes met hers.

"Is it . . ."

This was so *hard*. And it was her own fault that it was.

"I was wondering," she began again, not quite looking at him, "if . . ."

He shifted his posture, clasping his hands behind his back. "What is it, Georgie?"

She looked up, because this was the sort of thing that deserved something more genuine than her gaze on the ground.

He deserved more.

"I would like to reconsider your offer of marriage," she finally said.

And then he said—

"Why?"

What the devil?

"Why?" she echoed. She had not thought he would question her. He would say yes, or he would say no, and she would carry on from there.

"Why," he repeated. "You were quite firm this afternoon." He frowned. "Yesterday afternoon, I suppose it is now."

"You surprised me," she said. It was certainly the truth, and surely it was best to be honest. "I should have taken the time to think before answering, but everyone has been so pitying and it has been awful, and all I could think was that you felt sorry for me, and wasn't that a terrible reason to ask someone to marry you, and I didn't want you to regret it."

But then she realized this wasn't quite what had happened. She took a deep breath and said, "No, that's not true. I wasn't thinking about you. I was thinking about myself, which isn't as selfish as it sounds, or at least I hope not, but it's a horrible thing to be pitied. It's just horrible. And I couldn't see past that."

Her words came out like a flood, but his expression remained even. Not emotionless, not unkind, just . . . even.

She wasn't sure if this scared her.

"What changed your mind?" he asked.

Finally, an easy question. "I got home and realized I was being an idiot."

One side of his mouth hitched up. Almost a smile. That had to count for something.

But he did not speak, which meant she had to, and

now that she'd managed to say the important part she wasn't sure she had anything left.

"I think . . . I think . . ."

I think I can make you happy. I know I will try.

I think if I go with you to Edinburgh I might find that I'm not the person I always thought I was.

Maybe I'm someone better.

"Georgie?"

"I will be a good wife to you," she said.

"That was never in any doubt."

"I was going to come see you tomorrow." She looked up at the sky as if she knew how to tell time by the stars. Stars that weren't even out. The clouds still hung heavy, but it didn't feel like rain. "Today, I suppose. I have no idea what time it is."

"I was planning to leave for Edinburgh."

"I was planning to come very early."

"Were you?"

She nodded. There was something teasing in his voice, and it left her with a feeling she could only describe as fizzy.

"I was. But then all this happened"—she waved her arm behind her, assuming he'd correctly interpret that to mean Freddie Oakes and his broken arm—"and then I saw you . . ."

This seemed to amuse him. "You saw me?"

"Tending to Freddie's arm."

"Technically," he said, "I saw *you* tending to Freddie's arm."

"You're making this very difficult," she muttered.

He crossed his arms, not in an angry way; rather, there was something almost sarcastic to it, as if the very motion said—*What did you expect?*

"You were practicing medicine," she said. It seemed far too formal a phrase for the moment, but she didn't know what else to say. And so she continued in her apparent quest to have the most awkward conversation of her life. "There was something very attractive about it," she mumbled.

"About practicing medicine?" he asked, and she couldn't quite tell if he was dubious or amused.

"You knew what you were doing," she said with a helpless shrug.

"You like a man who knows what he's doing?"

"Apparently I do."

His eyes settled on hers, and she could not look away. She didn't *want* to look away.

"Well, then, Miss Bridgerton," he said. "I suppose I will ask you again."

Her breath caught. It wasn't a surprise. She'd known he would renew his offer; he was too honorable a man to refuse her. But she had not anticipated just how anxious she would feel, regardless.

He took her hand. He had not done that the first time around.

"Georgiana Bridgerton," he said, "will you marry me?"

She nodded solemnly. "I would be honored."

And then . . . nothing.

They just stood there.

"Right. Well," Nicholas said.

Georgie swallowed. "That settles it."

"Indeed."

She rocked on her feet, wondering how on earth she felt more awkward now than she had when she was actually asking him to marry her.

Or rather, when she was asking him to ask her to marry him. Which was quite possibly worse.

Finally, he broke the silence. "It's almost dawn," he said.

She looked to the east. There was no pink or orange to be found, but at the edge of the horizon, the sky was a lighter shade of blue.

"I should go," she said, without actually making a move to do so.

"Right." He brought her hand to his lips. "You should know that I am not a wealthy man. My family is, but I, myself, am not."

"I don't care." It was the truth. And while Nicholas might not be wealthy in the manner of an earl or a viscount, he would certainly never be poor. As his wife, she would want for nothing important.

"I will work for a living," he continued. "Some might call me a cit."

"No one whose opinion matters to me."

He held her gaze for a few more seconds, then murmured, "It is almost morning."

"You should kiss me," she blurted out.

His grip tightened on her hand.

"Isn't that what people do?" she asked, trying to cover her embarrassment.

He, too, looked a little uncomfortable, which made her feel better. "I suppose it is," he said.

"I've never kissed anyone," she whispered. "Freddie tried, but . . ."

He shook his head. "It wouldn't have counted, even if he succeeded."

"No, I suppose not." She swallowed nervously, waiting.

Waiting.

Why was he just looking at her like that? Why didn't he kiss her?

Maybe this was up to her. He had been brave when he asked her to marry him. Now it was her turn.

She rose onto her tiptoes, leaned forward, and touched her lips to his. She lingered there a little longer than she thought she was supposed to, and then set herself back down.

Well. That was that.

Her first kiss.

All in all, it wasn't very exciting.

She looked up at him. He was gazing down at her in a manner that was utterly inscrutable.

She cleared her throat. "I don't suppose that was your first kiss too?"

He shook his head. "No. But my kisses have not been legion."

She stared at him for a moment, then burst out laughing. "Your kisses have not been legion? What on earth does that mean?"

"It means that I have not had many of them," he ground out.

And she realized—*he was embarrassed.*

Maybe. She wasn't sure.

But it made sense if he was. Theirs was a stupid society, she was coming to realize. Men were supposed to have experience before they married and women were meant to be pure as snow.

Georgie had accepted this as the way things were, but after all that had happened in the last few weeks, she was fed up with the whole thing. It was the same hypocrisy that led the *ton* to celebrate Freddie Oakes while she was deemed soiled.

Very well, maybe they had not *celebrated* him, but his reputation had taken no hit.

"I'm sorry," she told him. "That was terribly rude of me. It was your wording that was amusing, not the sentiment behind it. Although, I must confess . . ."

"Yes?" he prompted.

Her cheeks were burning, but still she admitted, "I'm *glad* you haven't kissed many women."

He started to smile. "Are you?"

She nodded. "You won't be much better at it than I am."

"We could try it again," he suggested.

"Now?"

"No time like the present."

"I'm not sure if that's strictly true," she replied. "At present we are hiding behind a tree in the shadows of my home, and it's, I don't know, perhaps five in the morning. We've just treated the broken arm of my sworn enemy, which necessitated my literally cutting the shirt from a man's body, and—"

"Georgie?" he interrupted. "Shut up."

She looked at him, blinking like mad.

"Let's try it again, shall we?"

Chapter 12

O nce the engagement was announced, it was remarkable how quickly it all moved forward.

Nicholas was impressed. Or rather, he would have been impressed if he had not been so frustrated. And overwhelmed.

But mostly frustrated.

That kiss . . . the one he'd been so suave in suggesting when he'd murmured *Let's try it again, shall we . . . ?*

Disaster.

He'd leaned down to kiss Georgie, and honestly he didn't know what had happened—maybe she'd jumped?—because his forehead knocked hers with enough force to make him lurch back in surprise.

He wouldn't say he saw stars. That seemed far too

grand a description for the jolt of pain that shot through his skull. Stars were a good thing, and this was . . . not.

He'd tried again, of course. He'd just spent the better part of twenty minutes in a rather uncomfortable state of arousal. *And* she had made it quite clear she wanted to be kissed. *And* he was going to marry her.

So yes. He was going to attempt another kiss. Frankly, he thought himself rather restrained considering he'd ridden from the farmhouse to Aubrey Hall with his future wife's bare legs wrapped around his thighs. She'd tried to preserve her modesty with her dressing gown, but that had lasted no more than thirty seconds.

Even when he kept his eyes forward (which he did, some of the time), thus avoiding a glimpse of the moonlight rippling across her pale skin, there was still the matter of her breasts, which had been pressed up against his back, and her hands, which had been pressed up against his belly.

Everything. Her everything had been pressed up against his everything, and by the time they reached Aubrey Hall he was hard as a bloody rock, which was no way to ride a horse.

Or dismount from a horse.

Or help a lady dismount from a horse. When he'd placed his hands on Georgie's hips it had been all he could do not to slide them down the length of her.

Instead he'd let go as if she'd caught on fire. Metaphorically speaking, it wasn't that far from the truth.

He'd clasped his hands in front of himself because *Good God*, what else was he supposed to do? He couldn't just stand there with his cock trying to bust out of his breeches.

But their first kiss had been uninspiring. And their second downright painful.

He'd pondered a third, but then the horse sneezed. On Georgie.

That was the end of it. The sun was close to rising, his ardor was cooled, and frankly, there were plans to be made.

He needed to go home, inform his parents that Georgie had accepted his proposal, and see to putting that special license to use. They'd be married in a day, maybe two, and he could be on his way back to Scotland. He wasn't precisely sure how he and Georgie would manage once they reached Edinburgh—he was quite certain he could not bring her to live with him in his rented boardinghouse rooms. His father had said something about renting a house in New Town, but surely such arrangements took time. Georgie might want to wait in Kent until they could secure a lease.

But this was not the time to make such a decision. He could bring it up later, when she wasn't in her dressing gown and he didn't still have a handkerchief in his pocket stained with whiskey and Freddie Oakes's blood.

They said their farewells—perhaps a little more stiffly than was warranted—and Nicholas remounted his horse.

"Wait!" Georgie called.

He turned his mount. "What is it?"

"How shall we tell them? Our families?"

"However you like." Honestly, he had not thought about it.

"Yours already knows, I imagine."

"Just my parents. And obviously they do not yet know you have accepted."

She nodded, slowly, the way he'd come to realize she did when she was thinking something through. "Will you come with me?" she asked. "When I tell them?"

"If that is what you wish."

"I do. They will have so many questions. I think it will be easier for me if you are there to share the burden."

"The very definition of marriage," he murmured.

She smiled at that.

"Shall I call upon you later this morning?"

"That would be most welcome."

And that was that. There was nothing romantic about

the moment, nothing to make his breath catch or heart leap or any of that nonsense.

Until she smiled.

His breath caught.

His heart leapt.

And he felt *all* the nonsense.

Georgie was eating breakfast when Nicholas arrived. It was as they'd planned; she wanted to make sure that her parents were both available when he arrived, and as the Bridgerton family tended to keep to a regular morning schedule, it seemed the best time for him to find them all in attendance.

She had not anticipated, however, that he would arrive with his own parents in tow.

"You're all here," she said with faint surprise when he leaned down to greet her.

"Surely you did not think I would come on my own." He quirked a brow, the expression oddly devilish on so serious a person. "If I am to share your familial burden, you must share mine."

"Fair enough."

He sat beside her. "Also, I couldn't stop them."

This made her grin, but for some foolish reason she hid this behind a sip of her tea.

The Rokesbys were regular visitors to Aubrey Hall, but it was somewhat unusual for them to make a call so early, and indeed Lady Bridgerton wore an expression of surprise as she rose to greet them. "Helen!" she exclaimed as she went to her friend's side. "This is unexpected. What brings you to Aubrey Hall this morning?"

"Ah, well, you know . . ." Lady Manston mumbled a string of nothings. Georgie was impressed. She knew Nicholas's mother quite well; she had to be bursting with the news.

"Is something amiss?" Lady Bridgerton asked.

"Not at all." This, however, was said with enough vigor and emphasis to cause the whole room to look her way.

"Mother," Nicholas said under his breath. He leaned out of his chair and took hold of her arm, gently tugging her away from Lady Bridgerton. He looked over at Georgie. "Where is Edmund?"

"He and Violet already left with the boys."

"Probably a good thing," he replied. "It's going to be chaos enough in a moment."

Lady Bridgerton looked from person to person. "Why do I feel as if there is a secret and everyone knows it but me?"

"*I* don't know it," Lord Bridgerton said genially, getting back to his breakfast. "If it makes you feel better." He motioned for Lord Manston to take a seat beside him. "Coffee?"

"Or champagne," Lord Manston murmured.

Nicholas's head whipped around. *"Father."*

Georgie bit her tongue to keep from laughing at his frustration.

"You're not helping," he warned her.

Georgie decided there was nothing to do but make her announcement. "Mama, Papa, I have something important to tell you."

Nicholas cleared his throat.

"That is to say, *we* have something important to tell you."

Georgie had not intended to draw out the moment. But there was something fascinating and delightful in watching the parents react—Lady Manston's giddy smile, Lord Manston's smug happiness. Her own mother's eyes widening as she realized what was happening. Her father, of course, remained clueless until Georgie announced, "Nicholas and I have decided to marry."

"Oh, that's *wonderful!*" Lady Bridgerton exclaimed, and Georgie did not think it was an exaggeration to say that her mother leapt across the room to give her a hug.

"This is the *best* news," Lady Bridgerton continued. "Oh, the very best. I could not have hoped for better. I don't know *why* I didn't think of it, except that Nicholas was not here, and it never occurred to me—"

"It does not matter how it came about," Georgie interrupted gently, "just that it is happening."

"Yes, of course," her mother said. She looked over at her husband. "We'll need a special license."

"Done!" Lord Manston called out, and Georgie could not keep her mouth from falling open when he whipped the document out of his pocket.

"I have it right here," he said. "We could get them married this afternoon."

Georgie tried to intercede. "I don't think—"

"Should we?" her mother said. "I mean, yes, of course, there is every reason to get it done and quickly, but would such haste be unseemly—"

"Who will know if it's unseemly or not?" Lady Manston put in. "No one knows when he asked her, and it's not as if anyone will think it's not in *some* response to the scandal."

"That's true," Lady Bridgerton mused. "It really is more of a we-must-make-the-best-of-it situation."

"I'm delighted," Lord Bridgerton said to no one in particular. "Just delighted."

Lord Manston leaned over and said something in his ear. Georgie was no lip reader, but she was fairly certain it was: "This was my idea."

Nicholas turned to Georgie. "Do you think anyone will notice if we leave?"

She shook her head. "Not even a little bit."

"We must make plans," Lady Bridgerton announced.

"No time for a grand wedding," Lord Bridgerton reminded her.

"I'm not talking about the wedding," she replied. "I'm talking about *after*. Where will they live?"

"Edinburgh, Mama," Georgie said, even though the question, while *about* her, had not been directed *toward* her. "Nicholas must return to school."

"Yes of course, but . . ." Lady Bridgerton let her words trail off, and she made a little motion with her hands that seemed to indicate that she expected everyone to understand what that meant.

"But nothing, Mama. I will go with him to Scotland."

"Darling," her mother said, "you don't want to go to Edinburgh right away."

Georgie kept her expression scrupulously even and matter-of-fact. "But I do."

"Don't be silly. Nothing will be ready."

"I don't mind."

"That's only because you don't know."

Georgie tried not to grit her teeth. "Then I'll learn."

Lady Bridgerton turned to Lady Manston as if to say, *Help me here.*

Lady Manston smiled brightly. "Lord Manston wishes to lease a house for you in New Town."

"New Town?" Georgie echoed. She didn't know much about Edinburgh, she realized. Nothing, really.

"It's the new part of town," Nicholas said.

"Oh, that's helpful," she muttered.

He shrugged. "It's true."

She scowled. "Really?"

"Some of Andrew's friends are involved in the planning," Lord Manston said. "It's all very progressive, I'm told."

Nicholas's older brother Andrew was an architect by training, if not by degree. Georgie had always enjoyed talking with him about architecture and engineering, and if he said New Town was the place to lease a house, she was sure he was correct.

This did nothing to mitigate the fact, however, that if one more person tried to tell her what she wanted, she was going to scream.

"Georgiana," Lady Manston said, "it will be very rough in Edinburgh."

"Rough?" Georgie echoed. What the devil did that mean?

Nicholas leaned forward, frowning at his mother. "What are you talking about? It's a perfectly civilized city."

"No, no," Lady Manston replied, "that's not what I meant. I'm sure it will be a lovely place to live. Eventually." She turned to Georgie. "You must understand—even once a suitable house is found, there will be much to do. Furniture to purchase, servants to hire."

"I can do all that," Georgie said.

"Georgie," her mother said, "I'm not sure you understand—"

"I can do all that," Georgie ground out.

"Only if you want to," Nicholas said. He was trying to be helpful, she was sure, but what she really needed was for him to put an end to all of this interference and insist that they travel north as a couple.

"I am not going to remain in Kent after I marry," Georgie said firmly.

"It *would* send an odd message," her mother acquiesced.

"I don't care about the message," Georgie said. "I care about myself. And Nicholas," she added hastily.

He nodded graciously.

"If I am marrying him, then I am marrying him. Boardinghouse and all."

Nicholas cleared his throat. "Actually," he said, "I'm not certain if ladies are permitted in Mrs. McGreevey's establishment."

"Even married ladies?" his mother asked.

"I honestly don't know. I never had cause to ask. But the current tenants are all male." He turned to Georgie. "I do want you to come with me to Edinburgh, but I'm not sure you will be comfortable in such an environment."

"We won't know unless we try," she muttered.

"They can have Scotsby," Lord Bridgerton suddenly said.

All eyes turned in his direction.

"Scotsby," he said again. "I'm sure I've told you about it. It's a small hunting lodge. Haven't been there in ages, but it's not too far from Edinburgh. I don't see why they can't stay there. Nicholas can travel in when he needs to."

"That is most generous of you, sir," Nicholas said, "but how far is it from Edinburgh, if I might ask?"

Lord Bridgerton frowned. "I don't recall precisely, but it can't be more than two hours."

"Two . . . *hours?*"

"By coach," Lord Bridgerton clarified. "Half that on horseback, I would think."

"Papa, that won't work," Georgie said, leaping in before Nicholas could protest. "Nicholas is very busy. He can't possibly be expected to travel an hour each way just to get to school."

"You have to go every day, then?" Lord Bridgerton asked.

"Most every day, sir," Nicholas said politely.

"I beg your pardon," Lord Bridgerton said. "I'd assumed it was mostly tutors and that sort of thing." He looked up at the room at large. "That won't work then."

"But Georgiana can stay at Scotsby," Lady Bridgerton said.

Georgie's head snapped up. "By myself?"

"You won't be by yourself," her mother assured her. "We're not going to let you go to Scotland without staff."

"I meant without Nicholas," she said.

"It's only temporary, dear," Lady Bridgerton said with a gentle smile. "Until Lord Manston can see to the house in New Town."

"We can find our own lodgings," Nicholas said firmly.

"When?" Lord Manston said. "You're always telling me how busy you are."

"Not too busy to find a place for my wife to live."

"Nicholas, dear," his mother said. "Please accept our help."

"I am happy to accept your help," he said. "Just not your control."

Silence.

"What Nicholas *means* to say," Georgiana jumped in, "is that we would prefer to make our own decisions."

Silence.

"What *Georgie* means to say," Nicholas began, but his tone was such that Georgie thought it best not to let him finish. She gave him a sharp elbow and fixed an accommodating smile on her face.

"Scotsby will make a fine temporary home until we figure out a more long-term solution," she said. She turned to Nicholas. "Wouldn't you agree?"

He looked unconvinced. "It depends on the definition of temporary."

"Obviously," she muttered.

"Regardless," Lady Bridgerton said, after watching this exchange with interest, "you will need some help, at least at the outset. I insist that you take Mrs. Hibbert."

Georgie looked at her mother. "Mrs. Who?"

"Mrs. Hibbert. She is Mrs. Brownley's sister."

"Mrs. Brownley?" Nicholas echoed.

"Our housekeeper," Georgie explained. She turned back to her mother. "I was not aware she had a sister."

"She is new to the area," Lady Bridgerton said. "Recently widowed. But she has experience and is looking for a position."

"Well, then," Georgie said. She couldn't *not* agree. Not if Mrs. Brownley's sister needed work.

"And we shall provide a butler," Lady Manston said.

Georgie blinked. "I'm not sure we need—"

"Of course you do," Lady Manston said. "And besides, it's Wheelock's nephew. You can't say no to Wheelock's nephew."

"Richard?" Nicholas asked.

"Yes. Wheelock has been training him for several months."

"But what if he doesn't want to move?" Georgie asked.

"Head butler positions don't open every day," Lady Manston said. "I'm sure he will want to snatch this up. And besides, Wheelock is originally from the north. But by all means, you can ask Richard yourself."

"Marian will accompany you, of course," Georgie's mother put in, "but I don't feel right sending *only* Marian. I believe Mrs. Hibbert has two daughters. They shall go, too."

"You can't separate a family," Lady Manston said.

"Certainly not."

Georgie cleared her throat. "This seems a rather large retinue for a student and his wife."

"Which is why you'll need a carriage," Lady Manston said. She turned to her husband. "You can see to the carriage. Whatever is best for cold weather."

"We'll have to send them with two," Lord Manston said. "They'll never fit everything in one."

"We don't need two carriages," Georgie protested.

"Of course not." He looked at her as if she were *very* silly. "One will return to Kent."

"Of course," Georgie murmured, wondering why she felt so chastised.

"But you'll need two drivers," Lord Manston continued, "and at least one spare in case one of them takes ill."

"And outriders," Lord Bridgerton said. "The roads are dangerous these days. You cannot be too careful."

"I'm afraid nothing can be done about a cook," Lady Bridgerton said. "You'll have to hire one in Scotland."

"We'll manage," Georgie said weakly. "I'm sure."

"The daughters of your housekeeper's sister," Nicholas's mother said to Georgie's mother. "Can any of them cook?"

Georgie turned to Nicholas. "Didn't you say you took the mail coach down?"

"Most of the way, why?"

"It's starting to sound very appealing."

He made a crooked grin. "That's because you've never ridden in a mail coach."

"We could take one and elope?" she said hopefully.

"NO!" roared her mother.

And his mother.

Georgie startled. She'd thought she'd been speaking under her breath.

"Banish the thought," Lady Bridgerton said.

"I was joking, Mama." Georgie turned to the rest of the table, rolling her eyes. "I was joking."

No one seemed to be amused. Except for Nicholas, who said, "I thought it was funny."

"It's a good thing I'm marrying *you*, then," she muttered.

"Tomorrow," he said suddenly.

"I beg your pardon?"

"Tomorrow." He paused, somewhat dramatically. "We will marry tomorrow. And leave immediately thereafter."

This was met with immediate resistance, the loudest of which came from his father who said, "Don't be daft, son. You can't pack a household that quickly."

Nicholas shrugged. "Then the next day. Either way, I'm leaving. I must get back. I'd rather not leave Georgie to travel north on her own . . ."

"She can't do *that*," his mother said.

He smiled. "Then we are agreed."

And somehow, they were. The parents who had just

been arguing that they couldn't possibly send them off to Scotland in under a week seemed to have no problem with two days' time when the only other alternative was one.

Georgie stared at him in wonder. He was *good*. She couldn't even begrudge his smirk. He deserved that smirk.

Two days. She would be married in two days.

Or to be more precise, she would be married and off to a new country where she knew absolutely no one except her soon-to-be-husband. She had to find a new home, set up a household, make new friends, learn new customs.

She *should* be nervous.

She should be terrified.

But she wasn't.

And as everyone talked around her, the parents making plans and Nicholas taking notes, she realized she was smiling. Grinning, even.

This was going to be grand.

Chapter 13

It wasn't going to be grand.

The wedding was lovely. The wedding breakfast delightful.

But the journey north . . .

No one was going to come out of it alive unless something was done about Cat-Head.

The other two cats were easy. Judyth had curled up in her basket like a proper feline and gone straight to sleep. Blanche had felt the need to demonstrate her contempt for all humans, so she'd spent a few minutes fussing and hissing before finally parking herself as deeply in the corner of the padded coach bench as possible.

But a furious Blanche Georgie knew how to handle.

Blanche would be sullen and resentful, but she was easily bribed with a nugget or two of cheese.

Cat-Head, on the other hand . . .

Cat-Head moaned.

Cat-Head howled.

Cat-Head made noises Georgie would not have thought possible outside purgatory or hell.

And while Georgie might have been able to withstand such torture on her own, the traveling party had grown to fifteen, and she wasn't sure how long she could inflict him on the others.

GRAOWWW!

Georgie peered nervously at Nicholas, sitting across from her in the carriage. He was doing an admirable job of hiding his flinches. Much better than—

GRAOWWW!

—Marian, Georgie's trusted maid, who seemed to have developed a tic in her left cheek.

GRAOWWW!

"Cat-Head, hush," Georgie said, patting him on the head. She didn't know why she thought that might make a difference. It wasn't as if she'd met with success the first one hundred and sixty-three times she'd said it.

GRAOWWW!

"How long have we been on the road?" Marian asked.

Georgie attempted a cheerful tone. "I'm not carrying a timepiece."

"I am," Nicholas said without looking up from his medical journal. "It's been three hours."

"That long?" Georgie said weakly.

GRAOWWW!

Marian's eye began to twitch.

Georgie gave Nicholas a hard stare, the kind where one widened one's eyes and jutted one's chin forward. It clearly meant *Do Something.*

He returned with the sort of expression where one widened one's eyes but instead of a jutted chin one tipped one's head to the side, as if to say a shrugful *What?*

Georgie jutted her chin.

Nicholas tipped his head.

They both widened their eyes.

"Is something wrong?" Marian asked.

GRAOWWW!

"Besides that," she muttered.

"Nicholas," Georgie said pointedly, "perhaps Marian would like a sip of your whiskey."

He blinked, then gave Georgie an expression she was fairly certain meant—*How was I to glean that from your buggy eyes and jutty chin?*

"Er, Miss—"

GRAOWWW!

"Miss Georgiana," Marian croaked. "I don't know how much longer I can—"

"Whiskey?" Nicholas asked, thrusting a flask in her face.

Marian nodded gratefully and took a swig.

GRAOWWW!

"Georgie," Nicholas said, "is there anything to be done?"

He probably deserved her admiration for lasting this long before saying anything, but three hours of constant cat-moaning had left her nerves well frayed. "If there were," she said peevishly, "don't you think I would have done it by now?"

GRAOWWW!

Marian drained the flask.

"Will it continue like this the entire trip to Edinburgh?" Nicholas asked.

"God help us," Marian muttered.

"I don't know," Georgie admitted, finally pulling her eyes off her maid, whom she'd never seen drink more than a quarter-glass of sherry. "I've never taken him in a carriage before. The other two are managing well enough."

"Are you sure about that?" Nicholas asked. "That one looks like its plotting your death."

Georgie peered down at Blanche. She'd been quiet for most of the trip, and Georgie had thought she'd resigned herself to the situation, but at some point during the past few hours the sun had shifted far enough to shed light on her position in the corner of the coach bench. Thus illuminated, it was now clear that Blanche's repose was really the stiffened *I-cannot-BELIEVE-you're-doing-this-to-me* stare of utter betrayal.

Georgie silently handed Blanche a piece of cheese.

GRAOWWW!

"Maybe that one would like some cheese, too," Nicholas suggested.

Georgie shrugged. At this point she was willing to try anything. "Cat-Head?" she said sweetly, holding the creamy nugget in her hand. Cat-Head scarfed up the treasure, and they all breathed a sigh of relief. He wasn't a particularly quiet eater; there was plenty of tongue-smacking and whisker-snuffling, but it was better than—

GRAOWWW!

"Can you give it more cheese?" Marian begged.

"I might have more whiskey," Nicholas said.

"We're not giving whiskey to my cat," Georgie said.

Nicholas and Marian exchanged a glance.

"We're not!"

No one rushed to agree.

"It can't be that much farther to London," Georgie said, with some desperation.

Nicholas peered out at the road. "An hour? Maybe ninety minutes."

"That's all?" Georgie said with forced brightness. "That's nothing. We can—"

GRAOWWW!

"Can you put it in a basket?" Marian asked.

Georgie looked down at Judyth, all fluffy and silver gray, still delightfully quiet in her wicker home. "I've only got the one basket."

"How is that possible?" Nicholas asked.

Georgie thought about that for a moment. "I don't know. We had three starting out. The other two baskets must have ended up in the other carriage. Or perhaps up top."

"Up top, you say?"

Georgie felt her expression turn glacial. "We are not putting Cat-Head on the roof."

Marian turned to Nicholas with a shake of her head. "We'd still hear it."

"It wouldn't be as bad," he mused.

Georgie honestly could not tell if he was being serious.

"Well, if you've only got the one basket," he said, "take the other cat out."

"But she's being so good," Georgie said, gesturing down. "She hasn't made a peep."

"Perhaps she's dead," Nicholas said.

"Nicholas!"

He shrugged. "It would free up the basket."

Georgie fixed him with an icy stare. "I am not going to dignify that with a response."

He shrugged again.

"And there's no guarantee that Cat-Head wouldn't howl if he was in the basket."

Nicholas held up a finger. "Response."

Georgie muttered something under her breath that would not have been considered appropriate for a lady of her station.

GRAOWWW!

"We're nearly to London," Georgie said, almost desperately. She was stroking the cat now with renewed firmness, moving to its cheeks, scratching them with just enough pressure that maybe he wouldn't be able to actually open his jaw . . .

But he tried.

Grrrrrrrrr.

"That was better, don't you think?" Georgie said.

Grrrrrrrrr.

"It sounds like it might combust," Nicholas remarked.

Grrrrrrrrr.

"It can't be healthy for it to hold it all in like that," Marian worried.

Georgie looked at her. "You want me to let go?"

"No!"

Georgie nodded and kept up with the cheek and chin scratching. "There you go, Cat-Head. It's not so bad."

Cat-Head did not seem to appreciate her efforts. *GRRRrrrrr*, he managed, and Georgie found she had to exert more pressure to keep his yawls trapped in his mouth.

"Good kitty," she murmured. "Good, good little kitty."

"Very bad kitty," Nicholas said. "The worst, really."

Georgie glared. "Good kitty," she practically growled. But Cat-Head's little jaw was straining.

GRRRRRrr . . .

Marian's brow knit with concern. "That sounds unsafe."

"No, I'm sure he—"

GRAAAAAAOOOOOOOOWWW!

Cat-Head let out a shriek of such unholy proportions that Georgie's hand popped right off his head. The noise rent the air, and the cat, clearly bursting with the need to let it all out, thrust its legs and head out like a stiff, fuzzy, orange pentagon, howling at the injustice of the world until . . .

He stopped.

The three human occupants of the carriage held their collective breaths.

"Is it dead?" Nicholas finally asked.

Georgie looked at him in horror. "Why do you keep assuming my cats are dead?"

"But is it?"

"I think he fainted," she said, peering down with concern. The cat was sprawled on its back, belly up, one paw thrown dramatically over its face. Gingerly, Georgie put her hand against his chest. "He's still breathing," she said.

Marian let out a sigh. Though *not*, Georgie thought, one of relief.

"Whatever you do," Nicholas said in a low voice, "do not move. If you wake that thing up—"

"It's a cat, Nicholas."

"If you wake that *cat* up," he amended, with no discernable remorse, "our misery will know no bounds."

Marian peered out the window. "Are we slowing down?"

Georgie frowned and leaned forward to look.

"Don't move!" Nicholas and Marian hissed.

"Are we here?" Georgie asked, making a great show of remaining in place.

"That depends on your definition of *here*," Nicholas murmured, "but assuming you meant London, then no, we're not."

The carriage came to a complete stop.

"Stay put," he said. "I'll find out why we've stopped."

Georgie and Marian watched as he hopped down. After a moment, Georgie said, "We can't be that far from our destination."

"No," Marian murmured. "We're meant to get there early evening. Lady Manston sent word ahead for the staff."

Georgie nodded, suddenly very aware of the flock of butterflies taking root in her stomach. The only good thing to have come from Cat-Head's caterwauling was that she hadn't been able to think about the night that lay ahead.

The plan was to spend the night at Manston House, in London. It was the logical first layover on the journey north, and it meant that Georgie and Nicholas would not have to have their wedding night at an inn.

They also would not have to spend it with their families, who were back in Kent. Georgie could not imagine spending her wedding night at Crake, knowing that Nicholas's family were all in their own bedchambers, just down the hall. The only thing worse would be spending the night at Aubrey Hall, with her own family right there.

"Can you see what's happening?" she asked Marian, who was now fully out of her seat and hanging out the open door.

"Mr. Rokesby is speaking with Jameson," Marian said.

"Jameson the groom?"

Marian nodded. "He looks peaked."

"Jameson or Mr. Rokesby?"

"Jameson," Marian confirmed. "Wasn't he meant to be riding ahead to London?"

"He *did* ride ahead to London."

"Well, he's back."

"That doesn't make any sense," Georgie countered.

Marian turned back to look at Georgie. "Sense or not, he's here and he's talking to Mr. Rokesby, and neither one looks pleased. Oh, hold up, here come Marcy and Darcy."

Marcy and Darcy were Mrs. Hibbert's twin daughters. Georgie wasn't sure how old they were—fifteen? Sixteen? They were riding in the second coach along with their mother and Wheelock's nephew (also called Wheelock). The traveling party was rounded out by two Aubrey Hall footmen serving as outriders, two

Crake footmen (also serving as outriders), an Aubrey Hall coachman, a Crake coachman, an Aubrey Hall stableboy, and Jameson, the groom from Crake who had ridden ahead to London.

"Do you know what's happening?" Marian asked Marcy.

Or Darcy, Georgie wasn't sure which. The two girls were wholly identical in appearance.

"Something about pestilence," Marcy-or-Darcy said.

"Pestilence?" Georgie echoed, instinctively starting to rise.

"Don't move!" Marian whisper-shrieked.

Georgie grumbled, but she did as bid. She didn't want Cat-Head to awaken any more than Marian did.

"What was *happening* in your coach?" one of the twins asked Marian. The other wandered off, presumably in search of more interesting conversation.

"The noise?" Marian asked. "It was the cat."

"There was no way they could hear him in the second coach," Georgie protested.

The young maid shrugged. "It sounded like the devil himself was riding up here with you."

"Again," Georgie said, not that anyone was listening, "I don't believe you could hear him."

Marcy-or-Darcy (Georgie was really going to have

to learn how to tell the two apart) poked her head in. "Did you kill it, ma'am?"

"No, I didn't kill the cat," Georgie snapped.

Marcy-or-Darcy looked unconvinced.

"I'm sure Mr. Rokesby didn't say anything about pestilence," Georgie said.

"Not Mr. Rokesby, ma'am," Marcy-or-Darcy said, "Jameson the groom."

"I hardly—I'm sorry," Georgie said. She could not go on like this. "Are you Marcy or Darcy?"

"Marcy, ma'am. You can tell us apart by our freckles."

"Your freckles?"

Marcy leaned farther in, although the effect was somewhat comical since her chin was on level with the floor of the carriage. "I have more than she does," she said, motioning to her cheeks. "See?"

"Perhaps one of you could consider wearing your hair differently," Georgie suggested.

"We used to do," Marcy confirmed, "but Mama said we must wear it back in proper tight buns now that we're in service." She bobbed a quick curtsy, as if only just then remembering that she was speaking with her new employer. Unfortunately for her, this caused her to thunk her chin on the carriage floor.

"Ow!" she let out.

In Georgie's lap, Cat-Head shifted position.

Everyone froze. Well, at least Georgie and Marian did. Marcy clutched her cheek with her hand and jumped up and down as she whimpered in pain.

"Is she bleeding?" Georgie asked.

"Don't move," Marian begged before turning back to Marcy. "Are you bleeding?"

"I think I bit my tongue."

Georgie gasped when Marian moved to the side and Marcy's head came into view. Marcy was trying to smile, but all that did was reveal blood-coated teeth.

"Oh, dear," Georgie said. The poor girl looked positively ghoulish. "You'd better fetch Mr. Rokesby. He will know what to do."

"He's a doctor," Marian assured her.

"He *will be* a doctor," Georgie corrected. "Soon."

Marcy scurried off, and Georgie continued to watch Marian as she hung out of the carriage to try to figure out what was going on.

"You might as well just get out," Georgie muttered. She looked down at Cat-Head, still asleep in her lap. "Since I can't."

Marian gave her a look, as if to get one last verification that Georgie didn't mind if she fled the scene.

"Go," Georgie said. "But see if you can find out why we've stopped!"

Marian nodded, then sat on the floor, dangling her legs out before hopping down. Georgie heard her land with an *oooff*, but she was clearly unhurt because she dashed off.

"Well," Georgie said, not quite daring to direct her soft comment at Cat-Head. "It's just you and me."

Blanche looked up and yawned.

"And you and Judyth," Georgie said, giving Blanche a little nod. "But if you can endeavor to make me forget you again, we'll all be happier."

Blanche gave her a disdainful sniff but she lay back down, clearly pleased that the death-stare she'd been directing at Georgie for the past few hours had had its intended effect—that was to say, the carriage had stopped moving.

But just as Blanche got settled, Cat-Head began to stir, and after a wide yawn it became clear that he was awake and planned to stay that way.

But again, they weren't moving, so at least he was quiet. Georgie set him down on the seat beside her and scooted toward the open carriage door. She might as well stretch her own legs now that she no longer had to hold Cat-Head still. Everyone else seemed to be walking about.

One of the Aubrey Hall footmen saw her in the doorway and rushed over to help her down. But before

Georgie could make her way to Nicholas—still in deep conversation with Jameson—Marian came dashing over.

"Oh, it's terrible, Miss Georgiana," she said, out of breath from running. "London is overrun with plague!"

Chapter 14

G od save him from hysterical women.

"London is not overrun with plague," Nicholas ground out, chasing after Marian before she started a riot.

"Not even a little bit?" the maid asked.

"Do you want it to be?" he asked, somewhat perplexed by the hopeful tone of her question.

"No!" She turned to Georgie. "My goodness, such a thing to say."

Nicholas resisted a retort, but only barely. In any case, his attention was diverted by Marian's next outburst.

"Brimstone and pestilence!"

He stared at her. "What?"

"It's what Jameson said," Marian explained.

"No," Nicholas countered, "that's not what he said." But technically that was almost precisely what Jameson had said. He'd just said it with a lot of swearing and not-fit-for-the-ears-of-ladies modifiers.

God save him from hysterical *men*.

He took a breath and turned to Georgie. "There are several cases of influenza at Manston House. Nothing approaching the level of brimstone. And certainly no plague."

"Well, that's a relief," she said. "Isn't it?"

"Inasmuch as it's better than black death, yes," he said dryly. "But influenza is no trivial matter. We will have to bypass London. There is no way we can stay at Manston House."

"Surely it cannot be so dangerous," Georgie said. "It's such a large building. We need not go near the affected section."

"Influenza is highly contagious, and we don't understand how it spreads. It is simply not safe, especially for you."

"For me?" Georgie's eyes widened, possibly from surprise, possibly from irritation. He could not tell for sure.

"It is a disease of the lungs," he told her. "You may not have had a breathing episode for several years, but you are almost certainly more susceptible than most to this sort of illness."

"Mr. Rokesby is right," Marian said emphatically. "Your mother would flay us alive if we took you to a house with such disease."

Georgie turned to Marian with a sharper expression than Nicholas was used to seeing on her face. "My mother," she said, "is no longer responsible for my welfare."

"No, but *I* am," Nicholas said, eager to be done with the discussion. "And we're not going to London."

He would not put Georgie—or any of the others—at risk.

It was odd. It had not been until Jameson had breathlessly informed him of the outbreak in London that Nicholas had felt the full weight of his new obligations. It wasn't just Georgie he was responsible for now. He was a man with a household.

"We need to help them," Georgie said. Then as if something had shifted inside her, her voice filled with emotion. "We need to help them, tend to them, and . . . and you're a doctor."

"I'm not a doctor yet," he reminded her.

"But surely you would know what to do."

"I know enough to know there is nothing I *can* do."

She gasped.

"No, no, I don't mean it like that," he said quickly. Good God, he *had* sounded fatalistic.

She made a questioning motion with her hands.

"Based on Jameson's report," he told her, "there is nothing I can do for them that is not already being done. A doctor has been called for, and the ill have all been given willow bark and bone broth."

"Willow bark?"

"It seems to help with fevers."

Her brow dipped into a vee. "That's so interesting. I wonder what the reason . . ."

He waited for her to finish her thought, but she just shook her head. "Never mind." She blinked, then looked up, her eyes suddenly bright and clear. "What now?"

"We press on," he said. "And find a place to spend the night."

"Will that be a problem?"

Nicholas let out a sigh. His father had sent a man ahead to reserve space at coaching inns along the route, but obviously no arrangements had been made for the first stop.

"We shall take our chances like everyone else on the road," he said. "I've gone back and forth to Edinburgh several times, and I've never had difficulty securing a room before."

Of course he'd never traveled with a wife, thirteen servants, and three cats.

Meow.

It was a delicate sound, quite unlike the howling they'd endured all afternoon. He looked at Georgie, his brows raised in question.

She shook her head. "That wasn't Cat-Head."

He sighed. "Of course it wasn't."

But she didn't hear. She was already hurrying back to the carriage, tending to the one she called Blanche.

Which was almost as ridiculous a name as Cat-Head, given that Blanche was almost completely black.

"Did anyone find the other baskets?" Nicholas asked as he followed Georgie to the carriage.

"I don't think anyone looked," Marian said, scurrying along after him. "Do you want us to?"

"No, best to be on our way. We'll find them for the journey tomorrow."

Marian nodded, but when he stepped aside to allow her to enter the carriage before him, she said, "If you don't mind, sir, I thought I might ride in the second carriage."

Georgie, who had already alighted, poked her head out. "Are you sure? It's smaller than this one, and you'll be three across on the seat."

"We will be just fine," Nicholas said, putting an end

to the discussion. Frankly, he'd been surprised when Marian had entered the lead carriage at their departure. Surely as newlyweds, they could expect to have the space to themselves.

Meow.

He sighed. Along with the cats.

At least the he-devil was quiet. Although the true test would come when the wheels began to—

GRAOWWW!

"I'm sorry," Georgie said.

Nicholas attempted a smile. "Nothing to be done."

She smiled in return, an expression that was one-part apologetic, one-part grateful, and one-part ready to tear her hair out.

GRAOWWW!

He fixed the cat with an icy stare. "You have no interest in romance, do you?" he muttered.

"What did you say?" Georgie asked, startled.

GRAOWWW!

He shook his head. Funny how it hadn't been until they were packing up the carriages and it became clear that Georgie was bringing her pets that he remembered that he didn't much actually like cats. His sister had had cats. They had been the most spoiled creatures on the planet, and they left fur everywhere.

GRAOWWW!

And some of them, apparently, liked to complain.

"Sorry," Georgie muttered. She picked up a shawl, and then—

His eyes widened. "Are you swaddling that cat like a baby?"

"I think it's helping."

GRAOWWW!

Well, it wasn't hurting, at least.

"There, there, Cat-Head," Georgie said. "We haven't much farther to go." She looked up at Nicholas. "Do we?"

He shrugged. He wasn't sure where they were going to spend the night. He'd instructed the driver to stop at the next reputable coaching inn, but if there wasn't room, they'd have to keep going.

Grrrrraow.

"I think he's falling asleep," Georgie whispered.

"Praise the Lord."

Georgie sighed. "Indeed."

By the time they finally stopped for the evening, Georgie was exhausted. She'd got Cat-Head to sleep, but then she'd had to hold him like a baby the rest of the trip. She'd tried to set him down once, careful to keep the swaddling tight and firm, but the minute he touched the bench, his eyes popped open and his howling began anew.

"No, no, Cat-Head," she murmured, desperately trying to settle him back down.

She then tried to keep her hold on him while at the same time setting him down on the bench. She felt ridiculous, all bent at the waist as she leaned over him, but if she could get him to fall back asleep in such a position, maybe he'd stay that way when she pulled her arms away.

"Pick him up," Nicholas had begged.

"He doesn't know the difference."

"He knows!"

"How can he know? I have my arms around—"

"He knows!"

She picked him up. He quieted instantly.

He knew.

Damn cat.

So she held him. The whole trip.

She held him when they stopped at the first inn, only to be told there were no vacant rooms.

She held him when they stopped at the second inn, where she waited while Nicholas and the drivers conferred for at least ten minutes, only to decide that they did not like the look of the other travelers.

Georgie was not exactly sure what that meant, but as they all had experience traveling the Great North Road and she did not, she decided to take their word for it.

It was late, though, much later than they would have normally chosen to retire for the evening, and she sensed that everyone was eager to put an end to the day's journey when they came to a stop in front of the third inn. Unfortunately, it proved only marginally more fruitful than the other two.

"Bad news, I'm afraid," Nicholas said when he opened the carriage door.

Georgie had been waiting in the coach, Cat-Head still swaddled in her arms. "Please don't tell me they are full."

"They're not, but they've only one room available. I'm afraid you shall have to share with the maids."

"All five of us? Will we fit?"

"The innkeeper says he can send up extra bedding."

"But what about you?"

"I shall sleep in the stables, along with the rest of the men."

"But it's our—"

Wedding Night.

The words hung unspoken.

"We shall make do," Georgie said firmly. Maybe it was for the best. Did she really wish to spend her wedding night in a coaching inn called The Brazen Bull?

"We could keep going," Nicholas said, "but it sounds like the other nearby inns are also full, and—"

"It's fine, Nicholas."

"The horses are spent," he said, "and I suspect we're all exhausted."

"Nicholas," she said again. "We will be fine. I promise."

He stopped talking finally, and just blinked up at her. "Thank you," he said.

"There is nothing to thank me for."

"You could be very ill-tempered about it all."

"I could." She smiled. "I still can." She held up Cat-Head. "Want a cat?"

"God, no." He held out his hand. "Let me help you down. We should make some haste. It's late, but I'm told we can still get supper. I've made arrangements for a private dining room."

The cats were handed off to the maids, the footmen saw to the luggage, and Georgie and Nicholas made their way across the courtyard.

The inn was at a busy crossroads, and after so long in the carriage, Georgie was unprepared for the sheer volume of humanity sharing the scene. Nicholas, however, seemed perfectly at ease. He strode forward with purpose, threading between strangers as he made his way to the front steps of the old Tudor building that now housed The Brazen Bull Inn. Georgie was thankful for him, or to put a finer point on it, for the crook in his elbow in which her hand was tightly tucked. She could have done without his legs being quite so long; she had to scurry like a mouse just to keep up.

But then he stopped suddenly a few feet from the entrance—Georgie had no idea why; she hadn't been paying attention—and she smashed right into him. Her arms flew around his midsection as she tried to keep hold of her balance. It was muddy, and the ground was hard—a fall would have been messy, embarrassing, and probably painful.

It was over in an instant, but the moment lengthened the way a blink can last forever. She felt her fingers spread against his firm belly as she regained her balance, instinctively pulling herself against him for stability. She felt her cheek press against his soft wool coat. She felt her breath catch.

"Are you all right?" Nicholas asked, and she felt him start to twist in her arms.

"I'm fine, I—" She stopped, realizing that she was hugging him. Her face was pressed into his strong back, cradled in a curve she hadn't even known was there.

"I'm fine," she said again, reluctantly loosening her grip. He finished turning, and they were face-to-face. How were his eyes so luminously blue, even now when the night air stole the color from the sky?

Was it just because she *knew* what he looked like?

She'd grown up around the Rokesbys; they all possessed those marvelous azure eyes.

But this felt different. *She* felt different.

"Are you sure?" he asked. And she realized his hand had covered hers. It felt . . .

Intimate.

She looked down at their hands, then back up at his face. She had known him forever, but suddenly the whole world was strange and new. He was holding her hand, and she was suddenly full of emotion and confusion and something she couldn't quite define.

"Georgie?" he said softly. "Are you all right?"

She smoothed out her breathing, and said, "Yes."

Then the moment was over.

But something inside her had changed.

It turned out that The Brazen Bull's private dining room was private only insofar as it was separated from the main dining room by a wall with a doorway in it.

But just a doorway. If a door had once resided there, it was long gone, and while the inn's other patrons respected the boundary with their bodies, the same could not be said for their words and conversation, which poured loud and bawdy through the air.

It made conversation a challenge, and Nicholas

almost wished they'd pressed for their meal to be had up in the room with the maids, but then he remembered that the maids had the cats, and at least one of those cats was probably howling, and frankly, he wanted nothing to do with it.

Uncharitable of him, perhaps, but it was the truth. Even the raucous singing wafting in through the doorway wasn't bothering him. Not that it normally would, but Georgiana was a lady and if he was hearing correctly, someone was extolling—in rhyming couplets, no less—the tongue-related talents of an unnamed, yet highly industrious, female.

He *should* get up and say something. But he was damned hungry, and the beef stew was surprisingly good.

Oh my sweet Martine, something, something quite unclean.

Nicholas grinned in spite of himself. *Martine.* She was probably French.

And hopefully imaginary, poor woman, if the lyrics were anything to go by.

He stole a glance at Georgie, hoping she wasn't too bothered by the coarse language. She had her back to the doorway, so at least she couldn't see the men dancing along in their clumsy jigs.

Georgie's brow was fixed into a frown. Nothing distressing, just that faraway look people got when their mind was somewhere else.

Nicholas cleared his throat.

She seemed not to hear him.

Nicholas reached forward and waved his hand in front of her eyes. "Georgiana," he said, his voice a little bit singsong. "Georgiana Bridgerton."

Rokesby, he realized with a start. Georgiana *Rokesby*.

He didn't think she noticed his mistake; instead, she seemed to be embarrassed that he'd caught her woolgathering.

She blushed. *Blushed!* And she looked . . . beautiful.

"Pardon," she murmured, looking down. "I was thinking on a dozen different things. This noise makes it hard to concentrate."

"Yes," he said, but what he was really thinking was that looking at *her* made it hard to concentrate. She was pretty, of course, she'd always been pretty with her strawberry blond hair and intelligent blue eyes. She was his wife now, he thought, and when he looked at her, it felt different.

And strangely, he wasn't so sure it was only because they were married. He had the oddest feeling that even if they had not stood before the priest that morning and said their vows, he would see something new every time his gaze touched her face.

She had become a discovery, and he had always had an endlessly curious mind.

She took a sip of her wine, then dabbed at the corner of her mouth with her napkin. Her eyes flicked over her shoulder at a particularly loud burst of laughter from the men in the other room.

"Are coaching inns always so noisy?" she asked.

"Not always," he replied. "But I find this quite soothing after the cat."

She let out a little snort of laughter. "I'm sorry," she said. "That was not well done of me."

"Who do you fear offending? The cat?"

"He tried his best," she said.

"He is a demon."

"Don't say that! He just doesn't like to travel."

"Neither do I," Nicholas said. "He's ruined it for me."

She gave him a look, lips pressed together and eyes both narrowed and thoroughly amused. "He will grow on you," she said primly.

"If I don't kill him first."

"Nicholas!"

"Don't worry," he said with purposeful blitheness. "It's not me you need to fear. The maids will surely crack first."

"Cat-Head is a very brave kitty."

At this he could only raise his brows.

"He was the one who attacked Freddie in the tree."

"That was *that* one?"

"He was brilliant," Georgie said, eyes flashing with the memory. "You would have loved it."

"After having seen what he did to Oakes's face, I'm inclined to agree."

"First he did this"—Georgie made a motion with her arms that did a surprisingly good job of demonstrating a cat jumping out of a window—"then he did *this*"—her arms rose past her face in a clawed vee—"and then he did *this.*"

Nicholas could not make out this last motion. "What is that?"

Her face split in a gleeful grin. "He wrapped himself over Freddie's face. Honestly, I don't know how Freddie could *breathe.*"

Nicholas started to laugh.

"I would draw it for you if I had any talent. It was the funniest thing I've ever seen. Or rather, it is now. At the time I was too terrified Freddie would fall from the tree. But oh my goodness, if you had seen it for yourself . . . He was shrieking, 'Get it off! Get it off!' and he was clawing at Cat-Head . . ."

"*Clawing,*" Nicholas gasped, because that was somehow the funniest thing he'd ever heard.

And then his laughter set her off, as laughter often did, and the two of them completely lost the battle for dignity. They laughed and laughed, until Georgie had to set her head on the table and Nicholas feared he'd strained a muscle.

"Well," Nicholas said, once he'd mostly recovered and Georgie had returned her attention to her meal. "I suppose I owe him a debt of gratitude. But you must admit, Cat-Head is a stupid name for a cat."

He watched Georgie pause, spoon lifted midway to her mouth.

"What?" he said. Because honestly, she had the oddest expression on her face.

She set her jaw and lowered her spoon. "Oh?" she said with calculated pacing. "A stupid name, is it? And I wonder whose fault that is."

Nicholas paused. This was clearly a question to which he was supposed to know the answer. "Edmund?" he guessed, because Edmund was usually responsible for such things.

"You, Nicholas. *You* named my cat Cat-Head."

"I named a cat Cat-Head." It came out more of a statement than a question.

"You named *my* cat Cat-Head."

"Surely you jest."

Georgie's mouth dropped slightly open, and she neatly laid her spoon back on the table. "Surely you remember Pity-Cat."

Nicholas had no idea what she was talking about.

"Mary's cat?" Georgie prodded. "Your sister's tabby from when you were at Eton . . ."

The memory came to him, then. It had been years and years before. He'd actually liked that cat. It was a scrappy little thing that liked to hide under his mother's skirts and nip at her ankles. She'd cry out randomly in surprise and yes, it was funny.

Then he frowned. *Pity-Cat?*

He shook his head. "That cat wasn't named Pity-Cat."

Georgie's whole face turned into a heart-shaped *I-told-you-so.* "No, Pity-Cat's name was Turnip, but then you and Edmund thought it was much more fun to say Turnippity, and—

"It *is* more fun to say Turnippity."

Georgie pursed her lips. He could tell she was trying not to laugh.

"I mean," he continued, "who names any breathing creature Turnip?"

"Your sister did. She names all her pets after food."

"Yes, well, let's be thankful Felix didn't let her name their offspring Dumpling, Pudding, or Bacon."

"One of her cats *is* named Dumpling."

He rolled his eyes. "It was only a matter of time."

Georgie rolled *her* eyes at that. "*I'd* named Cat-Head Patch."

"Why?"

"Have you ever looked at him?"

Not really. "Of course I have."

Georgie's eyes narrowed.

"Although *mostly* I've listened."

She rolled her eyes again.

He snickered. "Oh come now, you must give me credit for that one."

"Very well, touché." And then she stared, waiting for him to set the conversation back on course.

"Very well," he acquiesced, "tell me the story. How am I responsible for your cat's ridiculous moniker?"

She needed no further encouragement. "As I said, *I'd* named him Patch. He has little markings around his eyes. Rather like how the broadsheets draw the Dutch sailors with the triangular patches over their eyes."

Nicholas skipped over the obvious question of how broadsheets depicting piracy occurring mere miles from Aubrey Hall made it out of the security of Lord Bridgerton's office and into the hands of an impressionable young girl, and instead merely said, "Just the one eye, I'd think."

She mock-scowled. "Yes, well, I thought it a perfectly proper cat name, but then you and Edmund came home for a few weeks after term and by the time you went back, Turnip went from Turnip to Turnippity to Pity-Cat, and somehow that led to you deciding that Patch ought to be Cat-Head."

"I have no recollection, although it does sound like something we would do."

"I tried to bring him back to Patch, but he wouldn't answer to it any longer. It was Cat-Head or nothing."

Nicholas was skeptical that cats answered to their names at all, but forbore to argue. "I'm sorry?"

"You are?"

"Shouldn't I be?"

She took a moment to consider this. Or at the very least, give the impression of doing so. "To be fair, I don't know that it was you as much as Edmund who led the naming brigade."

"Regardless, how about I stay out of the naming of our children, then?"

He wasn't sure where the thought had come from, or why on earth he'd said it out loud, but the words *our children* seemed to shut down the feels-like-old-times familiarity with the swiftness of a guillotine.

He supposed it was a lot to joke about when they had not even shared a wedding night.

Then, a quirk in her cheek, Georgie raised her gaze to his. There was playfulness in her eyes as she said, "You trust me not to name a child Brunhilda then?"

"Brunhilda's a fine name," he replied.

"You think so? Then I'll—"

But whatever she might have said was cut off by the sound of a door slamming open followed by a panicked male voice shouting, *"Is there a doctor in the house?"*

Without thinking, Nicholas rose to his feet.

"What do you think . . ." Georgie murmured, and she followed him to the doorway. In the main dining room they both saw a man—a groom by the looks of him—covered in mud and blood.

"We need a doctor in the stables!" he cried.

"Let me assess this situation," Nicholas said to Georgie. "You should take the rest of your meal in the room."

"But—"

He looked at her. "You can't stay here on your own."

"No, that's not what I meant. I should come with you. I can help."

And in that moment, he knew deep in his core that she could. And that she wanted to. And she'd be helpful. But—

"Georgie, they need me in the stables."

"Then I'll go with you to the stables. I can—"

"Georgie, women aren't allowed in the stables."

"That's ridiculous." She smoothed her skirts, making every indication that she planned to follow him. "I'm in the stables every day."

"You're in Aubrey Hall's stables. These are public stables."

"But—"

"No," he said, because he could not imagine trying to keep an eye on her welfare and tend to an injured man at the same time. "I'll send a footman or groom back to escort you to the room where the maids are."

"But—"

"You cannot come with me to the stables," he said firmly.

"But I . . . I . . ." For a moment she looked lost, as if she could not decide what to do. But finally she swallowed and said, "Very well. I was almost done eating, anyway."

"You'll go straight back to the room?"

She nodded. But she didn't look happy about it.

"Thank you." He leaned forward and gave her a quick kiss on the cheek. "I likely won't see you until morning. I'm spending the night in the stables, anyway. Once I'm done, I might as well just settle in for the night."

She let out a tiny sigh. "Good night, then," she said. "I guess—"

"Straight back to the room," he said one more time. The last thing he needed was to worry about Georgie's welfare.

"Yes," she said impatiently. "I'm going. You can watch me if you want."

"No, I trust you. I've got to go. I think Wheelock's got my medical bag, and—"

But she wasn't listening. She couldn't. He was already out the door, his feet carrying him faster than he could finish his sentence.

He turned around one last time. "Go," he said. "Back to the room. Please."

And then he ran off, feeling rather like he was about to save the world.

Chapter 15

G eorgie was not in a good mood when she woke up the following morning. She knew she shouldn't be annoyed with Nicholas for insisting that she go back to the room the night before while he tended to whatever injury awaited him in the stables, but surely the very definition of emotions meant that they were not always rational.

Also, she was tired.

One very small room, one rather lumpy bed, five women (each with a long braid), and three cats—*comfortable* was not a word anyone had spoken the evening before.

Sam (the groom who hailed from Aubrey Hall) was sweet on Darcy, and he'd brought a hammock from the stables and strung it from the rafters. He'd offered it to

Georgie first of course, but he'd brought it for Darcy, and while Georgie did look at it with curious longing, she did not take it.

So Darcy had been in a hammock, and Marcy had— at her mother's insistence—slept on the floor, but that had still left three women in a bed that had been meant for a cozy two. Georgie had woken up with Marian's elbow in her armpit and an unpleasant taste in her mouth.

And no abatement of the frustration from the evening before.

Now, as the women made their way through the busy loading and unloading areas in front of the stables, she looked for Nicholas. If she could not help him with his medical work, she could at least force him to tell her all about it.

But Nicholas was nowhere to be seen.

"Mr. Rokesby," Georgie said to one of the footmen as she handed Judyth's basket up to Marian. "Where is he?"

"He's sleeping, Mrs. Rokesby, ma'am."

Georgie stopped with one foot on the blocks. "He's sleeping? Still?"

"Yes, ma'am. He only finished up with the injured man a few hours ago."

"My goodness, what happened?"

"I'm not sure, ma'am, but there was quite a lot of blood."

Another footman appeared at her other side. "It was a broken leg, ma'am. The sort where the bone comes through the skin."

"A compound fracture," Georgie said. She might have been showing off. No, she was definitely showing off.

"Er, yes."

"Will he be all right? The man with the broken leg?"

The footman shrugged. "Hard to tell, but if he's not, it won't be Mr. Rokesby's fault. He was a proper hero, ma'am."

Georgie smiled. "Of course he was. But, er . . ." What to do? She was in charge now, she realized. It was an unfamiliar sensation. Unfamiliar, but not, she was relieved to discover, unpleasant.

She cleared her throat and drew her shoulders back. "We'd planned to get an early start."

"I know, ma'am," the first footman said. "It's just that he was so tired. We wanted to wait until as late as possible to rouse him. He's got cotton stuffed in his ears and he tied his cravat around his eyes so it's not surprising he's still sleeping, but . . ."

"But?" she prompted.

The first footman looked at the second footman and

then into the carriage. The second footman just looked at Georgie's shoe, still perched on the step.

"But?" she prompted again.

"But we're really quite nervous about the cat."

Georgie paused for a moment, then stepped down. "Would you please take me to him?"

"To the cat?"

She forced her expression into one of utter patience. "The cat is already in the carriage. I would like to see Mr. Rokesby."

"But he's sleeping."

"Yes, you'd mentioned."

The three of them stood for an extended moment in awkward silence. The first footman finally said, "This way, ma'am."

Georgie followed him to the stables, where he stopped at the entrance and pointed. Over on the left side a single hammock still hung, a fully clothed Nicholas barely discernable in the low light. His arms were crossed over his chest, and his eyes were covered by his cravat.

She wanted to hug him.

She wanted to strangle him. If he had let her help the night before he wouldn't be so tired.

This wasn't, however, the time to be petty.

She turned on her heel and strode back toward the carriage. They could delay their start by an hour. Nicholas needed his sleep, and it went without saying that no one was going to get any rest inside the carriage. Holding Cat-Head like a baby seemed to help, but it didn't keep him completely quiet.

She paused, peering back over her shoulder into the stables. She couldn't quite see Nicholas any longer, but she could picture him in the hammock, swinging slightly with each breath.

He'd looked so comfortable. She hated to wake him. It was really too bad—

"Ma'am?"

She looked up. One of the footmen was regarding her with concern. And no wonder. She'd been standing there for what had to have been a full minute, frozen in thought.

"Ma'am?" he said again.

A slow smile spread across her face. "I'm going to need some rope."

Nicholas awoke with a start. It was unnerving to open one's eyes and see nothing, and it took him a moment to remember that he'd tied his cravat over his eyes the night before. He unwrapped his makeshift sleeping mask and yawned. Christ, he was tired. The hammock had been more comfortable than he'd have anticipated, but as he'd been settling into it the night before, all he'd been able to think was that he really should have had the opportunity to sleep in a bed with his wife.

His wife.

He'd been married a day and he'd barely even kissed her.

He was going to have to do something about that.

He looked around. His was the last hammock hanging and the stable door was wide open. The sky was a bright English white. Blue would have been cheerful, but white without rain he'd take.

His feet hit the ground just as one of the Crake footmen appeared in the doorway and waved at him.

"Good morning, sir," the footman called. "We're just about ready."

"Ready?" Nicholas echoed. What time was it? He reached into his pocket for his watch, but before he could take a look, the footman said, "Mrs. Rokesby has been very busy."

"Arranging for breakfast?" Nicholas asked. It was half eight, much later than he'd meant to start his day.

"That, and the, er . . ." The footman frowned. "You should really see for yourself."

Nicholas wasn't sure whether to be curious or scared,

but he decided to go with curious until convinced otherwise.

"She's right clever, she is," the footman said. "Mrs. Rokesby, I mean."

"She is," Nicholas agreed, although he could not imagine what cleverness she'd managed to display at half eight in the morning at The Brazen Bull Inn.

He made his way to the stable door and stopped short. There in the middle of the driveway were the two carriages, surrounded by a small crowd of onlookers.

Who all seemed to be watching his wife.

Georgie was standing on the main carriage's step, dressed for travel in a plum-colored frock, her gingery hair unadorned by a bonnet.

"Yes, like that," she said, calling out instructions to some unseen person within. A pause, and then: "No, not like that."

"What is going on?" Nicholas asked the first person he came across.

"Strangest thing I ever did see."

Nicholas turned and blinked, only just then realizing that the man with whom he was speaking was not a member of their traveling party. "Who are you?" he asked.

"Who are you?" the man countered.

Nicholas motioned toward Georgie. "Her husband."

"Really?" The man grinned. "She's something." And then he started to laugh.

Nicholas frowned. What the devil?

"Been watching her for a quarter of an hour at least."

Nicholas decided he did not like this man. "Have you now?" he murmured.

"If she makes this work . . ." The man shook his head with admiration before turning to face Nicholas head-on. "You wouldn't happen to be heading north?"

"Why?" Nicholas asked suspiciously.

His new best friend took this as yes. "Do you know where you're stopping? I'm desperate to know how it turns out. We're taking bets on it."

"What?"

"Or we would be, if we could be assured we'd hear the results. Don't suppose you're planning to make a stop at Biggleswade? Could you leave word at the King's Reach and let us know how it works out?"

Nicholas gave the man one last irritated glance and stomped off to Jameson, who was standing closer to Georgie.

"Jameson," he said, perhaps a little more gruffly than he'd intended. "Why has a crowd of spectators congregated around my wife?"

"Oh, you're awake!" Jameson said. "Good morning, sir."

"Is it?" Nicholas asked. "Is it?"

"We all hope so, sir. Mrs. Rokesby is certainly trying her best."

"But what is she doing?"

"A little higher!" Georgie called. "Right, good. Now tie a knot right there. Make sure it's tight."

GRAOWWW!

Nicholas had almost forgotten the particular horror of that sound. "Where is it?" he asked in a desperate voice. Good Lord, he had not slept well. Or rather, he had not slept much. He could not bear to ponder another full day in the carriage with the beast.

"We found its basket," Jameson said, pointing to a wicker basket currently resting on the lead carriage's footboard. "It doesn't seem to like it, though."

GRAOWWW!

Nicholas resolutely turned his back on the cat. "Would I be correct in assuming that Mrs. Rokesby's current machinations have something to do with the cat?"

"I would hate to spoil her surprise, sir."

"Almost . . ." they heard Georgie say, followed by, "Perfect!"

She poked her head out. "We—Oh! You're awake."

Nicholas gave a little bow. "As you can see." He glanced around the crowded courtyard. "As everyone can see."

"Oh, yes." Her cheeks turned slightly pink, although it seemed to be more with pride than embarrassment. "We seem to have garnered a bit of an audience."

"One can only wonder why."

"Come in, come in," she urged. "I must show you my masterpiece."

Nicholas took a step forward.

"Wait!"

He stopped.

She held up a hand. "One moment." Then, looking past him, she said, "Could someone hand me the cat?"

There was no question which cat she was referring to. One of the grooms retrieved Cat-Head's basket and handed it to one of the maids, who handed it up to Georgie.

"I will be ready for you in just a moment," she said. Then she shut the door.

Nicholas looked at Jameson.

Jameson grinned.

GRAOWWWOOOWWW!

Nicholas frowned. That didn't sound quite right. Not that anything that cat did sounded right, but this sounded more wrong than usual.

GRAAAAAOOOWWWAAAOOOWWW!

Nicholas looked at Jameson. "If she doesn't open the door in five seconds, I'm going in."

Jameson shuddered. "Godspeed, sir."

There were sounds of a tussle, followed by another howl, slightly muffled. Nicholas took a breath. Time to save his wife.

GRAaaa . . . Graaaa . . .

Meow.

Nicholas stopped short. That sounded almost . . .

Happy?

Meow.

"She did it," Jameson said, in a statement that could only be described as reverent.

Nicholas looked at him, and then back at the carriage.

Georgie opened the door. "Do come in," she said, the very model of a gracious hostess.

With equal parts trepidation and curiosity, Nicholas ascended the steps to the carriage, only to be met with the sight of—

"Is that a hammock?"

Georgie nodded excitedly.

"For the cat?"

"It's my design. But of course I could not have put it together without Sam's help."

Nicholas turned and blinked at the heretofore unnoticed groom, who was crouched at the far end of the carriage, looking inordinately proud of himself.

"It was all her idea, sir," the groom said modestly.

Nicholas could only stare. First at the groom, then at Georgie, then at the orange cat, who was suspended in a loose webbing of rope.

"I think he likes it," Georgie said.

Nicholas wasn't so sure about that. It was true that Cat-Head sounded almost content, but he *looked* ridiculous.

And ridiculously uncomfortable. All four of his legs had been poked through holes in the webbing and hung down like furry twigs. Its face was squished but visible through another gap, a thick piece of rope supporting its chin.

"Is he going to choke?" Nicholas asked, looking over at Georgie with concern.

"No, I think he's comfortable. Feel him." She grabbed his hand and placed it under Cat-Head's belly. "He's purring."

Nicholas looked at Sam. Why, he wasn't certain. But surely someone still possessed a shred of sanity. "Are we certain it's not just indigestion?"

"No, no," Georgie said, "that's definitely a purr. Although you do bring up an important point. He will need to relieve himself at some point."

"We will all need to relieve ourselves at some point," Nicholas said, somewhat dazedly.

"Yes, of course. It's just that it's a bit, er, complicated to get him into it."

"And out of it, as well?"

"I haven't yet made the attempt," she admitted.

"Let's hope we figure it out before his needs become urgent."

Behind him, Sam let out a little snort of amusement.

"But what do you think?" Georgie asked.

He thought she'd gone mad, to be honest, but she was so damned proud of herself he was never going to say that.

"I think it's ingenious," he said. Which was also true. It was ingenious *and* she'd gone mad.

"I wasn't sure if he would like it," Georgie said with palpable excitement and pride. "And I still don't know what will happen once we start moving, but it was worth a try."

"Indeed."

"After all, you looked so comfortable in your hammock this morning."

"Me?"

"I didn't want to disturb you. Everyone said you worked so hard last night. You'll have to tell me about it later today."

"You modeled this on me?"

Cat-Head made an odd noise, but it wasn't a howl.

"He sounds . . ." Nicholas searched for the correct descriptor. "Not happy, exactly."

"But better than yesterday," Georgie said brightly.

"Absolutely." Nicholas said this with utter conviction. It couldn't possibly be worse.

Grrrmphamow.

Nicholas moved his head for a better look. It was possible that the cat's change in volume may have been due to a simple inability to open its mouth. But as long as it could breathe . . .

"Shall we be on our way?" Georgie said.

Sam scooted to the door. "Yes, ma'am."

But no sooner than he had hopped down, Marian appeared in the doorway.

"Are you riding with us today?" Georgie asked.

Nicholas gave the maid a long, hard stare.

"Er, my things are here," Marian said, nervously motioning to a small satchel on the rear-facing bench.

Long. Hard. Stare.

"But I can ride in the other carriage," Marian said very quickly.

Nicholas gave the maid an almost imperceptible nod.

"Are you sure?" Georgie said. "I think the cat will be better behaved than yesterday."

"I . . . ah . . ."

Nicholas did not take his eyes off Marian's face. She, in turn, was trying very hard not to look his way.

"I think . . . I think I had better . . ."

Marian accidentally caught his eye. His brows rose.

"I should like to get to know Mrs. Hibbert better," Marian blurted out. "And Marcy and Darcy."

"Oh," Georgie said. "I suppose that makes sense."

"Also"—Marian cast a wary eye toward Cat-Head— "that looks unnatural."

Georgie frowned. "Technically speaking, I suppose it *is* unnatural."

Nicholas looked at the cat. In all honesty, it was hard to look away.

Meow.

"Time to go," Nicholas announced. Someone had to make a decision. He handed Marian her bag. "We'll see you at the next stop."

And then, before anyone could make a noise of protest—even Cat-Head—he shut the door.

"Gah, finally," Nicholas muttered.

"Is everything all right?" Georgie asked. She sounded . . . not nervous exactly. Maybe curious.

"Nicholas?"

Maybe a little nervous.

"You should sit down before we start moving," he said.

"Oh. Yes. Of course." She sat, although not where he'd wanted her to.

"You don't get sick riding backward?" he asked.

"What? Oh. No. Not really."

"Not really?"

They started moving. They held their breath, but Cat-Head didn't make a sound.

"Not much," Georgie amended.

"Then sit over here." He reached out, took her hand, and pulled her over to the forward-facing seat. "I don't bite."

He didn't let go of her hand.

She blushed. "I thought you'd want room."

"There's plenty of room."

She gave a little tug, and he reluctantly let go of her hand; he supposed she needed it in order to get herself settled.

They moved slowly through the village, Nicholas and Georgie both keeping a wary eye on the cat.

But it didn't make a sound.

"Unbelievable," Nicholas murmured.

"I wasn't sure it was going to work," Georgie admitted.

"You may very well be a genius, Mrs. Rokesby."

She turned to him and smiled.

And again, all he could think of was the sun, and the way he felt happy when it broke through the clouds on a long gray day.

"Georgie?"

Her eyes lit with curiosity.

"I'm going to kiss you now."

Because honestly, it was past time.

Chapter 16

In a way, Georgie knew what he was going to say before he said it. There was something in his eyes, in the way he looked at her and covered her hand with his before he spoke. And of course it was crazy that they hadn't kissed, not properly.

They were married. They were *supposed* to kiss each other.

Georgie just wasn't sure it was supposed to feel . . .

Or that *she* was supposed to feel . . .

She looked at him.

She looked at Nicholas, at the man she'd known her whole life, the man she'd only recently stopped thinking of as a boy. She couldn't seem to catch her breath, or look away from his mouth, or wonder what it might feel like if his lips touched hers.

And she thought about the fact that she'd taken his name. She had pledged herself to him for better or for worse, till death did they part. It was supposed to be holy, but what she was feeling right now wasn't spiritual, it was base and it was carnal, and it thrilled her even as it terrified her, and—

"Georgie?"

His voice. It did things to her. This was new.

"Georgie?"

She dragged her gaze from his mouth to his eyes.

"You're thinking too much," he murmured.

"How do you know?"

His lips curved. "I just do."

"I think you know me," she whispered.

This seemed to amuse him. "I've always known you."

She shook her head. "No. Not like now."

"Not like I *will*," he vowed.

Mere inches separated them, and then slowly, softly, his lips touched hers. At first it was the softest brush of skin. Then his hand touched the back of her neck, and it was all she could do not to melt into him then and there. His tongue traced the seam of her lips, and what had started as a hint of a kiss turned into something deeper.

Hotter.

Georgie gasped at the unexpected rush of sensation, and when her lips parted, the kiss grew even more intimate, more luxuriant.

She hadn't known that a kiss could involve more than just a touch of the lips. Or that she could feel it everywhere, across her skin, in her blood, in the very center of her soul.

"Nicholas," she murmured, and she heard the wonder in her voice.

"I know," was his response. "I know."

She felt his hands move to her back, but it didn't matter if he was pulling her against him because she was already pressing forward. This need within her—she didn't fully understand it. All she knew was that she wanted this. She wanted to be closer.

She wanted *him*.

She kissed him back—or at least she thought she did. She'd never kissed anyone before, not like this. She could only assume she was doing it right because he seemed to like it.

And she knew *she* liked it.

Tentatively, she brought one of her hands to his hair. Surely at some point in her life she'd touched it before, but suddenly she had to know—*right now*—what it felt like between her fingers. Was it soft? Springy? Both? His hair had always had the tendency to curl, just a little bit, and she was gripped by the most foolish desire to find one of those almost-ringlets and give it a little tug, just to see how quickly it would spring back into shape.

But first she just wanted to touch him. To feel his warmth, and to revel in the knowledge that he wanted her just as much as she wanted him.

It was a heady, giddy feeling.

It was glorious.

"Georgie," he murmured, and she heard the wonder in his voice.

So she said, just like he had, "I know."

He smiled. She felt it against her skin when his lips trailed across her cheek to the line of her throat.

She tipped her head back, shivering with delight as his lips found the hollow above her collarbone. She didn't know . . . she'd had no idea . . . if anyone had told her . . .

Meow.

"Nicholas," she whisper-squealed. He was doing something utterly shocking and delightful, and—

Meow.

Maybe if she ignored it . . .

Meow.

She made the mistake of looking up.

Cat-Head.

Staring at her with freakish intensity.

"What's wrong?" Nicholas murmured, his lips still warm against her skin.

"Nothing," Georgie said in a firm voice. She shut her eyes.

Grrra—

"Stop!" she said, her eyes flying back open.

Nicholas jerked back.

"No, not you!" She clutched his shoulder. "Don't you stop."

He stared at her in confusion. "What is going on?"

"Mee-OW."

Georgie glared at the cat. Without a doubt, that was the smuggest *meow* she'd ever heard.

"Did you hear that?" she asked.

Nicholas kept kissing her, moving to a particularly lovely spot near her ear. "Ignore him."

"I can't."

"Try harder."

Georgie turned her head, giving Cat-Head the cut direct.

She heard an indrawn kitty breath, and then—

GRAOWWW!

"No," Nicholas practically moaned. "No no no."

Georgie looked back up at the cat. "Stop that," she hissed.

Cat-Head gave a little cat shrug.

Georgie turned back to Nicholas.

GRAOWWW!

"What?" She whipped back around.

Cat-Head purred.

"You slippery vixen," she breathed.

Nicholas went mostly still. "Are you talking to me or the cat?"

Georgie disentangled herself from her husband's arms and sat up so she could give Cat-Head a full-on glare. "Enough."

"I really hope it's the cat," Nicholas remarked.

"He only makes that awful noise when you're kissing me."

"What if *you* kiss *me*?"

"Nicholas," she groaned.

"Not that I wish to defend the beast," he said, "but he did howl for at least six hours yesterday. And we were not, as I distinctly recall, kissing."

"Yes, but that was different. He wasn't in the hammock."

Nicholas ran a hand through his hair and looked up at the ridiculously trussed cat. "To be fair, it's hard to see how the hammock is helping."

"He's being quiet right now. And also, I don't have to hold him."

"True," Nicholas murmured. He sat back, and they

both watched Cat-Head, swinging gently as the carriage sped along the turnpike.

"This is actually interesting," Nicholas murmured. He leaned forward, eyeing the cat with a shrewd expression. "We should test the hypothesis."

A statement Georgie found baffling. "What?"

He immediately shifted into academic mode. "A hypothesis is a theory made on the—"

"I *know* what a hypothesis is," she cut in. "I just don't know what you mean about testing one."

"Ah. Right, well. As you know, the hallmark of scientific investigation is the rigorous examination of hypotheses. A theory is only a theory until you conduct an experiment to prove it."

Georgie regarded him with suspicion. "What is your theory, precisely?"

"Technically," he replied with a tip of his head, "it was *your* theory."

"Mine?"

"That the beast is trying to stop us from kissing."

"That's not exactly what I said," Georgie pointed out. "And at any rate, I doubt it's true. He's just not that clever."

"Clever or not," Nicholas muttered, "he is the spawn of Satan."

"Nicholas!"

"When we get to Scotland we're getting dogs."

"Not so loud," Georgie warned. "Judyth will hear you."

He gave her a *you-must-be-joking* look.

"She *is* very clever."

Nicholas stared at her for a long moment before executing a particularly sardonic combination of head-shaking and eye-rolling.

"You're the one who wishes to conduct a scientific experiment on my cat."

He looked pointedly at Cat-Head, still hanging from the hammock like an odd, furry plant. "*I'm* conducting experiments?"

"It worked, didn't it?" she said. "He was completely quiet."

"Until I kissed you."

"Well . . . Yes."

His eyes lit with anticipation. "Now it's time for *my* experiment."

"You're scaring me a little," she said.

He waved this off. "May I kiss you?"

Georgie was a little surprised—and to be honest, perhaps a little disappointed by the clinical tone of his voice. But she couldn't think of any reason to say no, so she nodded.

Nicholas touched her chin, drawing her close. Their lips met, and once again, she melted into him. The mere touch of his mouth on hers seemed to set her fingers tingling, and her body was—

GRAOWWW!

"I knew it," Nicholas grunted. He whipped around, glaring at the cat.

Georgie blinked. "What?" She sounded dazed. She *felt* dazed.

"Damned, meddling . . ."

There were other words, but his voice went too low for her to hear them.

"Look how innocent he looks," Georgie said. She reached out and scratched Cat-Head's smushed little face. "There's no way he's purposefully sabotaging us."

"Facts are facts, Georgiana. Your cat is a demon."

She sputtered with laughter. There was simply no other possible response.

"Can I turn it?" Nicholas asked.

"The cat?"

"Is there any way to turn the hammock so he's not facing us?"

"Ehrm, no, I don't think so." Georgie grimaced, looking over her contraption again. "Not unless we take him out and face him the other way."

This, she did not want to do. It had been a struggle to get Cat-Head into the hammock in the first place, and she had the scratches to prove it.

But she also really wanted to continue kissing her husband, so she said, "We could move."

He looked at her.

She pointed. "To the other side."

"I thought you said you get sick on the rear-facing bench."

"Not if you're kissing me."

"That makes no sense whatsoever," he said.

She smiled. "I know."

He looked at her. He looked at the rear-facing bench.

He looked at Cat-Head, smirking down at them both.

"Off we go!" He grinned and hopped over to the other side of the carriage, pulling her along with him.

Georgie tumbled onto the seat, laughing as Nicholas landed on top of her.

"Much better," he growled.

This just made her giggle more. "I didn't realize this could be so much *fun*."

"You have no idea," he murmured, nuzzling her neck.

She pulled back, just far enough to look at him with a mischievous smile. "I thought you said your kisses had not been legion."

He growled again, his weight settling on her in a thrillingly possessive manner. "I know enough to know I'm going to enjoy our wedding night immensely."

"Just you?" she teased.

His eyes sobered, and he brought her hand to his mouth. "Georgie, I promise you that I will do everything in my power to make it a pleasant experience for you."

He looked so serious; it made her smile. It made her want to make him smile. She reached up and touched his cheek. "Surely more than pleasant?"

He paused before saying, "It can be difficult for a woman the first time."

She stared up at him. Could he be speaking from experience? "But you haven't . . . I mean . . . Not with a woman who hasn't . . ."

He shook his head. "No. No, of course not. But I . . ." He cleared his throat. "I've spoken with people."

Georgie touched his cheek. He looked terribly embarrassed, and she loved him for it. She supposed some women wanted a husband with leagues of experience. Leagues of experience with leagues of women.

Ugh.

She *liked* that Nicholas had not been with many women before her. She didn't want him comparing her to other women. And after the way society had treated her following the whole Freddie Oakes affair, she'd decided that if it wasn't good for the goose, the gander could damn well do without too.

"Georgie?" Nicholas said with soft amusement. "Where'd you go?"

"Hmm?"

He kissed the corner of her mouth. "You look far too serious right now."

"Just thinking."

"Thinking, eh? You shouldn't be thinking."

She could not help but smile. "No?"

"If you have the capacity for thought, I must not be doing a very good job of this."

"No, not at all, I—Oh!"

His hand continued to do devilish things to the back of her knee. "Like that, did you?"

"Where did you learn this?"

He grinned and shrugged. "Making most of it up as I go along."

Georgie sighed, then sighed again. Because this was really just the loveliest way to pass a long carriage ride.

And lucky for them, they had all day.

Chapter 17

By the end of the day, Georgie was in a mostly wonderful mood.

Mostly.

Cat-Head's hammock had held for a stunning five hours. Five glorious, lovely hours of kissing, then napping, then kissing again. And somewhere in the middle of all the napping and the kissing, Nicholas treated her to an incredibly detailed, thoroughly exciting, gruesomely recounted tale of the previous evening's compound fracture.

Georgie was riveted. She wasn't quite as immune to the gore as she might have liked—her stomach lurched when Nicholas described how he slid the bone back into place, but only a little, and she was sure it was something she could get used to with a little practice.

She said so to Nicholas, and he admitted that he felt the same way when he was first beginning his studies. Some of his classmates had even fainted. They had taken a ribbing, but apparently it was all quite normal and to be expected. Almost a rite of passage for any new group of medical students.

Georgie was not used to tales of men fainting. Whenever someone gossiped about someone swooning it always seemed to be a woman. She'd long suspected, though, that this had less to do with a so-called weaker constitution and more to do with corsets. As someone who knew quite intimately the sensation of losing one's breath, Georgie could not imagine who had thought it was a good idea to strap people into garments that squeezed the ribs, compressed the lungs and generally made it impossible to do anything that required energy or movement.

Or breathing.

The case of her sister and the fire at court was a prime example. Billie was the most athletic and coordinated person Georgie knew, male or female. She had once ridden a horse backward, for heaven's sake. If she couldn't manage to walk through a room in hoops and a corset without setting someone on fire, Georgie could not imagine who could.

Very well, hundreds of girls had made it through presentation at court without committing accidental arson, but Georgie was sure that not a one of them had been the least bit comfortable in her gown.

At any rate, no one ever talked about men fainting, so Georgie was not-so-secretly delighted to hear that more than one of them hit the floor the first time they saw a body cut open.

It seemed wrong to her that women could not be doctors. Surely a woman doctor could do a better job treating female patients. She *had* to have a better familiarity with the female anatomy than a man did. It was simple common sense.

She'd said as much to Nicholas. He'd looked over at her with a considering sort of expression, then said, "You're probably right."

Georgie was already leaning forward, girding herself for an argument. When none came, she sat back, momentarily speechless.

"What is it?" Nicholas asked.

"It has just occurred to me that most of the time, adages become adages because they are true."

This made him grin, and he turned more directly to face her. "What do you mean?"

"You took the wind right out of my sails."

His smile grew. "Is that a good thing?"

"It is for you." She, on the other hand, didn't quite know what to do with herself.

He laughed. "Did you expect me to argue that women should not be allowed to become doctors?"

"I didn't expect such a wholesale capitulation."

"It isn't capitulation if I was never on the other side of the issue," he pointed out.

"No, I suppose not." She thought about that for a moment. "I've never heard you express an opinion on the subject, though."

"It's not something to which I've given much thought," he admitted with a shrug. "It doesn't affect me directly."

"Doesn't it?" She frowned. His statement bothered her, although she could not precisely put her finger on the reason why. "If you worked alongside women," she said, thinking aloud, "you might view your patients differently. You might see the entire world differently."

He regarded her for a long moment, then said, "This conversation seems to have taken a very serious turn."

She nodded slowly, looking down at their hands when his fingers found hers. He gave a little tug, and she let herself be pulled into his embrace.

"I don't want to be serious right now," he murmured.

Nor did she, not when he was whispering naughty words against her neck.

And that was how the morning went. Kissing and conversation, conversation and kissing. It was enough to make a woman think that a two-week journey by carriage might actually be something to look forward to.

But all too soon it was midday, and the traveling party came to a stop. And so did everything wonderful—including Cat-Head's success in the hammock.

Georgie *had* to take him out. It would be unconscionable to leave any living creature like that for more than a few hours at a time, no matter how comfortable he seemed to be.

All three cats had a little break, as did most human members of the traveling party, and then they all piled back in to their respective carriages. Judyth and Blanche curled up in their baskets (Blanche only after being bribed with an extra piece of cheese), but Cat-Head was having none of it. The sound he made when Georgie attempted to put him back in his hammock . . .

"Good night," Nicholas exclaimed. "Are you gutting him?"

Georgie turned and glared, even as Cat-Head pushed against her forehead with his right front paw. "Do you want to try?"

"God no."

Georgie moved the paw from her forehead and slid it through the appropriate hole in the hammock webbing, only to be rewarded with a yowl and another paw, this one under her chin. "I don't know why he's making such a fuss," she grunted, dislodging the second paw from her person. "He was perfectly fine this morning."

Nicholas rubbed his chin. "Do you think he can remember that far back?"

The look Georgie gave him was not particularly warm.

"You yourself said he's not very bright."

"He's bright enough to remember this morning," she retorted.

Nicholas did not look swayed.

And thus began the second half of the day's travel.

After suffering through nearly an hour of ungodly howling, Georgie finally found a position that Cat-Head seemed to sanction, and she spent the next three hours rocking him like a baby. At one point Nicholas offered to take over for her, but Cat-Head had clearly decided it was Georgie or no one, and after five minutes, it was agreed that it was best for everyone's sanity if Georgie took him back.

By the time they reached their designated stopping point in Alconbury, Georgie's arms were so tired her muscles were shaking. And if the physical discomfort wasn't enough, she was full of inner turmoil. Every time she looked at Nicholas she remembered how they had spent the morning. She shouldn't have felt shy, but she did, and—

No. She didn't feel shy. That's not what this was.

She waited for another burst of clarity, another eureka moment that might define this strange, conflicted feeling in her chest, but none was forthcoming.

All she knew was that she had *feelings*.

About Nicholas.

For Nicholas?

No. That was impossible. She'd known him her whole life. It was illogical to think that everything between them would change just because they'd placed rings on their fingers. It had only been a day, for heaven's sake.

"Georgie?" the man in question murmured.

She looked down. He'd already exited the carriage and was holding out his hand to help her disembark. He looked tired, although not nearly as tired as she felt.

"Let's get something to eat," he said as she put her hand in his.

She nodded, letting him help her down. Her feelings—whatever they were—were going to have to wait. Firstly, because she could not be certain of the nature of *his* feelings, and she was not prepared to ponder the possibility of one-sidedness, and secondly—and more urgently—she was so hungry she would have happily eaten an entire cow.

Cooked, of course. She wasn't a complete savage.

It was late enough when they arrived that everyone decided to eat right away, and she and Nicholas were led to what was clearly the second nicest spot in the dining room, at the end of a long table, scarred by use, but thankfully clean. A sour-faced couple and their sour-faced son sat at the other end of the table, which was closer to the fire. They looked to be almost done with their meal, but Georgie was too tired and hungry to wait for them to vacate their seats. She'd be warm enough at the far end of the table.

"Are you hungry?" Nicholas asked as he held out her chair.

"Famished. And you?"

"The same." He took his seat across from her and set his hat on the table beside him. His hair was askew, with bits and pieces sticking out in unexpected directions. It would never do in a formal drawing room, but here on the road she found it charming.

"I'm half ready to eat the meat off their plates," he said with a tip of his head toward the family at the far end of the table.

But when a youth came by with cheese and a basket

of bread, Georgie watched Nicholas stop following the food with his eyes as soon as he got a glimpse of the boy's forearm.

"That's a nasty burn," Nicholas said. He reached for the boy's sleeve. "May I?"

The boy started to snatch his arm away, but he couldn't due to the bottle tucked under his arm. He quickly set it on the table, then tried to pull his too-short sleeve down as he took a step back.

"It's nothing, sir," the youth said, shooting a look over his shoulder. "I'll be back with the rest of your food in a moment." He gave a quick bow, said a "sir" and a "ma'am," and fled.

Georgie watched Nicholas fix his gaze on the doorway through which the boy had disappeared. She watched him take a deep breath, look at the spread before him, hungry eyes flitting from the bread, to the cheese, and to the bottle of wine.

And then again at the door.

And back to the bread, which he started to reach for, then stopped. It was as if he only had enough energy to do one thing, and thinking about the boy meant he couldn't figure out what to do with the bread.

He looked hungry . . . and resigned.

Georgie wanted to kiss him.

"He'll be back in a moment with soup," she said.

Though to be honest, she had no idea if soup or the boy would be forthcoming. They waited, inexplicably leaving the food untouched, until a nervous-looking young woman came with two steaming bowls. She set them on the table and turned to leave, but Nicholas caught her with a "Mistress?"

The woman had to stop and turn. "Sir?" She bobbed a quick curtsy to Nicholas, but she looked as if she wanted nothing more than to run.

"The boy who was just in before you," Nicholas said. "His arm—"

"He'll bide, milord," the woman said quickly.

"But—"

"Please, sir," she said, her voice dropping to a nervous whisper. "Mr. Kipperstrung, he don't like us tending to nothing but work until after the meal's been cleared away."

"But the boy's arm—"

An older man—Mr. Kipperstrung, Georgie presumed—emerged from the door to the kitchens and made great show of planting his fists on his hips. The young woman turned back to the table and made more of a show of slicing the bread that sat between Georgie and Nicholas.

"Martha!" Mr. Kipperstrung gruffed. "Dinnit be justen thand." His words made no sense to Georgie, but his intent was clearly to summon Martha away from their table.

"Martha?" Georgie said quietly. "If you please, how did the boy burn his arm?"

Nicholas looked at Georgie and for the life of her she couldn't tell if he was being stern, encouraging, or something else entirely. All her life she'd felt confident that she could read him, or at least his general mood. Now that she'd gone and married him, it was as if he was a stranger.

"Please, ma'am," the woman practically begged while making a mess of the bread. "We'll be turned out."

Georgie tried to meet her eyes, but Martha turned back to the bread, slicing another two ragged pieces before setting down the knife.

Georgie then looked at Nicholas. Was he going to say something? Should *she* say something? Was it even their place to do so?

Nicholas let out a breath, and for a moment he seemed to sink further into his chair.

Then, with a weary inhale, he stood up.

"Milord?" Mr. Kipperstrung called out. "Did Martha make a mess of the dinner? She's as useless as her—"

"No, no," Nicholas said, and Georgie watched him spread a smile across his face that did not reach his eyes. He patted Martha on the shoulder as he stepped deftly around her. "She's neat and quick. My wife and I are most grateful."

The burly man did not look convinced. "You need only tell me and I'll have 'er—"

Nicholas did not let him finish. He held up a hand, then turned to Martha and said, "If you please, my wife is hungry and tired. Would you see her to her room and make sure she has whatever she requires?"

And before Georgie could say, "Now wait just a moment," to Nicholas, he'd started for the door.

"My good man," he said in a tone that Georgie thought almost pompous, "I am a doctor, and the boy I saw a moment ago has a burn on his arm in which I am quite interested."

Mr. Kipperstrung let out a loud snort. "'Tis but a scratch, milord. He's a clumsy boy, and he's lucky I keep him. He needs to learn his job proper and he won't get hurt."

"Nevertheless," Nicholas said, his voice just slightly clipped. "I haven't treated a burn of that nature in quite some time, and I could do with the practice. After all, it's not like we can go and burn people for the purpose of healing them later."

Georgie choked on a *highly* inappropriate bubble of laughter. That last sentence had been for her benefit, of that she was sure.

Mr. Kipperstrung seemed not to know what to say, especially as Nicholas was already walking smoothly past him. In fact, he only seemed to regain his power of speech once Nicholas had already disappeared through the doorway, and even then, all he could do was splutter and stomp after him.

Several moments of extended silence followed. Georgiana blinked. Then she blinked again. Had she just been completely dismissed?

"What just happened?" she said out loud.

Martha eyed her warily, clearly not sure whether the question was rhetorical.

Georgie set down the spoon she only just realized she was still holding. She looked up at Martha.

Martha managed the weakest of smiles. "Should I take you to your room?"

Georgie shook her head, murmuring to herself, "I can't believe he just left me here."

"I . . . ah . . ." Martha wrung her hands, watching the kitchen door as if she expected flames to shoot forth at any moment.

"I could help, you know," Georgie said. She looked at Martha. "He didn't even ask."

"Ma'am?"

Georgie stood.

"*Ma'am.*" Now Martha sounded a little panicked.

"Please take me into the kitchen."

"What?" Martha's face drained of color. "I mean, are you sure?"

"Entirely so," Georgie said in her best *I-am-a-woman-of-means-and-I-shall-not-be-crossed* voice.

It was a somewhat new voice for her, but she'd had very good role models.

"But ma'am, it's the kitchen."

"I assume that is where Mr. Kipperstrung just took Mr. Rokesby."

"You mean the doctor?"

"The very same."

"Oh, no, ma'am," Martha said. "You don't want to go there."

Which made Georgie quite sure there was no place she'd rather be.

Georgie held her smile firmly in place. "I rather think I do."

"But you're a *lady.*"

This didn't seem to be a question, so Georgie did not answer it. Instead she started to make her way around Nicholas's now abandoned chair. Martha looked fit to cry.

"If you please, ma'am, my lady." Martha scurried forward, practically throwing herself between Georgie and the door. "The doctor—your husband, he said—"

"I believe he said something about whatever my needs were."

"Your meal . . ." Martha said weakly. "I could carry it up."

There was a resounding crash from the kitchen. Martha made an awkward step toward the door just as Nicholas strode back through it, ducking to clear the doorway with a limp boy slung over his shoulder.

"Georgie!" Martha called out in what was clearly concern and surprise.

That stopped Georgie cold. "Excuse me?"

"Georgie," Martha said, pointing at Nicholas.

"His name is Georgie?" Nicholas asked Martha.

"Me clotheid brother," Martha said, using the colorful Scottish modifier without a lick of a Scottish accent.

"And his name is Georgie?" Georgie asked Martha.

Martha nodded.

"My name is Georgie," Georgie said, her palm flattened on her chest.

Martha looked aghast. Whether she was horrified at the prospect of a lady with a man's name or at a lady suggesting a tavern maid call her by said name—this was unclear.

She also seemed entirely unaware she was making such a dramatic face.

Georgie, on the other hand, suddenly realized she

no longer felt even a little bit tired. There was no way Nicholas was going to get out of letting her help this time.

The other Georgie picked that moment to groan.

If Nicholas reacted to the noise, neither Georgie saw it. "Martha," he said, "your brother is going to be fine. But I can't fix his arm in the kitchen."

"Why not?" Martha said, swinging her head around looking for—

Mr. Kipperstrung, who burst through the doorway in an incongruous cloud of flour. "Why not?" he demanded.

Nicholas clenched his teeth, and Georgie could see that he was losing his patience. "Why not here?" she asked cheerfully, swinging her hand across the expanse of the table. When no one responded, she lowered her arm, and less-than-deftly started to sweep the leftover mess from the sour-faced family that Martha hadn't been able to get to yet.

"Wait," Nicholas said. He looked surprised when this actually worked, and everyone stopped what they were doing and looked at him. He shook his head slightly and then maneuvered Boy-Georgie to the other end of the table.

"What happened?" Georgie asked.

Nicholas gave her a brief glance before turning back

to his patient. "He fainted the moment I touched his arm."

"He tried to tell me it didn't hurt," Martha whispered.

"May I have a small pot of hot water and some clean linen?" Nicholas asked the proprietor.

Mr. Kipperstrung stared, mouth agape. "Me, fetch water?"

Nicholas smiled. "Yes, please. If you will."

"How can I help?" Georgie asked with cheerful eagerness.

"Honestly?" Nicholas asked her.

She nodded.

"Feed me."

Chapter 18

It was only when Nicholas climbed the stairs to his room at the Alconbury Arms that he realized two full hours had passed.

Georgie had been amazing. Spectacular. True, she'd looked at him as if he might be a lunatic after he'd asked her to feed him, but only for a moment.

Once she'd realized what he was about, she gave him a businesslike nod and turned to the food on the table, ripping off small bits of bread, cheese, and something he hoped was sliced beef. Piece by piece she popped the food into his mouth so that he could keep his hands free to work on Boy-Georgie.

When he'd asked her to take Jameson and go back out to the carriage to hunt for his personal medical supplies she hadn't balked that he was sending her away from the area, she just did it, then came back and continued to give him food while he assessed the situation and began the initial debridement of the wound.

Georgie had rolled her sleeves up to match his and waited for him to need her. She wiped his brow, helped remove bits of burned skin from the area he was working on, and, when he asked, held the candle closer. She even caught a drip of wax with her bare hand.

But once she'd got involved with tending to the boy's arm, she'd forgotten to keep up with supper. He'd forgotten, too, but this was typical. Hunger, the passage of time—none of it seemed to interfere with his concentration when he was with a patient. Only his hair falling in his face (which Georgie held back), and the waning of the light (which Georgie fixed with a second candle) interrupted his systematic attention to the boy's arm.

It was not as simple an endeavor as he'd first thought. The burn was more than a day old, and no one had cleaned it properly. Bits of dirt and dust had embedded themselves in the tender skin, and Nicholas thought it a minor miracle that there was no sign of infection. He worked carefully and methodically—he liked this type of medical care; there was great satisfaction to be had when one could see results as one went along—but it took time, especially when he was trying extra-hard not to cause the boy any more pain.

When he'd finally got it down to just some minor burning at the edges of the main injury, Nicholas looked up from Boy-Georgie's arm to Girl-Georgie's face and saw that she was literally falling asleep.

"Darling," he whispered.

She jerked and opened her eyes.

"You should go up to bed."

"No," she said blearily, shaking her hand. "I'm helping you."

"And you've been indispensable," he assured her. "But I'm almost done. And you're dead on your feet."

She blinked and looked down. At her feet, he could only presume.

He smiled. He couldn't help it.

"Don't you need the candlelight?" she asked.

"There are still people about," he said. "Someone else can hold it. Go on. I will be fine, I promise." And then, when she did not look convinced, he said, "I would not let you leave if I were not sure I could manage without you."

This seemed to mollify her, and she yawned. "You're certain?"

He nodded. "Go. You'll want some time to yourself before bed, I'm sure."

"I'll wait up," she promised.

But she didn't. Wait up, that was. Nicholas had no

doubt she'd tried, but he'd been stuck in the dining room much longer than he'd expected. As he was finishing with the boy's wound, Martha came forward shyly and asked about a lump on her elbow. Then Mr. Kipperstrung confessed to a terrible earache, and Mrs. Kipperstrung—Nicholas still could not quite believe there *was* a Mrs. Kipperstrung—pulled him aside and asked if he might take a look at her bunions.

Bunions. Ah, the romance of medicine.

By the time he entered his room, he was bone tired. He moved quietly; he suspected Georgie would not be awake when he opened the door, and indeed, she was lying on her side, one hand near her face, her chest rising and falling softly with each breath.

"It seems that we're to be denied our wedding night once again," he murmured. He barely made a sound; it was really no more than a movement of his mouth. But he wanted to say it, to feel the words on his lips. He wanted to stroke her hair, too, to brush aside the wisps that tickled her face. But he did not want to wake her. He needed her, but she needed sleep more, and he suspected that he did, as well.

Nicholas did not know if he could make their first time perfect, but he was determined to try, and he knew this did not mean mauling her while they were both so tired they could barely function.

He looked down at Georgie, asleep in a moonbeam across her pillow. In all of their families' matchmaking, a more contrived visual could not have been concocted. The moonlight through the window was romantic, and his sleeping wife's long plait falling off the side of the bed was oddly inviting. Nicholas was gripped by a whimsical urge to lift her braid and put it on the pillow next to her.

He could not imagine what it was like to have so much hair one had to contain it before bed. Nicholas had never grown his hair long; it simply wasn't his style, and frankly, it seemed more of nuisance than it was worth. His brother Andrew had once worn his past his shoulders, but he'd spent nearly a decade at sea as a privateer, and apparently queued hair was an expected aspect of the role.

Nicholas liked Georgie's hair. He'd never seen it down, or at least not since they were children. But even pulled back, the color was an undeniable beacon of warmth. It was red, but not *red*, not in the way one usually thought of redheads. Which was to say, it wasn't orange.

They'd napped a bit in the carriage, and during one stretch while she was dozing and he was not, he'd peeked down at the strands, marveling that each was somehow a different color—red and brown and blond and even a few he'd swear were white, and they all combined to make something he could only describe as the morning dawn on a winter's day.

He changed into his nightshirt and crawled into bed, taking care not to disturb her. But as he drifted off, it occurred to him that there was nothing more welcome on a winter's day than that first glimpse of sun, that promise of warmth. And even though he'd tried so hard to give her the space she needed to sleep, his body felt the pull of hers, and he moved. He curved behind her, and his hand found hers, and he slept.

Georgie came awake slowly, one sense at a time. The cool morning air on her face, the pink of the sunlight filtering through her eyelids. She felt impossibly cozy and cocooned under the quilt, and even as her brain slowly rose through her sleepy fog, she wanted to burrow in, to press herself into the warmth, into the strength.

Into Nicholas.

Her eyes flew open.

He was in bed with her. Which shouldn't have been shocking, except that she had no memory of how he'd got there. What had happened the night before? Nothing intimate, surely. They'd helped the boy, the other Georgie, and then Nicholas had insisted that she go up to the room and get ready for bed. He'd thought she'd want some privacy to get ready. She'd thought him so considerate. And then . . .

She must have fallen asleep.

She closed her eyes again, abject in her embarrassment. What sort of bride fell asleep on her wedding night? Or the night after the wedding night, as her case was. But it didn't matter. She was still a terrible wife.

She stayed like that for several seconds, trying to hold herself utterly still. What was she supposed to do now? Wake him? Surely not. Should she try to slip out of the bed? His arm was thrown over her waist. Could she move it without disturbing him?

Could she move *herself* without disturbing him?

She gave it a little test, edging forward just a smidge.

Gremmremph.

As noises went, it was sleepy. And adorable. And she wished she could actually see him, but they were both on their sides, and she was facing away, and if her miniscule motion elicited his sleepy mumble, she'd surely wake him if she tried to turn.

But maybe if she moved just a *little* more. And then a little more after that, inch by inch until she could slip out from under his arm. Then she could turn. She could see what he looked like when he slept. Was he a quiet sleeper, or did his dreams play out on his face?

Were his lips closed, or did he hold them ever-so-slightly open? And what of his eyes? Had she ever truly looked at him when they were closed? No one held a blink for long enough for someone else to remember the expression. Did he still look like a Rokesby if she could not see the electric blue of his irises?

She pushed herself forward again, wiggling across the sheets, using all of her concentration just to move an inch. And then she waited, because it wouldn't do to move too quickly. She needed to be sure he'd settled back into sleep before she moved again.

And maybe she also needed one last moment before leaving the bed, because nothing had ever felt quite so perfect as his hand on her hip.

She sighed. She loved his hands. Big and strong and capable, with flat square nails. Was she mad to find a man's hands so attractive?

Then she felt him move, a yawning, stretching motion, the kind one made when one wasn't quite yet awake. "Georgie," he said, his voice sleep-slurred and husky.

"Good morning," she whispered.

"Georgie," he said again. He sounded a bit more lucid this time. And happy.

"You were sleeping," she said, not really knowing what to do with herself. "I didn't want to disturb you."

He yawned, and she took the moment to rise from

the bed, but his hand tightened on her. "Don't go," he said.

She did not leave the bed, but she did sit up. "We probably need to get ready. It's—" She looked around. If there was a clock, she didn't see it. "I don't know what time it is."

He rustled in the bed behind her, and out of the corner of her eye she saw him sit up and look toward the window. "It's barely dawn," he said. "The sun is still very low on the horizon."

"Oh."

What was he really trying to tell her? That she didn't need to get out of bed yet? That he didn't want her to get out of bed?

"I love the dawn," he said softly.

She should turn around. He was right there behind her, close enough that she could feel the heat from his body, even beyond the hand that still rested on her hip. But she was nervous, and she felt oddly misplaced, and she wasn't sure what she was supposed to do.

And no one liked not knowing what to do.

"You were asleep when I came in last night," he said. "I didn't want to disturb you."

"Thank you, I mean—" She shook her head, just a little, in that way people did when they weren't sure what to say. "I mean, thank you," she said again. Not that it sounded much different backward. "I was very tired." She turned to face him. She was a coward if she didn't, and she did not want to be a coward. "I meant to wait for you."

He smiled. "It's all right."

"No, I don't think it is."

"Georgie," he said, affection coloring his voice. "You needed to sleep. Hell, I needed to sleep."

"Oh." Did that mean he did not want her? That didn't seem to make sense after the hours they had spent in the carriage. He'd kissed her like he wanted her. He'd kissed her like he wanted *more*.

He tucked a strand of her hair behind her ear. "Stop thinking so hard."

She frowned at him, taking in the amusement in his azure eyes. "How do I stop thinking so hard?" she asked, with perhaps just a touch of peevishness in her voice. This was easy for him. Or if not easy, at least not quite so complicated and new.

He gave a shrug. "I don't know, but I swear if you think any harder, steam will start coming out of your ears."

"Steam. Really."

He grinned. "Smoke?"

"*Nicholas.*"

"You'd be surprised what they teach us these days in medical school," he said, his expression oh-so-innocent.

"Apparently so."

His fingers walked their way up her thigh, crossing to her hand, and then up her forearm. "I'd like to kiss you again," he said softly.

She nodded. She wanted that, too, but she wasn't sure how to put it into words. Or even into action. It wasn't that she felt frozen—that was far too cold a sensation to describe what had come over her body.

But she was still. Utterly motionless save for her breath, which had, in opposition to everything else, begun to quicken. She didn't know how to move; she'd lost the ability to do so. All she could do was react, and once he touched her . . . really touched her . . .

She wasn't sure what would happen, only that it would be like nothing she'd ever known.

He sat up, his nightshirt gaping a little at the neck to reveal a sprinkling of chest hair. It seemed so intimate, especially since she, too, was dressed in the loose white muslin of sleep.

"Georgie," he said, and his hand came to her cheek, part caress, part entreaty. He leaned in, and she leaned in, and they kissed.

It was exactly how it had been in the carriage.

And at the same time completely different.

He groaned her name again, and his other hand came up so that he was cradling her head, holding her close as he explored. The kiss was deep, and it was hot, and it stole everything from her in a way that made her just want to give more.

The entire moment was a contradiction—the same but different, stealing but giving. It was all so new to her, and yet he seemed to know exactly what to do.

How did he know how to do this? How to move and touch and give and take in exactly the right way to make her simmer with desire?

"Tell me what to do," she whispered.

"You're already doing it."

She did not see how this could be the truth, but she wasn't sure she cared. She just kept kissing him, doing what felt right and trusting that he would tell her if it was wrong.

He touched her leg, his hand trailing delicious shivers along her skin. "You tell *me* what to do," he whispered.

She felt herself smile. "You know what to do."

"Do I?"

She drew back, feeling the confusion on her face. "Haven't you done this before?"

He shook his head.

"But—but—you're a man."

He shrugged, the very picture of nonchalance. But his eyes didn't quite meet hers. "Everyone has to have a first time."

"But—But—" This made no sense. Men of their society sowed their wild oats before they married. It's what they did. It was how they learned. Wasn't it?

"Do you mind that you're my first?" Nicholas asked.

"No!" Goodness, that had come out with a bit more force than she'd intended. "No, not at all. I'm merely surprised."

"Because I'm such a rogue?" he said with a self-deprecating quirk of his brow.

"No, because you're so good at it."

His mouth slid into a wide, naughty smile. "You think I'm good, do you?"

She covered her face with her hands. Dear God, she was blushing so hard she was going to burn her palms. "I didn't mean it that way."

"Oh, I think you did."

She made a vee with the fore and middle fingers of her right hand and peered through the space. "Maybe just a little?"

"Just a little bit good?" he teased. "That's not much of a compliment."

"Do you see how embarrassed I am?"

He nodded solemnly.

"And you have no remorse."

Again with the solemn nod. "None."

She snapped her fingers back together.

"Georgie," he murmured, gently prying her hands from her face. "If I'm any good at this, as you say, it is only because I'm with the right person."

"But how do you know what to do?" she asked suspiciously. Because if he didn't . . . well, they were going to be in trouble. She'd been counting on him being the one to move things along.

"All I've done thus far is kiss you," he said, "and I must confess, I have done that before."

Her eyes narrowed. "With whom?"

His lips parted with surprise, and then he let out a bark of laughter. "Do you really want to know?"

"Wouldn't you want to know if it were me?"

He didn't answer right away. "I'm not sure," he said.

"Well, I am. Who was it?"

He rolled his eyes. "The first time was—"

"It was more than *once*?"

He poked her lightly in the shoulder. "Don't ask questions if you don't want the answers, Georgiana Bridgerton."

"Rokesby," she reminded him.

"Rokesby." His eyes softened. "So you are."

She touched his shoulder, letting her fingers trail seductively over his nightshirt to the warm skin of his neck. "Although . . ."

His voice hitched. "Although?"

Her eyes met his. A strange womanly thrill zipped along her skin. "Some would say," she said slowly, "that I'm not truly a Rokesby yet."

He kissed her, once, and lightly, whispering his words against her lips. "Then I suppose we will have to do something about that."

Chapter 19

Nicholas had never planned to remain a virgin so long. He had certainly never explicitly thought to himself—*I shall not lie with a woman unless we are wed.*

He had no moral objection to sexual congress before marriage, no religious one, either. Perhaps a medical objection—he knew far too much about syphilis to find attraction in indiscriminate intercourse.

But he'd never made a conscious decision to hold onto his virginity until he lay with his wife. It was more that the opportunity never seemed to present itself. Or at least not the right opportunity, and the thought of doing the deed simply to have it done had never sat well with him.

If he made love to a woman it should mean something. It didn't have to mean they were married. It didn't even have to mean he was in love. But it ought to mean more than the ticking of a box.

Maybe things would have been different if he'd done it when he was young, when all his friends were foolish and immodest and eager for pleasure. It might have happened—hell, it probably *would* have happened—his first year at Cambridge had it not been for an ill-timed head cold. A group of his friends had gone out carousing, and they'd ended up at a high-end brothel. Nicholas had meant to be with them, but he'd taken ill the day before, and thought of adding a hangover to his congestion was more than he could bear.

So he'd stayed in his rooms, and his friends were taught the so-called ways of manhood. He'd listened to their boasts because—well, because he was nineteen years old. Did anyone think he *wouldn't* listen?

But he'd also thought he might learn something. Then he realized that none of his friends had a clue what they were talking about, and if he wanted to really learn something he ought to ask a woman.

He never did, though. Who would he ask?

But he kept listening, and over the years men talked and boasted, usually when they were slightly—or extremely—intoxicated. Most of it was utter shite, but every now and then he'd hear something that made him think—*That makes some sense.* And he'd file it away in his brain.

Because he'd want that information eventually. When he did finally make love to a woman, he wanted to do a good job of it.

That time had finally come, and now, as he kissed his wife, he realized that he was nervous. Not because this would be new for him, but because it would be new for her. He *knew* he was going to enjoy it. Hell, he was damn near certain he was about to have the best morning of his life.

But he wasn't sure he could make this the best morning of *her* life. He wasn't even sure he could make it pleasant, or fun, or without pain.

Although come to think of it, if this wasn't good for Georgie, it wasn't going to end up being the best morning of Nicholas's life after all.

If ever there was a time to excel at one's studies, this was it.

"What is it?" she whispered.

He had been staring at her for so long, he realized. He'd made her uneasy.

"I want to know you," he said, his voice soft with desire. "I want to know every inch of you."

She blushed at that, the faint pink of emotion shimmering across her face and neck.

He kissed her brow, then her temple, then the tiny indentation near her ear. "You're perfect," he whispered.

"Nobody's perfect," she said. But her voice was shaky, as if the reply was automatic, an ingrained attempt to bring levity to a moment that was disquieting in its intensity.

"Perfect for me," he murmured.

"You don't know that."

He smiled down at her. "Why do you keep saying such silly things?"

Her eyes widened.

"You"—he kissed her nose—"are"—and now her mouth—"perfect"—her mouth again, but this time with a growl—"for me."

He gazed down at her again, pleased with his handiwork. She blinked several times in rapid succession, and he could not help but feel delight that he'd managed to so thoroughly discombobulate her. It was hard to tell if her expression was one of surprise or desire—maybe a combination of the two or maybe something else altogether—but her lips were parted and her eyes were wide, and he wanted to drown in them both.

How could he have lived his entire life knowing her and not knowing he needed *this*?

Never had he seen anything as beautiful as Georgie's skin, pale and luminous in the early morning sunlight.

Her nightgown had not been designed to entice; it was a basic, utilitarian thing, much like his own, but as he slid the hem up her slender legs, inch by tantalizing inch, he was grateful for it. At some point in the rushed wedding plans, he'd heard her mother bemoan the lack of a proper trousseau. He wanted to see Georgie in French silk and Belgian lace, but not yet. He didn't think he could take it.

"You have to tell me what you like," he said.

She nodded, her eyes shy.

He touched her thigh, his large hand skimming over the front before he gave it a gentle squeeze. "Do you like that?"

"Yes."

His thumb slid from position, stroking the soft skin of her inner thigh, ever careful not to stray too high.

She wasn't ready for that yet. And maybe he wasn't, either. If he touched her there, felt the heat of her, he might explode.

He had to make this last. He was as hard as he'd ever been in his life, and despite this being new, he felt the primal instinct of man rising within, hard and fast. He wanted to claim her.

He wanted to mark her as his.

The need was so fierce and intense he barely recognized himself.

When he spoke again his voice was shaky. "What else do you like?"

She looked at him as if she couldn't believe he was even asking. "Everything," she whispered. "I've liked everything you've done."

"Everything?" he said in a low growl. It was almost embarrassing how much he liked hearing that.

She nodded shyly. "I really like it when—"

"What?" he asked urgently. He had to know.

"When you kissed me," she whispered, bringing her fingers to skin just below her collarbone. "Here."

He sucked in his breath. *Here* was where the swell of her breast began. *Here* was a short journey to the pink tip he was aching to discover.

Here was an excellent place to begin a journey.

He replaced her fingers with his mouth, his tongue drawing lazy, sensual circles on her skin. She arched toward him, moaning with pleasure, and the sound stoked the fire that was already raging inside him.

"You're so soft," he murmured. Had her skin ever been touched by the sun? He wanted to explore her, every inch of her. He wanted a map of her body, and he wanted it drawn on his own.

Dear God, where were these thoughts coming from? He was a scientist, not a poet. And yet when he kissed her—her lips, her cheek, her neck—he could swear the world broke out into song.

Her nightgown tied at the neck with a simple bow, and he gave it a little tug, watching as the loop of the bow grew smaller and smaller until it eventually popped free. He didn't think the gown was meant to be lowered over her body, but the loosened neckline gave him access to a wider expanse of her skin. He kissed one of those newly revealed spots, and then another.

And then another, because he couldn't seem to resist a single inch of her.

Her nightgown couldn't be lowered any further, so he moved his lips over the muslin, skimming along her plump breast until he found the peak.

She gasped.

He took it in his mouth, and she gasped again, but this time it was louder, colored by a moan of pleasure.

"Do you like that?" he asked, thinking he might very well die if she said no.

"Yes."

He took her other breast in his hand, playing with her nipple through the fabric of her nightgown. She writhed beneath him, breathless in her desire.

He felt like a god.

"I didn't know they were so sensitive," Georgie said.

This surprised him. "You've never touched them?"

She shook her head.

"You should." Nicholas nearly came right then, just thinking about her touching herself.

"Is it the same way for you?" she asked.

It took him a moment to realize what she was asking, but once he caught her meaning, he sat up and whipped his nightshirt off so quickly he was stunned it did not tear.

"Touch me," he said.

Or he might have begged it.

She reached up and touched her fingertips to his chest, starting at the center before trailing lightly to his nipple. He shuddered, and she snatched her hand away.

"No," he said, barely recognizing his voice. "I liked it."

Her eyes met his.

"I want it," he said.

She reached up again, and this time her touch was more sure. It wasn't that she suddenly knew what she was doing—he had a feeling neither of them did—but she was secure in the knowledge—bold, even—that she was bringing him pleasure.

It was a mighty aphrodisiac, that. He knew it, too. Every time she moaned with delight, his own body burned in response.

"Can I kiss you?" she asked.

"Please."

She sat up, her head tilting as she regarded him. The curiosity in her eyes was mesmerizing; she seemed to be studying every line and plane of his chest. It was odd to be the object of such intense scrutiny, but he could not fault her for it; he wanted to do the same. And if it made her more comfortable in their marriage bed, he would stay there for hours.

She could explore him at will.

Honestly, he could not imagine a lovelier torture.

He held his breath as she leaned forward and touched her lips to him. His muscles jumped beneath his skin, but he held still. His heart was pounding, and it felt as if his soul was straining against his body. He wanted to grab her, push her down against the mattress. He wanted to lay his body atop hers, make her feel the heat of him, the weight.

He wanted her to understand what she did to him, to know that in this moment he was hers to command.

And at the same time he wanted to dominate her.

He drew a shaky breath, the sound of it rushing past his lips like a gasp, and she looked up.

"Am I doing it right?" she asked.

He nodded. "*Too* right."

"Is that possible?"

"You're killing me, Georgie."

"But in a good way?" she murmured. It was barely a question; she was clearly growing confident in her feminine prowess.

He nodded again, taking her hand and bringing it to his lips. "I want to see you," he said.

She didn't say anything, but her eyes flared, and a pale blush washed across her cheeks.

"Will you let me?" he whispered.

She nodded, but she didn't move. She needed him to remove the nightgown for her, he realized. She was not yet so bold.

He bunched some of the thin cotton in his fingers, never taking his eyes off hers as he slowly lifted the gown over her head. Her lower body was still concealed by the bedsheets, but the rest of her was bared to him.

Gloriously.

"You're gorgeous," he said.

She blushed. Everywhere. But she didn't try to cover herself.

He wanted to touch her breasts, to cup them in his hands, but even more he wanted to feel them pressed against his bare skin, so he gathered her in his arms and kissed her again.

And again.

And again, holding her tight as he lowered her to the bed. He pressed his pelvis against her, his blood jumping in his veins as he asked, "Do you feel what you do to me?"

She nodded, but she looked unsure, so he said, "It changes when aroused. Gets bigger. Harder."

She nodded again, but again, her eyes held questions, so he touched her cheek and said, "Do you know what happens between a man and a woman?"

"Yes," she said. "My mother told me, and then Billie did."

For some reason this made him smile. "And how did their accounts compare?"

"My sister was far more frank."

"And encouraging, I hope."

Georgie's mouth curved into a tiny smirk. "Very much so. Although she said—" She cut herself off with a little shake of her head.

"Tell me."

"No." She shook her head, but she was smiling as she did so. "I can't."

"What did she say?"

"I can't. I just can't."

Nicholas brought his mouth to her ear. "I can get it out of you, you know. I have my ways."

And while she was twisting to get a look at his face

again, he brought his fingers to her ribs and gave a little tickle.

She shrieked.

"I thought I remembered that you were ticklish," he said.

"Stop. Oh, please stop."

"Tell me what Billie said."

"Oh my—Nicholas, stop."

"Tell me . . ."

"All right, all right."

He stopped tickling, but he didn't move his hand.

She looked pointedly down.

"Not removing the threat just yet," he murmured.

"You are the worst."

He shrugged, wondering what spectacular god was granting them this much laughter in their first marriage bed.

Georgie pressed her lips together in a peevish expression before saying, "She told me that I will be certain that it won't work, but that I would be wrong, and it would."

He considered that. "Why is that embarrassing?"

"Because she said I would be certain it would not fit," she ground out.

"Why is *that* embarrassing?"

"It just *is*."

He rested his forehead against hers. "It'll fit."

"How would you know?" she retorted.

And then he started to laugh. He laughed so hard he could no longer hold himself up and he fell against her, his full weight pressing her down. He laughed so hard he eventually had to roll off of her and onto his back.

He laughed so hard he didn't even realize he was crying until she wiped away his tears.

"I wasn't trying to be funny," she said.

"That's what *made* it funny."

She scowled. Or rather she tried to. He saw through it.

"It'll fit," he said again.

"You know this because you're a doctor?"

He slid his hand to the juncture of her thighs. Even without venturing into her folds, he could tell she was hot. And growing wet.

"I know this," he said, "because you were made for me."

She gasped a little, arching her back when he touched her more intimately. "And were you made for me?" she asked, her voice barely a breath.

He stroked her, every manly part of him puffing with pride and delight as she grew slick. "Let's think about that," he murmured. "You're the first woman *I've* lain with. So yes, I think I was."

Her eyes flared, and he took advantage of her de-

light by slipping one finger inside her. She was tight—
tight enough that he understood why she might think
his cock might not fit, but he was a patient man. His
body might be screaming for release, but he was more
than happy to continue with his current ministrations,
stroking and caressing until she was ready for his inva-
sion.

"Do you feel that?" he asked, his voice husky with
desire. "Do you feel how wet you are?"

She nodded.

"That's to make sure I fit. Your body changes too."

Her face lit with an expression of wonder. It was
almost intellectual. Maybe it *was* intellectual, or maybe
it would have been, had she not been in the grips of her
own desire. He realized that his words did just as much
to arouse her as his touch, and so he brought his lips
to her ear and said, "When I touch you like this, you
grow softer. And wetter. It means you're getting ready
for me."

She nodded shakily.

"Do you feel empty?" he asked.

Her brow creased with confusion.

"Like you want more," he whispered. "More here."

He slid another finger inside her.

"Yes!" she gasped.

"Yes, you feel empty?"

"I did."

"But not now?"

She shook her head.

"You will." He moved his fingers and was rewarded by another rush of heat. "You'll want even more."

"Another finger?"

He smiled deviously. "Is that what you want?"

"I don't know."

"Shall we try it?"

She nodded.

He slid another finger in. "As you command, my lady."

"Oh my God!" she shrieked. But it wasn't with pain. He could see that on her face.

He could bring her to completion like this. It had not occurred to him that he could do so; truly, he'd only been trying to ready her body for his entry. But if she climaxed, if she experienced the womanly "little death" he'd heard so much about, surely that would make their inevitable joining all the more pleasurable, wouldn't it?

"You like being stretched, don't you?" he murmured.

It took her a moment to speak, but when she did, her words were clear. "I do."

"Do you like it when I move like this?"

Her breath became shallow.

"I'll take that as a yes."

"Nicholas . . ."

"Do you like this?" He crooked one finger, tickling her on the inside.

She liked it. She didn't say anything. He suspected she couldn't. But it was clear she liked it.

He moved his thumb, caressing her outer lips, the little bundle he'd heard was so sensitive. "What about this?" he whispered devilishly.

Her lips parted and she began to pant. Somewhere in it all, he saw her nod.

"More?"

She nodded. Urgently.

"Someday I'll kiss you there," he said, his words the naughty lyrics to the song of his fingers. "I'll take my tongue and—"

"Oh!"

She arched beneath him, her body coiling tight. Her inner walls spasmed around his fingers, and dear God he almost came all over her right then.

"What *was* that?" she gasped.

"The French call it *le petit mort*."

"I can see why."

He slid his fingers out of her, and her eyes flew to his. "Now I do feel empty," she whispered.

He moved into place.

"I think you're going to fit," she said.

He nodded. "Oh yes."

Her body was more than ready for him now, her muscles still warm and flushed with pleasure. Three strokes and he was fully seated, and all he could think was that this was the best thing he'd ever felt in his life.

And he hadn't even started to move.

"Does that hurt?" he asked, all the while thinking *please say no, please say no.*

"No," she said. "It feels very strange, but it doesn't hurt." She looked up. "Does it hurt you?"

He grinned. "Oh no."

"What happens now?" she asked.

He put a little more weight on his elbows as he started to move. "This," he said.

Her eyes widened with surprise.

"Please tell me if it hurts you," he begged, because he knew that her words were the only thing that could possibly have slowed him down at that point. His hunger for her was taking over, and he just wanted to pound into her, to make her feel him. He wanted to mark her, to claim her, to know that it was his body inside of her and only his, that he was the one to bring her such plea-sure, that he was the one who would—

He came so fast he didn't even see it coming.

He let out a cry as he slammed forward, again and again and again until he didn't think there could be an inch of her womb that wasn't coated with his seed.

And then he collapsed.

He couldn't believe he had waited so long to try this.

Except he could. Because it would never have been like this with another woman.

It was Georgie.

There was only Georgie.

Chapter 20

Three weeks later

Georgie had been none too pleased at how quickly Nicholas had left Scotsby following their arrival. They'd had one evening together.

One.

Mrs. Hibbert had prepared a simple but lovely dinner. She'd fussed and apologized that it was all she was able to pull together for their first night in the newly opened home. She assured them there would be proper menus moving forward. Georgie had not minded. They could have had tavern fare of brown bread and end-of-the-night soup for all she cared. She just wanted to be with Nicholas.

Alone.

The trip north had been glorious. It hadn't seemed to matter that Cat-Head howled half the time or that Sam's affection for Marcy (or was it Darcy?) hadn't been returned, and then it was, and then not, and then—well, honestly Georgie had no idea what had happened except that there seemed to be an awful lot of drama surrounding it all, culminating in Mrs. Hibbert giving her daughter a tongue-lashing to end all tongue-lashings, only to discover she'd told off the wrong girl.

Georgie noticed none of this. She'd been lost in a blissful haze of new love, of shared conversation and laughter, of soft, quiet moments, and nights of erotic discovery.

Marriage, she'd decided, was turning out to be a most splendid institution.

But then they'd reached their destination.

Georgie had known that things would change. She just hadn't anticipated how fast.

One night. That was all.

She'd had a proper bath, which had been nothing short of bliss after so many days of traveling. She'd even washed her hair, a process that for her took an inordinately long time. She'd always been envious of her sister Billie, who could scrub her hair clean, apply a bit of apple cider vinegar mixed with lavender oil to her wet, straight tresses and then simply comb it out and be done with it.

For Georgie, however, there was no simple about it. Her curls were tight, overly plentiful, and of a delicate texture. Taming them was, as Marian said, "a minister's own penance." Her hair had to be dried very carefully, or else she'd wake the following morning with a bramble on her head.

Or she could just braid it. It didn't turn out as nice as when she so carefully combed, treated, and air-dried it, but it was a lot quicker. And had she known that Nicholas was leaving the next morning, that's what she would have done so that she might join him sooner in their new bedroom.

She smiled, despite her current ire. He'd been undone when she let her hair down for him, all damp and silky. It had been quite the most innocently executed move; her pins had simply loosened under the weight of it. She reached up to fix it, doing what she did when alone: tossing her head upside down, shaking it out and then flipping the whole mass of it back. She'd never *not* resented her curly hair quite as much as when he gathered fistfuls of it in both hands, uttered "Jesus," and pulled her to him.

They'd made such a mess of her hair that night Marian had nearly made the sign of the cross when she saw her the next morning. Georgie might have laughed—Marian wasn't even Catholic—but she was in far too despondent a mood to muster humor.

Nicholas was gone.

He'd awakened her to say good-bye, at least. A gentle kiss to her cheek and then a soft shaking of her shoulder. Georgie had looked up at him sitting on the side of the bed, gazing down at her as shafts of weak sunlight drifted down from the high window.

She'd smiled, because such a sight would always make her smile now, and she'd shamelessly scooted herself up to sitting and pressed her naked body to his clothed one and then—

And then he said his horse was saddled and he'd be off as soon as he kissed her. He'd been playful and sweet, but the reality of his oh-so-imminent departure was like a cold, wet wind.

He kissed her, and he was gone.

And he'd stayed gone for almost a week.

Georgie had pouted off and on for days. There had been a lot to do, so she stayed busy, but she did not like that he'd left her behind.

Yes, she knew she could not go with him to Edinburgh, at least not yet. He was still living in a rooming house, one not suitable for women.

And yes, she was fully cognizant of the fact that he hadn't *left* her. He had to go back to school. As was necessary. He was a student, and he'd already missed several examinations.

And yes, *fine*, she'd known this was coming. It wasn't a surprise, and she had no right to be petulant.

But she was. She was in a new place, a new country for heaven's sake, in what felt like the wilds of Scotland, and even though she knew Nicholas had behaved exactly as he must, she felt abandoned.

So she'd thrown herself into getting Scotsby up and running. Georgie had never quite subscribed to the belief that idle hands really were the devil's playthings, but busy ones usually worked well to keep one's mind off the unpleasant.

But there was only so much to do. Mrs. Hibbert had also taken up the task of getting the house in order, and to be frank, she was better at it than Georgie. Furthermore, it was Georgie's aim to *not* be living at Scotsby very long—weren't they planning to lease a house in Edinburgh, after all? How much work did she really wish to put into a house that would soon sit empty?

She was bored.

And she was lonely.

And Nicholas was hours away, learning all sorts of interesting things.

Now, nearly a week after he'd left for Edinburgh, she tried not to look impatient as she waited for him to return. There was no getting around *feeling* impatient, but she didn't need to be obvious about it.

As it turned out, when one was the mistress of a house it was not as easy to blend into the woodwork as when one was merely the daughter. At Aubrey Hall she'd curled up on a window seat with a book, or retired to her room and no one thought twice.

Scotsby was much smaller, though. And as the only family member in residence, she had the undivided attention of the staff.

All of them.

It was impossible to get a moment of true solitude. Georgie had tried to feign not feeling well, but the looks of concern were immediate and obvious. Clearly her mother had sent them all off with strict instructions not to endanger her "delicate health."

So that hadn't worked.

But it was finally Friday, the day Nicholas had said he'd return. He had no classes on Saturday or Sunday (although he'd warned her this was not always the case), and he'd promised to ride home that evening. Georgie had no idea what time to expect him. By her calculations it could be anywhere from four hours past noon into the late evening.

She hoped it was on the early side. The cook Mrs. Hibbert had hired from the village was a veritable fount of dire stories of highwaymen and mischievous fairies. And while Georgie was not too worried about fairies, the idea of highwaymen did make her concerned for Nicholas's status as a solitary rider.

Maybe he should have used the carriage.

It would have made his journey all the more slower, though.

Georgie sighed. She was literally waiting by the window.

"I am pathetic," she said to no one in particular.

No, she wasn't pathetic. She was just lonely. Which was startling in its own way. She'd always been content when left to her own devices. Certainly she enjoyed gatherings with friends and family, but she'd never been the sort of person who could not get along on her own. She *liked* the quiet. She *enjoyed* solitude.

She just hadn't realized it was possible to miss someone quite so much.

At nine that evening she was back at the window, back to feeling pathetic. To her credit, she hadn't been there all day. After feeling sorry for herself earlier that afternoon she'd got up and found some mostly unnecessary household tasks to complete. Then she'd had her supper. She was hungry, and she knew Nicholas would not want her to wait.

But now she was back to waiting for him. The days were still growing longer; they were almost to the solstice, and the sun would not set until nearly ten. And it would not be true dark until a good hour after that. Although Scotsby was in a fairly wooded area—it did make the night seem darker than it really was.

But apparently the old saying about a watched pot was true, because the minute Georgie got up to use the chamber pot was the minute Nicholas rode into the drive, and he was already in the front hall by the time she'd come back from her room.

"You're home!" It was all she could do not to throw herself into his arms. She would have done, had he not looked so tired.

And wet. It wasn't raining at Scotsby, but clearly it had been somewhere between there and Edinburgh.

"I'll have Marcy draw you a bath," Georgie said, reaching for his hat before Wheelock-the-younger could take it. "You look terribly cold."

"Summer in Scotland is like winter anywhere else," Nicholas said, giving a little shiver as he shrugged off his coat.

"How was your week? Did you learn anything new?"

He looked at her with faint surprise. She supposed he was not used to such interest in his studies. "Yes, of course," he said. "We've been focused on the proper- ties of circulation primarily. Plus a bit on—"

"And did you meet with the land agent?"

Nicholas handed off his coat to Wheelock, who'd practically jumped in front of Georgie to get it. "The land agent?"

"For the house," Georgie said.

"The house," he repeated.

"In which we might live."

He blinked.

She told herself that he was tired. That she must be patient. So she said, "In Edinburgh. Surely you don't want to remain at Scotsby any longer than we must."

"No, of course not. It's only I hadn't the time."

"Oh." Georgie followed him into the dining room. This was not what she'd been hoping to hear.

Nicholas looked around. "Is there anything to eat?"

"Yes, of course, we've been keeping it warm for you." Georgie motioned to a chair. "Sit."

He did, and she took a seat next to him. "Lamb stew," she told him. "It's very good. With freshly baked bread and raspberry trifle for dessert. I'm sorry I did not wait for you."

"No, no, don't be silly. I was delayed."

Georgie waited while Mrs. Hibbert brought out supper. Then she waited while Nicholas ate a few bites. But then she couldn't wait any longer. "So you didn't even contact him?"

He looked at her blankly.

"The land agent," she reminded him.

"Oh, yes." He wiped his mouth. "Sorry, no."

Georgie did her best to keep her disappointment off her face. He was busy, she reminded herself. He was learning how to save actual lives.

Nicholas reached forward and took her hand. "I'll do it this week, I promise."

She nodded, then managed to wait five whole seconds before asking, "Once you do contact him, how long do you think it will take to find a house?"

"I don't know," he said with the beginnings of impatience. "I've never leased a house before."

"But didn't your father say he was sending notice ahead? So he'll be expecting you."

"It's possible."

"Perhaps by the time you meet with him it will all be settled."

Nicholas scrubbed a hand through his hair. "Honestly, I don't know. I'm dead on my feet, Georgie. Can we talk about this tomorrow?"

She smiled tightly. It felt like all her smiles were tight this evening. "Of course."

He ate, and she watched, and then, because the silence was making her itchy, she asked, "Did you learn anything new this week?"

He looked at her. "Didn't you already ask me that?"

"You didn't answer."

"You didn't give me a chance."

"I'm sorry," she said, unable to keep all traces of sarcasm from her voice. "I was preoccupied by the fact that you haven't been to see the land agent."

"I'm sorry I was too busy to see to it," he snapped. "I spent the entire time dealing with everything I missed traveling down to Kent for *you*."

There it was. The expectation of gratitude. She'd almost forgotten that she'd been waiting for it.

"Thank you for marrying me," she said, shoving her chair back so she could stand. "I am sorry it has made your life so difficult."

"For God's sake, Georgie. You know that's not what I meant."

"I know it's not what you *thought* you meant."

"Don't put words in my mouth," he warned, rising to his feet.

"I knew this would happen."

He rolled his eyes so hard she wouldn't have been surprised if he saw his brain.

"I'm going to bed," she said. She walked to the door, hoping he'd try to stop her, hoping he'd say something, say anything.

"Georgie, wait."

She turned just as he laid his hand on her arm.

"I don't want to go to bed angry," he said.

Something inside of her softened. "Nor do I."

"I don't even know why we're angry."

She shook her head. "It's my fault."

"No," he said, and his voice was firm even as his weariness seemed to cloak them both. "No, it's not."

"I missed you," she said. "And I was bored. And all I wanted was to hear that I would be able to move to Edinburgh so I could be with you."

He pulled her into his arms. "That's all I want too."

A part of her wanted to ask why, then, hadn't he gone to see the land agent, but she knew that would be petty. He was exhausted, and he had every right to be.

"I don't want you to feel grateful that I married you," he said.

"But I do," she admitted.

"Fine, then. Feel grateful."

She drew back. "What?"

"If you want to feel grateful, feel grateful."

She blinked. This was not what she'd expected him to say.

Then he took her hand and raised it to his lips. "But I get to feel grateful too."

That was when she knew. She loved him. How could she not?

"Can we go to bed now?" he asked. "I'm so tired. I don't even know how I'm still standing."

She nodded, not quite capable of words. This feeling—this love—it was still too new. She needed to give it time, to see how it felt.

"Can we talk about all this in the morning?" he asked. "The house? The land agent, moving to the city? Can we talk about it all later?"

But they didn't. Talk about it, that was. They were distracted—delightfully so, Georgie had to allow—but that meant that when Nicholas returned to Edinburgh Sunday night, nothing of import had been discussed or settled. And Georgie found herself looking ahead to another week of very little with which to occupy herself.

"There aren't even books in this house," she despaired to Marian two days after Nicholas had departed.

"It's a hunting lodge," Marian said. She looked up from the socks she was darning. "Do men read when they hunt? I thought they just went around and shot things."

"We need books," Georgie said. "We need books, and we need paper and ink, and honestly, I'd settle for embroidery right now."

"There's no thread," Marian admitted. "None that's suitable for more than mending. We didn't bring any up from Kent."

"Why not?" Georgie asked testily.

"You don't like to embroider," Marian reminded her.

"I was starting to like it," Georgie grumbled. She'd liked when she'd made all those even identical stitches. That had actually been, well, maybe not fun, but certainly rewarding.

"I suppose we could pick flowers," Marian suggested. "Orrrrrr . . . We could *look* for embroidery thread. Mrs. Hibbert found a bolt of muslin in the storeroom the other day. Very fine quality, and never used. Who knows what else is hiding there."

"I don't want to embroider," Georgie said.

"But you just said—"

"That's it," Georgie announced, because the last thing she needed to hear was an accounting of all her contradictions. "We're going shopping. First thing tomorrow."

"In the village?" Marian gave her a dubious look.

They'd been to the village. It was charming. And without shops.

"No. We'll go to Edinburgh."

"Us?"

"Why not? We have a carriage. We have a driver."

"Well . . ." Marian frowned. "I don't know. I suppose I thought we were meant to remain here."

"Meant by whom?" Georgie retorted. "Aren't I the lady of the house? To whom must I answer?"

"Mr. Rokesby?" Marian said.

"He's not here."

Georgie's volume was such that Marian's face took on an expression of faint alarm.

"He's not here," Georgie repeated, this time with a bit more modulation. "I'm in charge, and I say we are going to Edinburgh."

"But we've never been to Edinburgh. Should we not go for the first time with someone who knows his way?"

"The only person we know who knows his way is Mr. Rokesby, and he's already there. Cheer up, Marian. This will be exciting."

But Marian did not look excited, and Georgie supposed this was understandable. Marian liked routine. It was part of the reason she and Georgie were so well suited. Until recently, Georgie's life had been nothing *but* routine.

"Tomorrow, you say?" Marian said with a sigh.

"Tomorrow," Georgie said firmly. She was feeling better already.

They left early the following day, and were at the outskirts of the city by ten in the morning.

"Oh, look, it's the castle!" Georgie exclaimed, pointing at the grand fortress on the hill right in the middle of the city.

Marian scooted along the carriage bench to get a better look. "Oh, my," she said with surprise. "It's right here." She looked over at Georgie. "Can we visit?"

"I don't know. I think it's used as a prison now."

Marian gave a delicate shudder. "Perhaps not, then."

"It may have other uses," Georgie said. "We can find out. But we don't have time today, anyway. We have far too much to do. Our first stop is the land agent."

Marian turned sharply to face her. "What? You can't do that. Not without Mr. Rokesby."

Georgie folded her hands primly in her lap. "He has failed to do it without me, so I must take the reins."

"Miss Georgiana"—Marian had not quite got used to referring to her as Mrs. Rokesby, and truth be told, Georgie had not quite got used to hearing herself referred to that way—"you cannot go to the land agent by yourself. It is not done."

"It has *not* been done," Georgie said with deliberate obtuseness. "That is true."

"But—"

"Oh, look, we're here."

The carriage came to a halt outside a tidy office front, and Georgie waited while Jameson opened the carriage door and secured the steps.

"I'm going in," Georgie said with steely resolve. "You may come with me, or you may remain in the carriage. But it will certainly be more proper if you come."

Marian let out a noise that was probably meant to be a sigh. "You will be the death of me," she muttered.

"Heavens, Marian. We're not going into a brothel."

Marian's mouth pinched into a line as she looked up at the sign hanging over the door. "Is Mr. McDiarmid expecting us?"

"Likely not," Georgie admitted. "But he will know who I am. Lord Manston has been in contact, I believe."

"You believe."

"I'm *sure*," Georgie said, looking over her shoulder as she stepped out into the street. "It was a figure of speech."

Marian still did not look convinced.

"He's probably wondering what has been taking us so long," Georgie said, giving the edges of her gloves a little tug so they fit smoothly over her fingers. "I wouldn't be surprised if he's already found a house."

"That would be exciting," Marian allowed. "Although you wouldn't want to try to take up residence today, would you?"

"No, no, that would be quite impossible," Georgie said briskly. Tempting, but impossible. For now, she simply had to focus on securing a lease. Everything else would follow.

With one last look at Marian, she marched up the steps and pushed open the door. "Let's get this done."

"Oh, that was brilliant!" Georgie exclaimed several hours later. She and Marian had settled into a table at the White Hart—practically around the corner from the anatomical theater where Nicholas sat for his lectures— and were sharing a pot of tea. "Wasn't it brilliant?"

Marian opened her mouth, but before she could say a word, Georgie answered herself. "It was brilliant."

Georgie faced the nearby open window and grinned up at the sky, which rewarded her with clear blue bliss. "We have a home!"

"We have a home at Scotsby," Marian pointed out.

"Yes, but now we have one in Edinburgh. Which makes so much more sense. Mr. Rokesby can't be riding back and forth every day."

"He *wasn't* riding back and forth every day," Marian said.

Georgie rolled her eyes. "You know what I mean. Scotsby is beautiful, but it's dreadfully inconvenient." She laid a hand on her breast. "I'm a newlywed. My place is with my husband."

"That is true," Marian allowed. Georgie watched as she fanned herself, still trying to calm her nerves. Georgie wasn't sure why the maid had been so overcome at the prospect of two women entering the land agent's office; *she* had found it exhilarating.

Mr. McDiarmid had not wanted to lease a house to her. He hadn't even wanted to show her a property. She needed her husband, he said. Or her father. Or her brother. Or someone who could make a decision.

"I assure you," Georgie had said with all the ice in her veins, "I am fully capable of making a decision."

Not that Georgie had much ice in her veins, but she'd seen her mother and Lady Manston in action. She knew how to fake it.

"Your husband will need to sign," Mr. McDiarmid had replied, his voice as mincy as pie.

"Of course," Georgie had sniffed. "But he is a very busy man. He has entrusted me to do all of the preliminary viewings so that he might weigh in only when truly necessary."

Marian had almost gone and ruined the whole thing right then, coughing until her eyes watered. Fortunately Mr. McDiarmid had been distracted enough getting her something to drink that he didn't hear Georgie when she hissed, "Stop that right now!"

Or when Marian said helplessly, "But Mr. Rokesby hasn't entrusted you do anything."

Honestly, Marian was the worst liar.

After another ten minutes of hemming and hawing, Mr. McDiarmid admitted that he had indeed received the request from Lord Manston, and he did have two properties in mind that might do for the young couple. But he absolutely, positively put his foot down at the idea of showing them to a lady without her husband. He absolutely, positively could not even entertain the idea until—

Georgie stood right up and announced that she would find a different agent.

It was remarkable how quickly they'd gone to see the first house after that.

Georgie had known instantly that it would not do. The floor was crooked, and it was painfully short on windows. But the second house—in the New Town Georgie had heard so much about—was perfect. Light, and airy, and ready to be leased fully furnished. The décor was not quite what Georgie would have chosen herself, but it was close enough. And if it meant she could move in sooner rather than later . . .

Blue was just as good as green for a sitting room. Honestly, she did not care.

"Have you had enough tea?" Georgie asked Marian, even though they'd barely been sitting for five minutes. "I want to go find Nicholas. Mr. McDiarmid said he can sign the lease today."

"He's going to be very surprised to see you," Marian said.

"But good surprised," Georgie said with more certitude than she actually felt. She didn't *think* Nicholas would be angry that she'd taken care of the house on her own. But he might not like her coming to Edinburgh without informing him ahead of time. Men were funny that way. Still, what was done was done, and she was eager to share her news.

Mr. McDiarmid had inadvertently shown her the location of the medical school, boasting of its proximity to the houses he was showing her, and so Georgie was confident she knew where she was going as she, Marian, and Jameson made their way to Teviot Place.

Nicholas had told her about the grand anatomical theater, about the steeply tiered seats looking down at the small stage at the bottom. He'd told her that sometimes the lecturer just spoke, but sometimes there was a dead body down there, cut open for all to see.

Georgie wasn't sure she wanted to see *that*, but she

was eager to see the room where her husband spent so much of his time.

It wasn't difficult to find the anatomical theater, but as it had well over a hundred men in it, all facing away from her as she peeked through the door, finding Nicholas from among the many was. Georgie was wearing a deep green day dress and a hat that wouldn't be called fancy in any drawing room, but in this place she was decidedly out of place.

And conspicuous.

But luck was on her side. The bench just outside the door was positioned such that if she leaned over the armrest she could hear almost everything. She didn't recognize half the words, but the context was helpful, and she was riveted.

"Did you hear that?" she whispered to Marian. Something about blood, and how much of it was in the human body.

Marian closed her eyes. "I'm trying not to."

Georgie leaned further. Now the lecturer was talking about why blood was red, and how bloodletting was frequently essential to restore balance to the nervous system.

"The body is an animated machine!"

Georgie looked down at her hands. "I suppose," she murmured.

"What are you doing?" Marian whispered.

Georgie shushed her, tipping her ear back to the open door. Drat, she'd missed something.

". . . *perform a variety of motions . . .*"

Georgie opened and closed her hands. All right. She could accept that.

". . . *and to communicate and interact with external bodies.*"

Well now, *that* just made her think of Nicholas.

"We're leaving," Marian declared.

"What? No."

"You're flushed. I don't know what they are talking about in there, but I *know* it is not appropriate." Marian stood up with alacrity, exchanged a few quick words with Jameson, who had been waiting on the other side of the hallway, and then ushered Georgie right out the building's door and into the courtyard.

Chapter 21

"Georgiana?"

Nicholas's heart had nearly stopped when he exited the lecture hall and saw Jameson waiting for him in the corridor. There was no reason why the footman should be here in Edinburgh, much less on the grounds of the medical school.

No reason except an emergency.

Jameson must have seen the panic on his employer's face, because before Nicholas could get out anything more than, "What are you—" Jameson blurted, "Nothing's wrong, sir!"

Still blinking with surprise—and yes, concern, even though he'd been assured there was no reason for it—Nicholas let the footman lead him out into the sunny courtyard where his wife waited.

"Georgiana?" he said again. She was chatting with her maid and must not have heard him the first time. "What are you doing here?"

"Nicholas!" she cried with clear delight. She jumped to her feet to greet him. "I have splendid news!"

His first thought was—*she's pregnant.*

Except that it was too soon. Not for it to have happened—their recent behavior was of the sort that pretty much guaranteed it *would* happen. But it seemed too soon for her to know. Maybe suspect, but not know.

And besides, it wasn't the sort of thing she'd tell him right in the middle of a busy academic courtyard.

He took her outstretched hands, still somewhat suspicious of the joy on her face. "What is it?" he asked.

"Oh, don't look so concerned," she said. "I promise, it's nothing but good news."

"I am concerned," he told her. "I can't help it. I was not expecting to see you here."

Not to mention that she'd never been to Edinburgh before. She didn't know her way around the city, and there were many areas that were not safe for a lady. Hell, there were many areas that weren't safe for him.

"I spoke with Mr. McDiarmid," she said.

"Who?"

Something impatient flashed across her face, but

then she seemed to shake it away. "Mr. McDiarmid. The land agent."

"Oh, yes." Damn it, he'd been meaning to go see the man for over a week. It was just so difficult to find time with all of his academic commitments. "My father's man."

"No, he's been in touch with your father's man," Georgie corrected. She gave his hands a tiny squeeze before tugging her own away. "I assure you, he's never met your father in person. If he *had*—Well, that's hardly here nor there."

Nicholas stared at her for a moment, but no, she didn't seem to have any intention of illuminating that cryptic remark. "Would you please just tell me what is going on," he said. Honestly, he didn't have the energy to guess.

"I found us a house!" she exclaimed.

"Why, that's won—"

But she was far too excited to listen to his congratulations. "He didn't want to show me anything at first," she said, probably not even aware that she'd cut him off. "He insisted that you be there, even though I told him that you were terribly busy, and if he wanted our business he was going to need to deal with me." She paused, rolling her eyes. "He's really not a nice man, but I put up with him since I just wanted to find a house."

"You leased a house?" Nicholas asked.

"I haven't signed anything of course. You need to do that. But I told him that you'd entrusted the search to me and that you would go along with whatever I chose." Her eyes narrowed a bit, and her lips pressed together before she added, "You'd better like what I picked out, because if you don't I'm going to look a fool and worse, that awful man will never do business with another woman again."

"It sounds as if women shouldn't want to do business with him," Nicholas said.

"I hadn't much choice, not if I wanted something right away. Besides"—she flipped her hand in the air in a *this-ought-to-be-obvious* sort of motion. "I don't know how to find another land agent."

They'd likely all be the same way, Nicholas thought. Most men would be willing to do business with a widow, who could sign her own contracts, but not a married lady. Not when her husband could so easily gainsay her.

"How did you get him to show you the properties?" he asked her.

She gave him a cheeky grin. "I told him I'd find another land agent."

He laughed out loud at that. "Brava," he told her. "I am impressed."

"You should be," she said pertly. She was clearly impressed with herself, and it was stunning how much Nicholas liked seeing that expression on her face.

"Can we go to his office now?" she continued, all brisk determination. "He said you could tour the property this afternoon. I've been crossing my fingers that you would be free."

"I am free, but I don't need to see it." Nicholas reached out and hooked her pinkie finger with his. "If you think it's suitable, I trust you."

She looked at him as if she could not quite believe his words. "You do?"

"Of course." He shrugged. "Regardless, it ought to be more your decision than mine. You'll be there more than I will."

"Then can we go sign the lease?" she asked, her face lighting with excitement. "He said he'd have it prepared, but I'll be honest—I'm not sure he meant it. I think he's half-expecting you to swoop in and give me a tongue-lashing for my impertinence."

"A tongue-lashing for your impertinence?" Nicholas murmured. "Intriguing."

"Nicholas!" Georgie exclaimed. Her eyes widened and she motioned with her head toward her maid, who was still seated on a nearby bench.

"She can't hear us," he whispered. "And she wouldn't know what I meant, anyway."

"That's almost as bad. I don't want her thinking you

don't approve of my actions." She drew back, just a tiny bit. "You do approve, don't you?"

"Of your taking care of the land agent so I don't have to? Hell, yes. I wish I'd thought of it." He touched her chin, tilting her face toward his. "But let me know ahead of time if you're going to do something like this again. I do like to know what you're up to."

"To be completely honest," she said, "it was a spur of the moment thing. I only decided yesterday." Her eyes turned shy. And maybe a little embarrassed. "I don't like to spend all week in the country without you."

"I'm sorry." He squeezed her hand. He didn't like leaving her at Scotsby, but he didn't see how there had been another option.

"You have nothing to be sorry for," she replied. "I knew what I was getting into. I just didn't know how much I wouldn't like it."

He leaned forward. Only about an inch; they were in public, after all. "Does it make me a bad husband that I like hearing that you're miserable without me?"

"I didn't say miserable," she said, with a little co-quettish tilt of her head.

"Humor me," he said. "I've been miserable without you."

It wasn't entirely the truth. Most of the time he was

too busy to be miserable, and when he wasn't too busy he was too tired.

But he missed her. At night, when he lay in his narrow boardinghouse bed, he longed to reach out for her, pull her close. And then during the day, at the oddest moments, he'd notice something—usually something odd or funny or unusual—and he wished he could point it out to her.

He'd grown accustomed to her presence in a way that ought to have terrified him.

But it didn't.

It only made him want more. And that started with getting the house in New Town sorted. "Where is Mr. McDiarmid's office?" he asked Georgie. "We'll take care of it right now."

Georgie grinned and pulled a scrap of paper from her reticule. "Here, I have the address written down."

He gave the words a quick look. "That's not too far. We can walk there. Give me a moment, and I'll make arrangements for Jameson and your maid. They'll need to find a suitable place to wait for you."

"It shouldn't take very long."

"No, but now that you're here, we should make a day of it. I can show you the city."

"Really? You don't have anything else you need to do?"

He had a mountain of things he needed to do. He was still behind on his studies, and he needed to prepare for a meeting later that week with one of his professors, but he could not see beyond Georgie's smiling face. His wife was here, and he wanted to be with her.

"Nothing that will not keep," he told her. "Come. Let's get that lease signed. Then we shall have some fun."

She placed her hand in his and grinned, and he had a sudden flash of memory. It was from when they were tending to Freddie Oakes, and she'd smiled at him, and it had made him want to grab the sun from the sky and hand it to her on a platter.

It was still true. One smile from Georgiana, and he thought he could do anything.

Be anything.

Was this love? This crazy, heady feeling, this sense of endless possibility?

Could he have somehow fallen in love with his wife? It seemed too fast, too soon, and yet . . .

"Nicholas?"

He looked at her.

"Is something wrong?" she asked. "You looked very far away."

"No," he said softly. "I'm right here. I'll always be right here."

Her brow creased with confusion, and he couldn't

blame her. He wasn't making sense. And at the same time, it felt as if the entire world was finally clicking into place.

Maybe this *was* love.

Maybe.

Probably.

Yes.

Ninety minutes later, Georgie was tiptoeing up the stairs in Mrs. McGreevey's Respectable Boardinghouse for Bachelors.

"We're not being very respectable," she whispered.

Nicholas put his finger to his lips.

Georgie giggled. Quietly. She couldn't help it. She felt positively giddy sneaking into Nicholas's rooms.

The meeting with Mr. McDiarmid had gone smoothly, although Georgie could not help but be somewhat miffed at how much more accommodating he had been with Nicholas than with her.

She kept her complaints to herself, though; there was nothing to be gained by voicing them. She wanted the lease signed, and she wanted it signed quickly. It was clear that the most efficient path to her goals was to sit quietly and play the deferential spouse.

She knew it wasn't the truth, as did Nicholas, and that was what was important.

Once they had all that taken care of, though, they still had a bit of time before she was supposed to meet Marian and Jameson for the ride back to Scotsby. Several hours, in fact. Nicholas had said that he would show her a bit of the city, but then they just happened to be walking past the boardinghouse, and Mrs. McGreevey just happened to not be anywhere in sight . . .

The next thing she knew she was giggling her way up the stairs.

"I feel so naughty," she whispered as Nicholas turned his key in the lock.

"You *are* naughty," he said. "Very, very naughty."

He leered at her and before she knew what was happening, the door was closed behind them and he'd tossed her onto his bed.

"Nicholas!" she whisper-shrieked.

"Shhhhh. You'll get me in trouble. I'm not supposed to have women here."

"I'm your wife."

He looked at her with a ridiculously innocent expression. "But think about how long it would take to explain that. All that time wasted when I could be doing *this*."

Georgie let out a little squeak. She wasn't sure if *this* referred to his hand on her thigh or his lips on her neck, but both were delicious. And she had no idea how she was supposed to keep quiet.

"What would happen if she found me?" she asked. "Would she ask you to leave?"

He shrugged. "No idea. It wouldn't be the worst thing. We did just sign the lease for a new house."

Georgie forced herself to be serious, if only for a moment. "It won't be ready for occupancy for at least a week. And as much as I would love to have you with me at Scotsby, you can't be riding back and forth every day. You'd be exhausted."

Nicholas gave her a quick kiss on the lips. "Then we'll just have to be extra quiet so I don't get caught."

"Well, yes," Georgie said. But now she was concerned. It was only for one more week, but Nicholas needed this room. "Surely Mrs. McGreevey would understand."

Nicholas groaned. "Why are we talking about Mrs. McGreevey?"

"Because I don't want you thrown out of your rooms."

"I won't be," he said, "because we're going to be so very, very quiet."

Georgie sucked in her breath. His voice was hot and seductive, and she felt herself melting into his embrace.

"Can you do it?" he murmured. He squeezed her thigh in a way they'd both learned she loved, his thumb skating dangerously close to her womanhood.

"Do what?"

"Keep quiet."

"No," she said frankly.

"Pity." His fingers went still. "I'll have to stop."

She grabbed his hand. "Don't you dare."

"But you're so noisy." He shook his head with mock resignation. "What am I to do?"

Georgie laid a bold hand on his member. Over his clothes, but he'd get the idea. "What am *I* to do?"

"Minx," he growled.

She squeezed. "Can *you* be quiet?"

He quirked a brow. "I can if you can."

She'd never been able to raise a single brow, so she did a silly almost-wink. "Well, I can if you can."

He stared at her for a long moment, and Georgie thought it a wonder she did not burst into flame. Or laughter. Then he stood.

"What are you doing?" she asked, scooting into a sitting position.

"I"—his hands went to his cravat—"am very quietly taking off my clothing."

"Oh."

"Oh?" he echoed. "That's all you have to say?"

She licked her lips. "I am quite pleased with your decision."

He finished untying the linen and whipped it off. "You are pleased with my decision," he restated.

"*Quite* pleased," she corrected.

He smiled. Devilishly. "Do you know what would please me?"

"I have my suspicions," she murmured.

His hands went to the buttons on his shirt. There were only three, but he needed them undone so that he could pull the garment over his head. Maybe Georgie should have been tending to her own clothing, but watching him strip with such slow deliberateness might have been the most arousing thing she'd ever seen.

He didn't speak, but he didn't need to. His eyes locked onto hers, and Georgie knew what he wanted. She brought her fingers to the bodice of her dress, to the silk fichu that filled the neckline of her gown.

Slowly, she tugged it free.

"I've become brazen," she whispered.

He nodded, his eyes flaring with desire before he pulled his shirt up and over his head.

"I can't do all the buttons," she said. She twisted, giving him just enough of her back so that she could still peer over her shoulder.

"A most impractical frock," he murmured. He sat next to her and began to work the buttons, one by one.

"I've always had help," she whispered.

He kissed the patch of her skin bared by the top few buttons. "I am ever your servant, Mrs. Rokesby."

Georgie shivered, wondering how his voice somehow

enticed her just as much as his touch. He was always such a gentleman, but when they were in the privacy of their marriage bed he said the naughtiest things . . .

He didn't just do things to her, he spoke of them with hot, needy words. He told her what he wanted, and when she wanted something, he made her say it too.

Somehow that was even more shocking. *Tell me what you want*, he'd say, and it was so hard to bring herself to do so. She wanted him to take charge, to take the decisions from her control, but he would not let her.

You have to say it, he'd say.

She'd shake her head, too embarrassed, but he would not allow her to get away with that. *Is this what you want*, he'd ask, touching her breasts. Then his hand would slip between her legs. *Is this?*

Even now, as they were trying to be so quiet, he whispered sinful words in her ear.

"I want to taste you."

She shivered. She knew what he meant.

"I'm not even going to take your dress off. I'm just going to crawl under your skirts, and lick you until you explode."

He started kissing his way down her body, taking his delicious time on her breasts. Then, he looked up, and good heavens, somehow that felt even more erotic—his eyes locked and burning on hers.

It was like she was the only woman in the universe. The only woman he'd ever see. The only woman he'd ever want.

"Well," he said, his voice husky with promise. "What do you say to that?"

She nodded. She wanted him so much.

His fingers crept beneath her skirt, but only just. "Not good enough, my darling."

"I want it," she whispered.

"What?" he asked, and in one quick movement, he was back over her, face-to-face. "You want what?" he pressed. "Tell me."

Her body felt electric. She didn't understand how speaking her desire could make her so desperate for him, but it did.

"I want you to taste me."

His eyes held hers for a long second, and then with an animalistic growl, he practically dove down her body, spreading her legs to his seeking mouth.

She almost screamed. She actually clamped one of her hands over her mouth.

He looked up with a cocky grin.

"Don't stop," she begged.

He gave a throaty chuckle and went back to work, torturing her in the most exquisite way possible.

He had done this before, and she still could not believe she had let him. No, that wasn't true. She believed it. She would probably let him do anything to her.

She just couldn't believe she had liked it so much. His mouth . . . there. It was so intimate. And then when he was done . . . when *she* was done . . . he always kissed her again.

And she tasted herself.

It was wicked, and it was carnal, and she loved it.

But he'd moved away from her sex and was now taking his sweet time, raining soft kisses on the inside of her thigh, never quite going back to where she wanted him. Where she needed him.

With a restless groan she parted her legs more widely, but all he did was chuckle against her.

"So impatient," he murmured.

"I need you."

"I know." He sounded very pleased.

She arched her back, thrusting her hips forward. "Now, Nicholas."

He nipped her, his teeth softly abrading her skin, so close to where she wanted him. "Soon, Georgiana," he said.

"Please," she begged. She didn't know how he knew how to make her want him so desperately, but she didn't care. She just—

"Oh!"

"Shhhh." His hand came up to cover her mouth. "We must be quiet."

But his tongue was stroking her at her very core, making lazy circles on the spot she'd learned was the most sensitive.

"Nicholas, I—"

He shushed her again, slipping a finger into her mouth, then groaned, when she started to suck it.

"My God, Georgie," he groaned against her. She could not imagine that he was feeling as much pleasure as she was, but there was something about sucking on his finger that made her feel so excessively wanton, so hungry for more.

His tongue began to move faster.

She sucked harder.

"Georgie," he moaned, his words vibrating against her.

She grew tighter, tenser.

He worked her with his fingers, sliding two inside, even as his mouth nibbled and licked.

She exploded.

No, she *came*. That was the word for it, he'd told her, at least one of them. And it made an odd sort of sense, because when she came, when he brought her to the point that she came, she felt as if she had arrived somewhere very important.

She could not have explained it, could not have defined it, except that she knew she was exactly where she was supposed to be.

With him.

With Nicholas. Her husband.

Home.

"Oh my," she sighed. She wasn't sure she could move. He might have melted her bones.

"I love feeling you when that happens," he said, moving up her body until his face was near hers. "It makes me want you even more."

He nudged against her, not in a demanding way, but rather just a little reminder. He was hard, and he still wanted her.

"I need a moment," Georgie somehow managed to say.

"Just a moment?"

She nodded, although in truth she had no idea. She was completely undone. Her skin was sensitized beyond belief. He was still touching her, lightly, just on her arm, but it made her shiver uncontrollably.

"What are we to do with you?" he murmured, a hint of laughter in his voice.

"I can't move."

"Not even a little bit?"

She shook her head, but she made sure to keep a teasing expression in her eyes. They lay side by side for a moment, squeezed together on his narrow bed, and finally Georgie said, "You didn't even undo your breeches."

"Do you want me to?"

She nodded.

He turned, kissed her cheek. "I thought you couldn't move."

"It might be possible to rouse me."

"Is that so?"

She nodded again. "I want you to be pleased, too."

His eyes turned serious. "You always please me, Georgie."

"But you didn't . . ."

His hand covered hers, and he rolled them both so they were face-to-face. "It's not a quid pro quo. I give to you freely."

"I would like to give to *you* freely," she whispered. Then she felt her face grow sheepish. "When I can move again."

"I can wait," he said. He kissed her on the nose, then on each closed eyelid, then on her mouth. "For you, my love, I can wait forever."

Chapter 22

"I don't understand bloodletting."

Nicholas looked at Georgie in surprise—nay, in shock.

Nay, in astonishment.

Because barely five minutes had passed since the most extraordinary sexual experience of his life—which perhaps wasn't that meaningful a descriptor considering he'd only started *having* sexual experiences a few weeks earlier—but still.

He was quite sure they had turned the earth on its axis. Weather patterns would change. Day would be night.

Hell, he would not have been surprised if they had created their own gravitational force. They might have pulled down the moon.

None of which explained his wife's sudden inquiry into the taking of blood.

"What did you just say?" he asked.

"Bloodletting," she said again, not looking the least bit interested in romance despite their current position, which was to say, naked in bed. In one another's arms. She shifted her weight so that she could look at him more directly. "I don't understand it."

"Is there any reason you should?" Nicholas hoped he was not condescending; he did not mean to be. But it was a complicated topic. Most laypeople did not understand the science behind it.

To be honest, he wasn't sure *he* understood the science behind it. He wasn't sure anyone did, just that it seemed to work. Some of the time, at least.

"Well, no," Georgie said, scooting out from under him so that she could lie on her side, head propped up on her hand. "Not really. But I heard a little bit of the lecture earlier today. It didn't make much sense to me."

"Today's lecture wasn't specifically about bloodletting," he told her. "It was just mentioned at the end as a disruptor of circulation."

She blinked a few times.

"Which *was* the topic. Circulation."

Again, she said nothing. And then, as if she'd decided she'd heard his words and found them irrelevant, she said, "Right. Well, here is the problem. I don't understand how, if men regularly bleed to death on battlefields, not to mention all the other people who bleed to death at other times, people think that the removal of blood from the body can be helpful." She stared at him for a moment. "It's clear that blood is necessary for survival."

"Ah, but is *all* of our blood necessary for survival?"

"Ah, but wouldn't you think that more is better?"

"Not necessarily. Too much fluid in the body is called edema, and it can be very dangerous."

"Edema?"

"Swelling," he explained.

"This is like that ecchymosis thing," she said with a slight curl of her lip. "Doctor-speak so the rest of us don't know what you're talking about."

"You mean a bruise?" he asked innocently.

She swatted him on the shoulder.

"You'll ecchymose me," he pretended to whine.

"Is *that* a word?"

"Not even slightly."

She chuckled, but then, ever tenacious, returned to the topic at hand. "You still haven't said—why *do* you bleed patients?"

"It's all about balance," Nicholas said. "Of the humors."

"Humors," she repeated skeptically. "This is accepted scientific fact?"

"There are some competing theories," Nicholas admitted. "And in some schools of thought bloodletting is falling out of favor. It depends a great deal on whether the physician is a devotee of heroic medicine or solidism."

This, she seemed to find too much to accept. "Wait just a moment. Are you telling me that there is such a thing as heroic medicine?"

"Some would say all medicine is heroic," Nicholas tried to joke.

"Stop that," she said impatiently. "I want to hear more about this. It seems very self-congratulatory for a branch of science to label itself *heroic*."

"I'm not entirely certain of the origin of the phrase," Nicholas admitted. "It is also known as heroic depletion theory."

"That's not off-putting at all," Georgie muttered.

"Likely why the more basic term has prevailed," he replied.

"But what does it mean?"

"It follows the idea that good health is achieved when the body's humors are in balance." He explained further: "Black bile, yellow bile, phlegm, and blood."

"All liquids," she observed.

"Precisely. Which is why the theory stands in contrast with solidism, which follows the idea that it is the solid parts of the body that are vital and susceptible to disease."

She frowned. He'd noticed she did this when she was in deep thought. He'd also noticed that he found this fascinating. When Georgie thought deeply on something, her face was in constant motion. Her brow might dip, or her eyes would dart from side to side.

She was not a passive thinker, his wife.

Then something occurred to him. "Were you ever bled?" he asked her. "For your breathing illness?"

"Twice," she told him.

"And did it work?"

She shrugged. "According to the doctor it did."

Nicholas did not find this reply satisfying. "What was his criteria?"

"For success?"

He nodded.

She looked at him frankly. "I'm not dead."

"Oh, for heav—"

Georgie cut him off with a shake of her head. "According to my mother, that is the ultimate proof of cure."

Nicholas smiled, although he didn't really think this was funny.

"But," Georgie continued, "I don't think that the bloodletting had anything to do with my getting better. If anything, it made me feel worse. It was exhausting. And it hurt."

"The exhaustion is to be expected. The body must work to produce new, healthier blood."

"—that is more in balance with the other three humors," she finished.

"That is the thought."

She frowned, and an odd, growly sound came from the back of her throat. She was impatient, he realized.

"How do we know I wouldn't have improved without the bloodletting?" she asked. "How do we know I wouldn't have improved *faster*?"

"We don't," he admitted.

Georgie's eyes met his and then held them in a piercingly direct manner. "Would you have bled me under the circumstances?"

"I can't answer that," he said. "I don't *know* all the circumstances. I don't know how labored your breathing was. Was it shallow, rapid? Did you have a fever? Muscle aches? Rigidity in your spleen?"

He paused for a moment, even though his questions were largely rhetorical. "It is dangerous to dispense medical advice when one does not have all the facts at hand."

"I'm not sure the *doctor* had all the facts at hand," Georgie muttered.

"He certainly had more than I do."

She dismissed this with a little snort. "But think about it," she said. "The difficulty was in my breathing. Whatever was wrong with me, it was in my lungs, not my veins."

"Everything is connected," he said.

She rolled her eyes. Hard. "You keep answering with platitudes that don't explain anything."

"Sadly, medicine is as much an art as a science."

She wagged her finger at him. "Another platitude."

"I didn't mean it as such," he said. "I swear. I *wish* we had more proof to guide our practices. I truly do. And I'm not sure I would choose to bleed a patient who was having difficulty breathing. At least not as a first measure."

"But when someone is having difficulty breathing," she said quietly, "there may not be time for a second measure."

A cold shiver passed through Nicholas, the kind one didn't feel so much as sense. He had never witnessed one of Georgie's breathing attacks. He'd heard about them over the years, though. He hadn't given them a lot of thought—it always seemed he found out about them well after the fact, when it was clear that she'd come through with no lasting implications. So he had not realized just how serious they had been.

And besides that, he'd been young. And not medically minded. Certainly not thinking like a doctor.

"Georgie," he said slowly, his thoughts coalescing as he spoke, "did your doctor ever suggest you might have asthma?"

"Oh yes, of course," she replied, with a tone and expression that suggested she found his question somewhat silly.

"No, no," Nicholas said. He had a feeling he understood her reaction. Many doctors—especially those who were not affiliated with a university and thus not as up-to-date on medical progress—used the word "asthma" to describe any sort of breathing malady. He explained this to her, then asked, "Did anyone ever use the term *spasmodic* or *convulsive* asthma?"

She thought for a moment, then gave an apologetic shrug. "I don't know," she said. "Not to me. Maybe to my parents."

"It's a very specific sort of breathing disorder," Nicholas explained, "one that manifests itself differently in different people."

"And this makes it difficult to diagnose?"

"Not that so much as difficult to treat. Different

people seem to respond to different treatments. The good news is it is rarely fatal."

"Rarely," she echoed, her voice flat.

"My late professor—he died just last year—wrote extensively on the subject."

At that she smiled. "How fortuitous."

"To be honest," Nicholas said, "he wrote extensively on almost every topic of medicine. His major life's work was the arrangement and classification of disease."

"In a book?" Georgie asked. "I should like to read that."

He regarded her with some surprise. "You would?"

"Wouldn't you?"

"I already have done," he answered. Dr. Cullen's tome was required reading of every medical student at the University of Edinburgh. Nicholas knew that some of his classmates had skipped the sections they were not interested in, but he had tried his best to give his full attention to the entire work.

Which hadn't always been easy. *Synopsis Nosologiae Methodicae* was, in a word, dense.

"Did you find it interesting?" Georgie asked.

"Of course. Well, most of it. I don't know that there is any doctor who finds every aspect of medicine interesting."

She nodded thoughtfully. "I think I would enjoy reading it."

"You probably would. Although you might like a different one of his texts better. It's less about the classification of diseases and more about how to treat them."

"Oh, yes, that does sound more interesting. Do you own this book?"

"I do."

"Is it here or at Scotsby?"

Nicholas glanced at his overflowing bookshelf, and then tipped his head in its direction. "It's right there."

She twisted to look, not that she could have possibly known which book he was motioning to. "May I take it back with me? Or will you need it?"

He smiled. "Not between now and when I next see you."

Her entire face lit with anticipation, and it occurred to Nicholas that she looked far more excited at the process of reading *First Lines of the Practice of Physic* than any medical student he'd ever seen, himself included.

"Thank you," she said, before snuggling into the pillow with a sigh. "It will give me something to do while you're gone."

"Is it so very dull, then?"

One corner of her mouth turned down—not sad, but

a little sheepish. "It shouldn't be. I have so much to do. But at the same time it feels like there is nothing *to* do."

"Nothing you *want* to do," he said.

"Something like that." She inched up a little on the pillow to look at him. "I *want* to set up our household. I think it will give me great joy. But that's not Scotsby."

"One more week," he said, giving her hand a squeeze.

She nodded, closing her eyes as she slouched back down into the pillow. "I wish I didn't have to go."

"As do I," he murmured. Although it had to be said, his bed was uncomfortable enough with only him sleeping in it. If she spent the night, neither of them would get any sleep. And not for the reasons he'd like.

"Do you know what time it is?" she asked. Her eyes were closed; she looked almost unbearably content.

Unbearable because he was going to have to rouse her from her position momentarily.

He reached over to his nightstand and checked his pocket watch. "We're going to need to leave soon," he said. "You're due back at the carriage in half an hour."

She let out a groan. "I don't want to go."

He chuckled, giving her a nudge.

"What if I remain here?" she asked, one eye popping open. "I will be quiet as a church mouse. You can bring me food, and I'll read your medical texts, and—"

"—and Mrs. McGreevey will likely have heart failure the next time she comes in to clean my room."

"She does that?"

"Every other day."

Now Georgie looked panicked. "Every other—"

"Not today," he cut in.

"Oh, thank goodness." She sat up, regrettably pulling the bedsheet up with her. "I was only joking about staying here, you know. Well, mostly only joking."

He chucked her under the chin. "It *would* make me far more eager to return in the evenings."

She rose from the bed to dress, facing his bookshelf as she pulled on her frock. She'd need help with the buttons, and he wondered how he'd make himself do them up when all he wanted was to kiss the tender skin on the nape of her neck.

"Don't forget to get the book for me," she said, oblivious to his hungry stare. "I don't know which one you mean."

"It's the green one, all the way to the left," he said, "but I'll get it for you." It still seemed strange to him that she'd want to read it, except . . . when he actually thought of it, it wasn't strange at all.

He'd never have thought that anyone not involved in medicine would wish to read such a thick text.

But not Georgie. For her, it made sense. Nicholas

wondered if there were any medical schools that accepted women. He had a feeling his wife would be an excellent student.

They finished dressing and made it out of the boardinghouse undetected. It was a warm day for Edinburgh, and the stroll to the carriage was most pleasant. Nicholas had one arm looped through Georgie's, and the other holding the thick textbook. They chattered about nothing of importance; they didn't need to. The air was bright and warm, and they were so comfortable and happy to be in one another's presence, that there was no urge to fill the silence with anything profound.

The carriage was waiting at the edge of Old Town, in a relatively quiet square. Jameson and the driver were sitting on the seat, sharing a loaf of bread, and it looked like Georgie's maid was waiting inside.

"There you are," the maid said, poking her head out when they approached. "It's getting late."

It wasn't, but Nicholas saw no reason to point that out. He waited for Marian to go back into the carriage, and then gave Georgie a boost.

But when she ducked her head to enter, he did not release her hand.

"Nicholas?" she said, gazing down at him with an expression of gentle amusement.

He looked at her. At her face, which was so familiar

to him. Or rather, it *had been* familiar. Somehow it had become new. Her eyes were the same, blue, merry, but not quite as bright as his own. Her nose—it was the same nose she'd always had. Same for her lips, and her hair, and every little thing about her, except . . .

She was new.

He was new.

They had just begun.

"I love you," he said.

Her eyes went wide. "What?"

"I love you." He brought her gloved hand to his lips. "I just thought you should know."

She looked about, her eyes not quite panicked, but maybe a little discombobulated, as if she were expecting someone to jump out at any moment and yell, "Surprise!"

"I love you, silly girl," he said.

Her lips parted. "Silly?"

"For not believing me."

"I—I believe you."

"Good." He smiled, waiting patiently for her reply.

She began to blink, and her mouth moved, just a little. She looked quickly over her shoulder at her maid; Nicholas wasn't sure why, perhaps it was a reflex. But then she turned back and said, "You love me."

"I do."

"Well." She swallowed. "I love you too."

"I'm very happy to hear it."

Her mouth fell open. "*That's* what you say in response?"

"You said, *What?*" he reminded her.

"I was *surprised.*"

He gave a little shrug. "I wasn't."

She gasped. "You—"

"Ah ah ah," he said, with a little step back to avoid the swat she had been about to land on his upper arm. "You don't want to do that. You love me."

Her eyes narrowed. It only made him laugh.

"You do," he said. "You can't take it back."

"I can't believe you told me *now,*" she said.

He hopped up onto the carriage step, one hand grasping the edge of the roof for balance, the other wrapping around her waist.

"Nicholas?"

"I couldn't wait," he said.

She flushed, smiling, then whispered, "Are we making a scene?"

"Do you care?"

She shook her head. "Do you?"

"Not even a little bit." He kissed her again. "But alas, I have to let you go. I don't want you on the roads after nightfall."

She nodded and he hopped down. "I'll see you on Friday evening," he said. "I'll leave for Scotsby just as soon as my classes are over."

Then he shut the carriage door, and watched it pull away. Damn, he was going to miss her.

Mr. McDiarmid had said they could occupy their new house at the end of next week.

Nicholas couldn't wait.

Chapter 23

Two days later, Georgie was back in Edinburgh.

She wasn't supposed to be there. Or rather, Nicholas wasn't expecting her. The plan had been for him to ride to Scotsby that evening, but Georgie had received a message from Mr. McDiarmid that there were additional papers to sign regarding the lease of their new house. She supposed Nicholas could have just taken care of this the following week, but truthfully, she'd been looking for an excuse to go back to the city.

She had it all planned out: She would surprise him again outside of class, they could see Mr. McDiarmid so Nicholas could sign the papers, and then they would travel back to Scotsby together in the carriage. Surely that would be more comfortable for Nicholas than to ride the whole way.

Now that she knew her way around Edinburgh—at least enough to get herself to the lecture hall—she was able to convince Marian that she did not need her accompaniment. Jameson would be with her; the driver, too. Plus, Georgie was no longer an unmarried maiden. She did not need chaperonage every time she left the house.

Not to mention that with Marian at Scotsby, Georgie and Nicholas would have the carriage all to themselves for the long ride home.

Georgie might be new to marriage, but she was not stupid.

But first there was the ride to the city. Georgie had never had difficulty reading in carriages, so she brought the medical textbook Nicholas had given her to help pass the time.

First Lines of the Practice of Physic by William Cullen, M.D. Thus far she'd only managed to get through the preface and the introduction. Fifty-two pages in all, though, so it wasn't as if she was being a layabout. The material was fascinating, but she'd never read anything like it before, and it required far more of her attention and time than her usual reading choices.

She'd also discovered that Nicholas had given her only the first volume. Of four.

She'd be reading this for months.

Then she thought of all the other books he had on his shelf at the boardinghouse. Had he read them all? Was it even possible for a human being to do so?

She wondered if Dr. Simmons, the man who'd treated her asthma back in Kent, read books like *First Lines of the Practice of Physic.* According to her copy, the original publication date was 1777. Dr. Simmons was easily in his sixties. He would have completed his medical training well before 1777. Had he continued his education on his own? Was he required to?

Who kept track of doctors once they finished their studies? Anyone?

Georgie had questions.

But these could wait. Instead, she busied herself with the book. She flipped to the first page of Part I.

Of Pyrexiae, or Febrile Diseases.

Fevers. This would be interesting.

She finished that page fairly quickly, then turned to the next.

Book One.

Wait, *Book One* of *Part One?*

She continued.

Chapter One.

She blinked. *Chapter One* of *Book One* of *Part One.*

Good heavens.

At least Dr. Cullen had broken his text into even smaller portions, most not even half a page long. The white space on the page seemed to make it easier to separate each topic in her mind. Chapter One began with portion eight, one through seven having been taken up with the introduction.

Out of curiosity she flipped ahead to the end of Book One. Two hundred and thirty-four separate portions!

How was it possible there were two hundred and thirty-four different things to know about fevers?

She was beginning to develop new respect for Nicholas's studies, which was saying something, as she'd already respected it a great deal.

Georgie read for about an hour, looking up every now and then to watch the countryside roll past her window. She couldn't help it. She needed to give her eyes a break. Maybe that was why Dr. Cullen had broken his text up into so many smaller portions. Maybe he understood that human beings couldn't focus their attention on such difficult material for more than half a page at a time.

How could something so interesting be so difficult to read? She was on portion forty-four, which began, somewhat discouragingly: "This may be difficult to explain . . ."

She sighed. It was also difficult to understand. Maybe she needed to take a rest. She closed her eyes.

Just for a moment.

Just for long enough to clear her mind for a few minutes before diving back into the textbook. Just a little nap until . . .

"Ma'am? Mrs. Rokesby?"

Georgie opened groggy eyes. Were they already in—

"Ma'am," Jameson said, looking up at her through the open carriage door, "we're here. In Edinburgh."

So they were.

Georgie blinked herself awake, rubbing her forehead inelegantly as she peered out the window. They were parked just outside of the university lecture hall. They wouldn't be able to leave the carriage there for a long period of time. The plan was for her and Jameson to get out while the driver took the carriage to the square where he'd waited earlier in the week.

"I'm sorry," she said as she gathered her things. "I must have fallen asleep."

"It was a smooth ride, ma'am," he said.

And a long book, she thought.

He held out his hand to help her down, and then, once the carriage had departed she turned to him and said, "You need not come into the building with me."

She was quite certain Jameson would rather stay outside. The last time they'd been within earshot of the lecture he'd gone a bit green about the gills. Marian had later told her that he'd confessed that he sometimes fainted at the sight of blood.

But he shook his head. "Begging your pardon, ma'am, but you can't go in by yourself."

"I will be just fine," she assured him. "I know exactly where to go. And there is a bench right outside the lecture theater. I can sit quietly while I wait for Mr. Rokesby to emerge."

Jameson did not look convinced. "I don't think Mr. Rokesby would approve."

"He won't mind at all," Georgie said, which was only a small fib. Nicholas would almost certainly prefer it if Jameson accompanied her, but he wasn't likely to be angry if he did not.

"I will be sitting right outside the room," Georgie continued. "If something happens, all I have to do is raise my voice, and Mr. Rokesby will come running."

But Jameson would not be swayed, so the two of them walked into the building together. Georgie brought the large green textbook with her, thinking it might make her look as if she was meant to be there.

Obviously she *wasn't* meant to be there—the University of Edinburgh accepted no female students—but maybe she'd look like someone's assistant, or a visiting dignitary.

Still unlikely, but she felt better with the book. Academic armor, so to speak.

They walked in, and Georgie took a seat on the bench, right next to the open door to the theater. Jameson stood across the hall, but she had a feeling it wasn't far enough away to keep him out of earshot because he started to look ill within minutes.

It wasn't surprising. Today's lecture topic had something to do with wound care, and the professor had just begun talking about worms.

And maggots.

Georgie wasn't sure she understood the relevance, but that was the least of her concerns. Jameson's skin had gone gray and pasty and he was clutching the wall. Surely he would do better outside. "Jameson," she whispered, trying to get his attention.

He didn't hear. Or possibly he needed to focus all of his energy on remaining upright.

"Pssst. Jameson!"

Nothing, but he swallowed a few times.

Georgie's eyes widened. This did not look good.

"Jame—" Forget that. She stood and hurried over. "Jameson, I think you shou—"

"*Urg uh blear . . .*"

Oh, God. He was going to—

". . . *uharff!*"

Everything—and Georgie meant everything—that was in Jameson's stomach came out of his mouth.

She jumped back, but she wasn't fast enough to avoid it all. It hit her shoes, and probably the hem of her dress, and—*Oh dear God he must have eaten fish.*

Her own stomach started to turn. Oh no . . .

"Oh, Mrs. Rokesby," Jameson groaned. "I don't think I can . . ."

Apparently he hadn't expelled everything the first time around because he heaved again, this time spewing the dregs of his breakfast.

Georgie clamped her hand over her mouth. The *smell.* Oh, God, the smell was making her sick, too.

"I have to go outside," he moaned.

"Go!" Georgie clutched at her own roiling belly. She needed him gone. If she could get away from the smell she might be able to keep her own breakfast down. "Please!"

He ran out, just as men poured forth from the lecture theater.

"What's going on?" more than one demanded.

"Is someone ill?"

"What is—"

Someone slipped in the mess on the floor.

Someone else crashed into her.

They *all* wanted to be of service, to be the doctor who would save the day.

"Are you ill, ma'am?

"Are you fevered?"

They kept pushing forward, and none of them were Nicholas, and she couldn't get away from the smell . . .

She tried not to breathe.

She took a gulp of air.

And another. But it smelled terrible, and she gagged.

And then she tried for another, but it didn't seem to come.

She gasped.

"Miss, are you—"

"Nicholas," she wheezed. "Where is—"

She couldn't breathe. She opened her mouth, and she thought she was pulling in air, but it wasn't reaching her lungs.

She couldn't breathe.

She needed air.

Everyone was so close.

She couldn't breathe.

She couldn't breathe.

She couldn't breathe.

406 · JULIA QUINN

Nicholas almost always sat near the front of the lecture hall. He had a sneaking suspicion that his eyesight was not what it once was—probably from all the close reading he'd had to do these past few years—and he'd found his attention was less likely to wander if he could see the expressions on his professors' faces as they lectured.

Today he was in the second row, which was why he was among the last to realize that something odd was happening just outside the lecture hall. Most of the students near the exit were gone by the time he turned around, and several more had jumped up from their seats and were hurrying out.

Nicholas shared a glance with the man seated next to him. They both shrugged.

"Do you know what's happening?" Nicholas asked.

"I think someone fainted in the hall," another student said.

"What was someone doing in the hall?" yet another asked.

Nicholas shrugged again. The hallway outside the lecture theater was usually vacant while class was in session. Sometimes a tardy student rushed through, hoping to slide into one of the back seats without being noticed, and he supposed that occasionally people waited on the bench for class to get out. That's what Georgie had done when she'd come a few days earlier, before her maid had insisted on waiting outside.

"Dr. Monro!" came an urgent holler.

The professor, who had been watching the exodus with visible irritation, set down his notes and bounded up the steep steps.

"Should we get up to help?" the man next to him asked.

Nicholas shook his head. "It's too crowded. We'd only get in the way."

And then, in the split second after he stopped speaking and before anyone else began, a panicked yell rang through the building.

"SHE'S NOT BREATHING!"

She?

Nicholas rose to his feet. Slowly at first, as his brain caught up with his legs.

She?

There were no women here. There were never women here, except when . . .

When Georgie . . .

He ran.

He tripped past the man sitting next to him, stumbling his way to the aisle.

Georgie was here. He didn't know how he knew, but he did. She was here, and she needed him.

He ran up the steps and pushed his way into the hall. A knot of people were surrounding someone on the floor.

"Out of the way," someone yelled. "Give Dr. Monro room!"

Nicholas shoved his way forward. "That's my wife," he said, even though he couldn't see her yet. "That's my wife."

Finally, he made it through the crowd, and there she was, sitting on the floor, gasping for breath.

"Lie her down!" Dr. Monro said. He spoke with the authority of a doctor who had been practicing for decades, who knew what to do.

Except the minute he lay her back, her body began to spasm.

"Stop!" Nicholas yelled. "She can't get enough air like that."

"Get him away from me," the doctor snapped.

Nicholas grabbed him by the arm. "She's my wife."

Dr. Monro turned to him with a sharp expression. "If you value her well-being, you'll back off and let me do my job."

Nicholas swallowed and took a step back, watching as his professor—one of the most well-known and respected doctors in Great Britain—began his assessment.

"She has a history of spasmodic asthma," Nicholas

said, hoping it was true. Everything Georgie had told him indicated this diagnosis. And that was certainly what he saw when he looked at her now. Georgie's inhales seemed more like gasps, her lungs convulsing as they tried desperately to fill.

Dr. Monro gave a curt nod.

"Sir," Nicholas said, "I believe she needs to sit up."

Georgie's eyes met his. He could see she was trying to nod.

The doctor grunted but helped ease her into a sitting position. Georgie took a gulp of air, but Nicholas could tell it wasn't enough.

Please, her eyes seemed to say. She thrust her hand out, toward Nicholas.

He shoved forward. Maybe the doctor needed room, but Georgie needed him.

"What did I just say?" Dr. Monro snapped.

"She wants my hand," Nicholas replied, fighting to keep his voice calm. "She needs comfort."

The doctor gave a single brisk nod, then said, "How often does she experience dyspnea?"

"Not often in adulthood," Nicholas answered. "Far more frequently when she was a child."

He looked to Georgie for confirmation. She gave a tiny nod. She was breathing more regularly now, but every exhale made a wheezy, whistling sound.

"It sounds as if she is improving, sir," Nicholas said. He looked at her carefully as he put an arm around her shoulders to support her. "Are you getting more air?"

Again, another tiny nod. "It's . . . better."

"I'm not satisfied yet," the doctor said grimly. "I've seen cases where the patient seems to improve but then relapses. Especially young women prone to hysteria."

"She's not prone to hysteria," Nicholas said stiffly.

"I know—what—" Georgie tried to say something, but she was having too much trouble catching her breath.

"Don't speak," Nicholas said. "You need a bit more time."

"But—he—"

"We need to bleed her," Dr. Monro said.

"What?" Nicholas looked at him in shock. "No. She's already improving."

"And this will hasten her recovery." He looked up at the crowd. "My lancets. Now!"

Several men scurried off. Dr. Monro took Georgie's wrist and started taking her pulse.

"Sir, no," Nicholas said. "She should not be bled."

His professor gave him a look of utter disdain.

"She's been bled before," Nicholas said. "It does not work."

He prayed this was true. He had not been there. He did not know the details. But Georgie had said it had not helped, and he owed it to her to trust her account of her own body, of her own health.

Dr. Monro ignored him. "We're going to have to cut her sleeve to access the veins in her arm," he said to the man next to him.

"You will not bleed her," Nicholas said forcefully. "It does not work."

"She's alive, isn't she?" Dr. Monro snapped.

"Yes, but not because she was bled. She said it made her worse."

The doctor gave a snort. "Patients are notoriously unreliable, especially when recounting events from several years earlier."

"My wife is not unreliable," Nicholas said. He looked at Georgie. She was still pale, but her color had improved, and her lips had lost that terrifying bluish tint they'd acquired when the doctor had had her lie down. "Are you feeling any better?" he asked her. "You seem to be—*euf!*"

One of the other medical students pitched forward and knocked into him. They were all still crowded tightly around, eager to watch the great Dr. Monro at work.

"Back off!" Nicholas barked at the crowd. "She needs space."

Georgie nodded. "They're too close. I need—"

Another whistling wheeze.

"Everyone, take a step back," Dr. Monro ordered. "I need room to work."

"She needs room to breathe," Nicholas retorted.

Dr. Monro gave him a sharp look before turning back to Georgie. "I have found that blood in the dominant arm has stronger circulatory properties," he said, not to her but to the students gathered round. He flicked his eyes toward Nicholas. "I assume this would be her right arm."

Nicholas gave a curt nod just as someone returned with a set of lancets. "But you will not be—"

"Excellent," Dr. Monro said. "Now then, observe my selected blade. You want to choose one that—"

"No." Nicholas jerked Georgie away.

"Mr. Rokesby," the doctor said, "I advise you to move away from your wife."

"No."

"Mr. Rokesby," Dr. Monro said sharply, "may I remind you that you are not yet a physician? And that your becoming one is predicated upon my approval? I will say it one more time. Move away from your wife."

Nicholas did not hesitate. "No," he said again. He gathered her in his arms and stood. "I'm taking her outside."

"The colder air will be too much of a shock," Dr. Monro said. "She needs to remain inside."

Nicholas ignored him. "Clear the way," he said to the assembled crowd.

"This is a bad idea," the doctor warned.

Nicholas didn't even look at him.

"If she dies," Dr. Monro said, "it's on you."

"You're not going to die," Nicholas said to Georgie as he strode down the hall.

"Not today, anyway," she said with a weak smile.

Nicholas gave her a tender smile. "I would scold you for such a joke, but under the circumstances, I'll take your humor as a sign of improvement."

She nodded, and when she exhaled, there was less of a whistling sound than there had been earlier.

"Please say I'm doing the right thing by taking you outside," he said.

"It was too crowded." She took a few breaths. Nicholas could see that she was focusing on slowing her inhales.

"And the smell," she added as he pushed through the front door.

Nicholas had noticed that, too. "Did you vomit?"

She shook her head. "Jameson."

"*Jameson* vomited?"

"It was the lecture. He's—" She coughed. "He's very squeamish."

"Good God," Nicholas muttered. "Remind me never to allow him near my offices when I become a doctor."

If he became a doctor. He did not know if Dr. Monro would make good on his threat. He wouldn't have thought him so vindictive, but he'd also never seen him so angry.

But Nicholas didn't care. Not at this moment, at least. He had Georgie outside, and if the city air was not as clear as he'd like, it was still a damn sight better than in the hallway outside the lecture theater, with dozens of men pressing in on every side.

Georgie's cheeks had even started to show the first traces of pink.

"Don't scare me like that again," Nicholas said. His voice trembled. He had not thought it would.

She reached up and touched his cheek. "Thank you."

"For not letting him draw blood?"

"For believing in me."

They sat on a stone bench beneath a tree, Nicholas still holding her scandalously close for such a public place. But he wasn't ready to let go.

"How are you feeling?" he asked.

"Better. Not quite right, but better."

"How long does it usually take to feel back to normal?"

She gave a helpless shrug. "I don't know, really. It's hard to say."

He nodded. And then, because he had to say it—

"I love you, you know."

She smiled gently. "I love you too."

"I'm going to tell you every day."

"I will be glad to hear it."

He frowned. Just a little. That was not *quite* the response he'd been hoping for. "And . . . ?"

She brought one of his hands to her mouth and kissed it. "And I will tell *you* every day as well."

"Much better."

"To think," she said, with what he could only describe as a mystified shake of her head, "you were right there under my nose, all these years." She looked up, her eyes suddenly wry. "Do I have to thank Freddie Oakes? Please say I don't."

"Freddie Oakes?" Nicholas echoed.

"He did bring us together."

Nicholas rolled his eyes. "We would have found our way. It just would have taken a little longer."

She let out a long breath, slow and sustained, and Nicholas was pleased to hear only the slightest remnants of a wheeze. "People are watching," she whispered.

He looked over at the building. The front door was open, and several of his classmates stood on the front steps.

"I'm fine!" Georgie called out. She waved, but then the exertion led to a little cough.

"Stop that," Nicholas scolded.

"They're worried. It's sweet."

"It's not sweet, it's intrusive."

"Can you blame them?"

Nicholas supposed not. She had collapsed in front of a group of medical students. There was no way they were not going to be curious.

"Why are you here?" he suddenly thought to ask.

"Mr. McDiarmid has more papers. I wanted to tell you, and then I thought we could ride back to Scotsby together."

"Forget the papers," he said. "Let's go home now."

"No! The sooner you sign, the sooner we can move into the new house."

"The house can wa—"

"The sooner we can be together," she cut in firmly.

He tapped one finger against her hand. "You do have a point there. But then it's straight to Scotsby. And you are remaining in the carriage while I deal with Mr. McDiarmid. I want you to rest."

"Yes, sir," she said with an uncharacteristically meek smile.

"And then when we're home it's more rest," he ordered.

She placed her hand on her heart. "I promise."

"Nothing too exerting."

Her brows rose. "Nothing?"

He groaned. He'd been looking forward to many exertions.

"I see Jameson across the street," Nicholas said. "I'll have him arrange to have the carriage meet us at Mr. McDiarmid's office. Do you think you can walk there?" They'd done the same walk just two days earlier; it was not far.

She nodded. "I think it will help, actually, as long as we go slowly."

Nicholas dashed off to give Jameson instructions, then returned to Georgie's side. Together, they walked through Old Town.

"Nicholas," she said.

He turned.

"I love you."

He smiled. "I love you too."

They took a few more steps, and then, with a little tilt of her head, she said, "I just wanted to say it first."

"Competitive, are we?"

"No," she said, a small pulse of amusement in her voice, "I just wanted to say it without saying, 'I love you *too*.'"

"Oh. Well, in that case, I love you, and I love you too."

"Who's competitive now?"

"Not me, surely."

"Well, then, I love you thrice."

"Does that even make sense?" he asked.

"I think it does, actually." She let her head rest on his shoulder. Just for a moment; they could not walk more than a step or two in such a position. "Everything about you makes sense," she said.

"That's hardly true."

"Everything about *us* makes sense."

She was on to something with that.

"Georgie?" he said.

She looked at him.

"I love you."

She grinned. "And I love you."

"Too?"

"Always."

He smiled. That would work.

Epilogue

A few years later

"Shouldn't the doctor be doing this?"

Georgie smiled and assured Mr. Bailey that she knew what she was doing. "Dr. Rokesby often asks me to stitch wounds," she said.

But Mr. Bailey was not appeased. He yanked his arm off the table, nearly causing her to reopen the small section of wound she'd successfully closed.

"I want the doctor," he said.

Georgie took a breath and once again plastered a smile on her face. She understood why patients wanted Nicholas. He was the esteemed Dr. Rokesby, and she—despite all the knowledge she'd acquired these past few years—was, and always would be, Mrs. Rokesby.

She liked being Mrs. Rokesby. She liked it a lot. But it would have been handy at a time like this to be able to spear Mr. Bailey with a withering stare and say, "I, too, am a physician."

Dr. and Dr. Rokesby. What a thing that would be. Alas, her inquiries at the University of Edinburgh had been met with incredulity.

Someday a woman would be granted a degree in medicine. Georgie was certain of it. But not in her lifetime.

Unfortunately, she was certain of that, too.

"Dr. Rokesby!" she called out. Nicholas was treating another patient in the next room, one with a much more serious condition than Mr. Bailey's lacerated arm.

Nicholas poked his head in. "Is there a problem?"

"Mr. Bailey would prefer that you stitch his arm," Georgie replied.

"I assure you, you don't," he said, directing his words at Mr. Bailey. "My wife is far more skilled with a needle than I am."

"But you are the doctor."

Georgie rolled her eyes in anticipation of what she knew Nicholas would say. They'd been through this before, and she knew it was the only way to convince men like Mr. Bailey, but still, it was galling.

"She's a woman, Mr. Bailey," Nicholas said with a

condescending smile. "Aren't they always better with needles and thread?"

"I suppose . . ."

"Let me see what she's done thus far."

Mr. Bailey showed Nicholas his arm. Georgie hadn't managed to get much done before he'd balked at having been placed in her care, but the five stitches were neat and tidy and, yes, better than anything Nicholas could do.

"Brilliant," Nicholas said, flashing Georgie a quick grin before turning back to Mr. Bailey. "Look at how even they are. You'll have a scar—there's no getting around that—but it will be minimal thanks to her skill."

"But it hurts," Mr. Bailey whined.

"There's no getting around that, either," Nicholas said, his voice finally starting to betray his impatience. "Would you like a shot of whiskey? I've found it helps."

Mr. Bailey nodded and grudgingly agreed to allow Georgie to continue.

"You're a saint," Nicholas murmured in her ear before returning to the other room.

Georgie bit back a retort before turning to Mr. Bailey with a purposefully bland expression. "Shall we resume?" she asked.

Mr. Bailey set his arm back on the table. "I'll be watching you," he warned.

"You should," she said sweetly. It was really too bad he wasn't the sort who fainted at the sight of blood. It would make all of this so much easier.

Twenty minutes later she tied off her knot and admired her handiwork. She'd done an excellent job, not that she could say that to Mr. Bailey. Instead she gave him instructions to return in a week's time and assured him that Dr. Rokesby himself would inspect the wound before deciding if it was time to remove the stitches.

He departed and she wiped off her hands and removed her smock. It was nearly six, certainly late enough to close the small clinic Nicholas had opened in Bath. They had loved living in Edinburgh, but it was too far from family. Bath wasn't exactly around the corner from Kent, but they'd both wanted to live in a proper town, and it was easy enough to visit home.

Besides, Georgie had discovered she liked having a little distance between herself and her family. She loved them and they loved her, but they'd never see her as a capable, grown woman. Her mother still went into a panic every time she coughed.

No, this was good. She looked around the clinic. This was where she was meant to be.

"Give him three drops every evening before bed," she heard Nicholas say as he walked his patient to the door. "And apply the poultice I recommended. If he's not feeling better in three days' time, we will reassess."

"And if he is feeling better?" a female voice asked.

"Then we shall all be delighted," Nicholas replied.

Georgie smiled. She could so easily picture his face, warm and reassuring. He really was an excellent doctor.

An excellent man.

The front door shut, and she heard Nicholas turn the lock. They lived upstairs, their rooms accessible by a stairway in the back.

"What are you smiling about?" he asked when he appeared in the doorway.

"You."

"Me? Good thoughts, I hope."

"I *am* smiling."

"So you are. Forgive me for not making the connection."

Georgie crossed the small room and stood on her toes so that she could give him a kiss. "I was just thinking," she said, "that this was where I am meant to be. And you"—she kissed him again, on the other cheek—"are who I am meant to be with."

"I could have told you that," he murmured. He leaned down.

And this time, *he* kissed *her*.

Chapter 21

"Georgiana?"

Nicholas's heart had nearly stopped when he exited the lecture hall and saw Jameson waiting for him in the corridor. There was no reason why the footman should be here in Edinburgh, much less on the grounds of the medical school.

No reason except an emergency.

Jameson must have seen the panic on his employer's face, because before Nicholas could get out anything more than, "What are you—" Jameson blurted, "Nothing's wrong, sir!"

Still blinking with surprise—and yes, concern, even though he'd been assured there was no reason for it—Nicholas let the footman lead him out into the sunny courtyard where his wife waited.

"What are you doing?" Marian whispered.

Georgie shushed her, tipping her ear back to the open door. Drat, she'd missed something.

"... *perform a variety of motions* ..."

Georgie opened and closed her hands. All right. She could accept that.

"... *and to communicate and interact with external bodies.*"

Well now, *that* just made her think of Nicholas.

"We're leaving," Marian declared.

"What? No."

"You're flushed. I don't know what they are talking about in there, but I *know* it is not appropriate." Marian stood up with alacrity, exchanged a few quick words with Jameson, who had been waiting on the other side of the hallway, and then ushered Georgie right out the building's door and into the courtyard.